ems should be returned on or before the last date
hown below. Items not already requested by other
orrowers may be renewed in person, in writing or by
elephone. To renew, please quote the number on the
arcode label. To renew online a PIN is required.
his can be requested at your local library.
Renew online @ **www.dublincitypubliclibraries.ie**
ines charged for overdue items will include postage
ncurred in recovery. Damage to or loss of items will
e charged to the borrower.

Leabharlanna Poiblí Chathair Bhaile Átha Cliath
Dublin City Public Libraries

Comhairle Cathrach
Bhaile Átha Cliath
Dublin City Council

Date Due	Date Due	Date Due
14/09/17		
1 0 OCT 2017		

A WHIFF
OF CYANIDE

Book 3 in the Hampstead Murders

GUY FRASER-SAMPSON

urbanepublications.com

First published in Great Britain in 2017 by Urbane Publications Ltd
Suite 3, Brown Europe House, 33/34 Gleaming Wood Drive, Chatham,
Kent ME5 8RZ
Copyright © Guy Fraser-Sampson, 2017

A CIP catalogue record for this book is available from the British Library.

ISBN 978-1-911129-76-9
MOBI 978-1-911129-77-6

Design and Typeset by Julie Martin
Cover by Author Design Studio

Printed and bound by CPI Group (UK) Ltd, Croydon, CR0 4YY

urbanepublications.com

The publisher supports the Forest Stewardship Council® (FSC®), the leading international forest-certification
organisation. This book is made from acid-free paper from an FSC®-certified provider. FSC is the only
forest-certification scheme supported by the leading environmental organisations, including Greenpeace.

A WHIFF
OF CYANIDE

A Whiff of Cyanide is the third volume of the Hampstead Murders. Readers are invited to sample the series in the correct order for maximum enjoyment.

CHAPTER 1

Hampstead village has a distinctive atmosphere all of its own, which derives partly from its elegant Georgian and Victorian houses, and partly from the knowledge that generations of writers, actors, artists and academics have graced their rooms over the centuries. It is as if a collective cultural consciousness, cosily eccentric and definitely left wing, has soaked gradually into the brickwork and is now exuded to be inhaled gently and appreciatively by the more sensitive passers-by, whether in the soft sunshine of a summer afternoon or the driving rain of a winter evening.

In the south-west corner of the Village, the imposing Georgian architecture of Church Row comes to an end with the parish church, internally a wedding cake confection of white, gold, pink and blue, and in whose graveyard is buried John Constable, of whose paintings an exhibition had, as our story opens, recently been mounted at Burgh House with unforeseen murderous consequences.

Beyond the churchyard, the traditional centre of Hampstead gives way to Frognal and the looming self-assurance of gigantic red brick houses built for wealthy and worthy nineteenth century families. Save for an hour or so each morning and afternoon, when the four-wheel drives of the country dwellers of Mill Hill, Wembley and Belsize Park disgorge or re-embark teenagers clad in the red and black striped blazers of University College School, Frognal is a tranquil sort of place. For most of the rest of the day, the calm is broken only by passing Filipina nannies, visiting masseuses and personal trainers, and the occasional delivery from Fortnum and Mason.

This particular autumn evening, it was that time of day when the good people of Frognal give themselves up to the traditional Hampstead ritual of the dinner party, a social custom which, rather like a gentleman walking on the outside of the pavement, may be in rapid decline in less well-bred parts of the country, but remains firmly entrenched as an institution within the London NW3 postal district.

A stroll up the driveway of one of the houses, about the only one not fitted with security gates and cameras, and a glance through a ground floor window would have revealed five people seated sociably around the early stages of a convivial meal, probably a starter featuring both goat cheese and rucola and 'drizzled' with an expensive variant of balsamic vinegar, for drizzling one's starter is a basic requirement of Hampstead culinary practice.

At the head of the table sat Peter Collins, for though he shared this house with two of the other diners he seemed automatically to be assumed to be the host, perhaps because he was significantly older than both of them, and as a confirmed Hampstead eccentric he took a very traditional view of a host's rights and responsibilities. It was he who with his long term girlfriend, Karen Willis, who was currently sitting next to him, had been visiting Burgh House when the murder had been discovered. In her case, since she was a newly promoted detective sergeant in the Metropolitan Police, this had turned out to be convenient, but something of a professional chore; in Peter's case, a minor irritant, since he had just sat down to tea in the Buttery.

Two of the other people sitting around the table were also police officers. Simon Collison was a detective superintendent, marked out by both the media and the police establishment as a high-flyer, a man to watch. One of the very few school-leavers each year deemed bright enough to be invited to study law at King's College London, he had been the Senior Investigating Officer on the Burgh House murder case, the second in quick succession on which the three of them had worked together. Bob Metcalfe was a detective inspector, the sort of dependable workhorse on whom any police force relies to shoulder the day to day burden of managing the logistics of a major investigation. He and Peter Collins had one thing in common, perhaps the only one other than that they lived in the same house, for he was also in love with Karen Willis.

It was this apparent anomaly which Caroline Collison, Simon's pregnant wife, was just now attempting to address with her customary tact and intuition.

"It's very kind of you to invite us to your house-warming," she ventured to the table in general.

There were the customary murmurs of deprecation which

such a conversational gambit tends to invite. She delicately masticated some drizzled starter and tried again.

"So, you're all living here together, then?"

The three of them looked at each other. Caroline read embarrassment, but also a resolution born of prior discussion.

"Yes," Collins confirmed mildly.

"Yes, we are," Karen Willis echoed more firmly, but with a distinct reddening of her cheeks.

"It's a *ménage à trois*, you see," Collins went on deliberately. "It was my idea, actually, based on some people my parents used to know."

"But it was my decision," Willis went on determinedly, "and Bob's of course."

She reached across the table impulsively and seized his hand.

"Dear Bob," she said warmly. "It was him that made it possible. He knew that if he'd asked, I would have stayed with him alone."

"But I also knew how unhappy that might make you," he said quietly.

Collison gazed awkwardly from one to another. He was in uncharted territory here, and anyway he wasn't sure how wise it was to get quite so deeply involved in the private lives of his colleagues. His wife, however, shared no such inhibitions.

"Why, what a wonderful thing to be doing," she exclaimed. "So sensible. It fits the situation exactly."

The situation, as she knew from previous tearful conversations with Karen Willis, was that she had fallen in love with Bob Metcalfe without falling out of love with Peter Collins, and without even understanding how such a thing could be possible. Nor had Caroline been able to enlighten her.

"We thought so, yes," Collins said quietly.

Simon Collison shifted uncomfortably on his chair. Was it his imagination, or did Metcalfe look equally awkward?

"Actually, Simon, I was looking forward to seeing you this evening," Collins said, changing the subject as if sensing their discomfort. "There's something I wanted to tell you: something that might amuse you, in fact."

"Oh yes?"

"Yes. You know that book I was writing on the Golden Age of detective fiction? Well, I've finished it."

"Oh, Peter, that is good news," Collison said warmly. "Many congratulations! What's it called?"

"I haven't quite decided yet," Collins replied with a slight frown. "Or rather, the publisher hasn't. They have the last word you know. I've suggested *Strong Poison* since it's about Golden Age poisoning cases and their links to real life crimes, but they may feel a bit uncomfortable about that."

"So might the estate of Dorothy L. Sayers," Caroline observed mildly.

"Er, quite," Collins acknowledged.

"Their counter-offer," Metcalfe interjected with a grin, "is *What's Your Poison?*"

There was a collective groan around the table.

"Yes, well," Collins said in donnish irritation, "hopefully we can arrive at a satisfactory compromise."

"What about *Notions and Potions?*" Caroline suggested.

"Too Harry Potter, I think," Willis replied as Collins grimaced.

"*Noxious Substances* sounds a bit more Golden Age," Collison proffered.

"Hm," Collins said, clearly unconvinced. "Actually, I've suggested *Strong Poisons.*"

"In the hope that the extra 's' will keep the estate's lawyers at bay, presumably?" Caroline asked in amusement.

"Yes, exactly," Collins responded with a smile. "You see the point of course, Caroline."

She smiled in turn. She was genuinely fond of Peter, as she was of all the Three Musketeers, as she referred to them, inspired no doubt by the three evangelists in the Fred Vargas novels of which she was inordinately fond. How wonderful that they had managed to resolve their difficulties, albeit in a somewhat unconventional manner, for she knew with a deep inner certainty that Peter would never have been able to manage on his own. Oh, he would drift through life alright, eating and sleeping, but it would be a very empty existence; he needed to inhabit his own little world, and he needed Karen to inhabit it with him, to make it whole.

"Apparently Warner Brothers tried to sue the Marx Brothers for using the word 'Casablanca' in *A Night In Casablanca*," Collison said.

"Really?" Metcalfe asked. "What happened?"

"Groucho had his brother Gummo, who also happened to be the family lawyer, write back threatening to sue Warner Brother for using the word 'brothers'."

Amid the ensuing laughter, Karen Willis got up to clear the starter plates and Metcalfe stood up to help her. When they returned with the main course, conversation was still taking the form of the sort of one-liner ping-pong which always seems to follow on from any random reference to the Marx Brothers.

"Have you told the guvnor about the convention?" Metcalfe asked Collins as he sat down again.

"Convention?" Collison echoed. "What this, Peter?"

"Oh, it's nothing really," Collins replied modestly. "It's just that my publishers happened to know that the annual conference of crime writers was due to take place in Hampstead this year – well, close to Hampstead anyway – and they've arranged a speaking slot for me. It seems their publicist knows the organisers."

"It's a real stroke of luck, isn't it?" Willis asked eagerly. "Apparently it's usually in Bristol, but the hotel there is being refurbished."

"Surely there's more than one hotel in Bristol isn't there?" Collison asked uncertainly.

"There is indeed," Collins concurred. "It's quite a thriving sort of place, so I understand, though not somewhere I would personally choose to visit, I suspect."

"Oh, Peter, really," Willis protested. "Don't be such a

snob. Why, I might have gone to Bristol myself. I had it on my UCCA form."

"Really?" Collins queried, raising his eyebrows in disbelief. "I never knew that. Well, well."

"What number?" Metcalfe asked her, intrigued.

"What do you mean?"

"Well, you get five choices don't you? And rank them from one to five?"

"Oh, I see what you mean. Well, five if you must know."

A fresh wave of laughter erupted.

"So what you're really saying then," Metcalfe clarified, "is that for a fifth choice university, Bristol's really not that bad."

"Not that bad at all, actually," Collison said with a chuckle. "At my school we were always advised to put Aberystwyth or Bangor, but I couldn't face it and chose UEA instead."

"Well, anyway," Collins said, with the air of a man dragging the conversation back to the point it had been at before he was interrupted, "I understand there are different factions within the crime writing fraternity, one of whom has always wanted the conference to be in London because that's where the greatest concentration of readers is likely to be."

"Sounds reasonable," Collison said judiciously.

"Well yes, except that apparently the other faction has never really wanted readers to come anyway. They see it as a convention for writers to speak to other writers. Even when it was in Bristol they never actually advertised it locally, so most members of the public never even knew it was taking place."

"Good Lord," Caroline said, aghast. "Do you mean it's just two or three days of writers telling each other how wonderful they all are?"

"So far as I can ascertain, yes," Collins admitted.

"But if this other faction has taken charge," Metcalfe observed, "then things may change. Writers may actually come face to face with Joe Public."

"Not so sure about that," Collins replied dubiously. "Apparently the London faction hi-jacked a committee meeting when a couple of the other tribe didn't show up and took the decision to switch the venue. The others were hopping mad when they found out, but were too late to change it because the booking had already been made and the notices had gone out."

"Goodness," Caroline exclaimed. "It sounds like something out of *Mapp and Lucia*, doesn't it? Warring factions and all that."

"It reminds me of that scene in *Gaudy Night*, actually," Willis said. "It's when Harriett says something like 'I'll tell any lie you like except to say that someone's beastly book is good when it isn't.' Do you remember? It sounds rather as if that's what this convention may be all about."

"Well," Collins said uncomfortably, "let's hope it doesn't come to that."

He gazed at her fondly nonetheless. The personae of Lord Peter Wimsey and Harriett Vane had always been part of their private world, to the extent that Peter frequently referred to Karen as 'Harriett' in conversation. Just once, though, during a previous investigation, what had always been a comforting fiction had threatened to intrude more dangerously on reality, and on Peter's mental health in particular.

"Weren't you writing something, Simon?" he asked. "Apart from your report on your last case, I mean."

"Still am," Collison said with a grimace. "I'm doing it with a chum of mine who teaches at business school. Not much fun, actually. Loads of stuff about span of control and organisational efficiencies. But hopefully when it's finished it'll be the sort of thing the Met are looking for."

"What's it about, exactly?" a curious Metcalfe enquired.

"Well, it was you who gave me the idea actually, Bob. Do you remember telling me about that management consultancy report the Met commissioned a few years back? Well, it seems pretty obvious to me that they didn't like its conclusions at all, because it's all been quietly shelved and never heard of again. I've got hold of it and I'm basically doing a hatchet job on it, but loaded up with all sorts of business school jargon."

"So, if you haven't finished it yet then you won't have come to any conclusions?" Metcalfe enquired.

Collison looked at him affectionately.

"Don't be silly, Bob. You start with the conclusions and then work backwards. Every management consultant knows that."

"I really don't understand why the Met had to spend so much taxpayers' money on a report like that," Caroline said as she laid down her knife and fork. "Somebody once told me that a management consultant is someone who borrows your watch to tell you what time it is."

"And then forgets to give it back, perhaps ...?" Willis suggested.

CHAPTER 2

Ann Durham eased herself into the armchair in her hotel room and noticed with distaste that the furniture at such establishments seemed to be growing narrower with each passing year. She rubbed her feet together with little jerky movements until she had succeeded in dislodging her shoes. They were expensive, which was all well and good, but new, which was not, for they were already hurting her. Thank goodness she had brought an older, less aggressive pair with her in her monogrammed designer luggage (aubergine, with the distinctive design of a brand which is often offered less convincingly on beaches in Thailand).

As she tried to settle her substantial thighs more comfortably within the restrictive confines of the chair, she considered her situation, and as she did so a scowl played across her face. It would be chivalrous to record that she had a face which looked as though it and scowls were generally strangers, but quite untrue. On the contrary, the tight line of her pursed lips hinted at the personality of a woman who was perpetually displeased with the actions of others, and not slow in making such feelings known.

The scowl was, however, for once not entirely unjustified, for the circumstances in which she found herself were indeed disagreeable. The doyenne of English crime fiction, a woman whose books had been adapted many times for television and translated into many different languages, she saw her position of natural leadership within the writing profession as being quite naturally accepted without question. Yet suddenly in place of servile acquiescence she found resistance, and even outright rebellion. Where once her wise and gracious leadership had been praised and welcomed, she now heard defiant whispers using ugly, unkind words such as 'tyranny' and 'dictatorship'.

Her mistake, of course, had been in not attending the final meeting of the organising committee, though at the time it had hardly seemed necessary. As Chair of the Crime Writers' Association (a role she had filled for many years) as well as every similar body, she was accustomed to her wishes, once made known, being accepted without question. Her presence in person should not have been required. Yet in the event some she had thought to be her friends, or at least compliant sycophants which was surely much the same thing, had seized the opportunity to rebel while the remainder had proved unequal to the task of facing down the opposition, as she would undoubtedly have done herself had she only been present, and able to enforce her implacable will.

Really, she thought, as though she didn't already have quite enough problems to worry about!

It was such a small point, they had pleaded with her afterwards, trying to justify their betrayal. A simple change of venue, and a decision which had been forced upon them anyway by the unexpected availability of the usual hotel in Bristol. Yet she saw it for what it undoubtedly was: the thin end of the wedge. The inflicting of what was as yet the smallest of cracks in the deepest foundation of her rule, but one which left unchecked would surely spread and risk undoing everything for which she had worked for so long.

Already it had begun. With the change of venue had come a sudden realisation (or at least, that is how it had been presented) that the rooms housing the sessions were larger than had been the case for all those years in Bristol, thus both justifying and necessitating the promotion of the convention to the public at large. She shuddered at the thought. The paying public were of course a tiresome necessity for any provider of goods or services and they were all very well in their place, but that place was in their homes reading her books or watching her television programmes, not thronging the halls of a writers' conference. When she met them at Book Festivals it was hardly a meeting at all in the true sense of the word, simply an hour or so of pre-arranged questions, all phrased so as to allow her to bring out, with all due modesty, her overall wonderfulness, followed by signing books for a gratifyingly lengthy queue of supplicants. The whole point of having had a sensible person like herself in charge of the arrangements year after year had been to avoid exactly this sort of situation; the horror of distinguished writers having to rub shoulders with the hoi polloi – and for three days, no less.

Now there were rumours of an election being held for the post she had held as of right for so long. While publicly she refused even to acknowledge the existence of such deranged fantasies (a stance which was assisted by no interviewer having as yet been so brave as to broach the subject), privately she felt intense irritation and a small but growing sense of foreboding.

While it was of course quite ridiculous that she should be forced into an election for a post which nobody could possibly fulfil anything like as well as she could, given her experience, expertise and warm personal skills, there was always the possibility that such an eventuality might indeed occur. While it was equally ridiculous that anyone might prefer her likely challenger (Tom Smythe – a pretentious little man whom she knew for certain had changed his name from Smith), there was always the chance that collective insanity might strike detective authors as a whole; already she was hearing blandishments such as 'time for a change', and 'a new approach'.

She snorted aloud at the thought of the creator of that dull little Inspector Naesby in Lewes, who plied his uninspiring trade among the antiques dealers of East Sussex, being elevated to a position so far beyond his abilities, to the ultimate detriment of the entire crime writing fraternity. Surely such an outcome was impossible? And yet ....

With a tut of exasperation she resolved to put on her comfortable shoes and head downstairs to stiffen morale among her supporters.

"A little touch of Harry in the night," she murmured purposefully.

At about the same time, Peter Collins was heading into the hotel, somewhat diffidently, since he was still getting used to the idea of being a writer, and this was his first formal outing as such. He introduced himself at the check-in desk and there was a gratifying little buzz of excitement as a plump and jolly young lady said 'oh yes, you're a speaker, aren't you?', found his name badge (a different colour to those on the main registration table, he noted) from a separate cache to the side, and escorted him across the crowded lobby of the hotel; she seemed almost to shoulder people aside as she did so, but perhaps she was just nimbler on her feet than might be expected, Peter mused. Suddenly he felt like a frail craft following in the wake of an ice-breaker. She broke free from the crowd and headed up a flight of stairs, sending a non-stop stream of loud conversational gambits over her shoulder as she did so.

On the first floor, Peter was led through a dazzling collection of books displayed for sale on trestle tables to a separate room which had a handwritten 'Speakers' Room' (with an apostrophe correctly employed, he noted approvingly) sign sellotaped beside the door.

"You can come here anytime," the girl hooted, now a little breathlessly after having combined climbing the stairs with constant chatter. "Now, I'm not sure if there's anyone ... oh, yes, look!"

She seized him by the arm and propelled him across

the room with surprising strength towards a rather imposing individual dressed in a three-piece suit cut from dark blue pinstripe, a gold watch chain stretched across his rather ample midriff. Given that everyone else in the throng through which he had just been led was very badly dressed (even by the standards of writers, as he would come to realise as he got to know the breed better), to say that he stood out would be an understatement. He had the air of an old style stockbroker come to advise on the family trust fund.

"Peter, this is Tom Smythe," she said. "Tom, this is Peter Collins. Can I leave you two to get to know each other? I really ought to get back to the desk. Gosh, we've never had a crowd like this before."

Without waiting for an answer she strode from the room. Peter just had time enough to notice that she was wearing a name badge which said "Fiona". He and the other man shook hands in that friendly but wary fashion which writers tend to employ before they have worked out whether you are a competitor or not.

"Can I offer you a coffee?" Smythe enquired, gesturing towards the refreshment table.

Collins's glance took in some plastic cups and a thermos flask, and he declined as graciously as possible.

"This your first time?" Smythe asked.

"Yes, my first time at any book festival, in fact. As a speaker, that is. Obviously I've been in the audience at quite a few, particularly crime ones."

"Ah, new to the game, eh?" Smythe observed cautiously. "What sort of stuff do you write, then?"

"I've written a book about poisonings, in fiction and real life," Collins explained, "but it hasn't actually been published yet, so I feel a bit of a fraud, actually."

Now that Smythe had established that he was in the presence of a creator of non-fiction, the atmosphere thawed considerably.

"Oh, my dear chap," he said expansively, "you don't need to worry about that. Why, there are people here who haven't had anything published for years. If you're a fraud, what does that make them?"

He laughed in a light, whinnying fashion.

Before Collins could think of anything to say in reply, his arm was grabbed, this time by Smythe.

"But whatever you do," he hissed conspiratorially, leaning closer, "don't refer to it as a book festival. Not if the old trout's around, anyway. As far as she's concerned, and so far as we are for public consumption, it's a writers' convention."

"Oh," Collins said, moving back instinctively and noting with relief that Smythe let go of his arm as he did so.

"What's the difference?" he asked disingenuously, for he understood all too well.

"The public, of course, old boy. At a writers' convention you're just talking to other writers, most of whom are jealous as hell of you anyway, because you're successful enough to be up on stage while they're not. It's just an ego-massaging exercise, with everyone saying how marvellous everyone else is. God knows why, because it's obvious that nobody means it."

"I see," Collins replied. "And a book festival?"

"Ah," Smythe said appreciatively, rubbing his hands together, "now you're talking, old man. The reading public. Lots of punters who've read your books – or just some of them, hopefully – and some of whom will actually buy some afterwards and queue up for you to sign them. That's all writers care about, you know, or should be anyway; selling books. Everything else is just an irrelevance, a distraction."

"Oh," Collins said, feeling it a somewhat lame response, "and who's this old trout you mentioned?"

"Queen Ann, of course. Ann Durham."

"Oh, Ann Durham," Collins enthused. "I'm a great fan of her Inspector Bergmann books. Vienna between the wars is such a marvellous setting, don't you think? An inspired choice, really."

"They're all right if you like that sort of thing, I suppose," Smythe said dismissively, "but what's she done recently? If you ask me, they were just a flash in the pan."

"She wrote six, didn't she?" Collins demurred. "Hardly a flash in the pan, surely? And they were all adapted for television."

"So were mine," Smythe said bluntly, "and I'm still churning them out, though God knows it gets harder and harder with each successive bloody book. But the last Bergmann book was published – what, twenty years ago? More?"

"More, I think," Collins conceded. "Of course she's written some other stuff since, but I have to concede that none of it was nearly as good."

While he was making this last remark he was thinking furiously about who this Tom Smythe might be, for surely from what he had said he was expecting Collins to know for exactly which televisions series, and thus which books, he was responsible. This might generally have been a safe bet, but in Collins he had encountered, though he did not know it, a man who watched little television and read almost no contemporary crime fiction.

Fortunately, Smythe was warming to another theme.

"On the subject of the old trout, I should mark your card, old boy," he said. "It seems like there's finally going to be an election for the post of Chair. Ma Durham grabbed it some time back and since then has somehow always managed to persuade the committee by sheer bloody force of will not to hold an election but simply to confirm her in the post for the coming year."

"Not really relevant to me, I'm afraid," Collins said quickly, for he hated anything that smacked even slightly of politics, "I'm only an associate member, so I'm not eligible to vote."

Smythe was however not so easily deterred.

"When's your book due out?" he demanded.

"In a few weeks," Collins admitted reluctantly.

"Well, you're OK then," Smythe purred. "Your associate membership automatically transitions to full membership on the publication date, and the vote won't be a for a month or two yet."

"Who else is standing?" Collins asked.

"Nobody officially at the moment because the election hasn't been called by the committee, but I don't mind admitting that I will be throwing my hat into the ring. I'm sort of the senior man as it were once you take Durham out of the equation."

"And how would you propose to do that, Tom dear?" enquired Ann Durham who had joined the group unannounced and unnoticed. "Murder, perhaps?"

CHAPTER 3

"So what happened then?" Willis asked, intrigued.

"Well, it really was the most amazing thing," Collins marvelled. "Just for a moment the most extraordinary expression flashed across his face. I've been trying to place it ever since. Dislike, certainly, but something stronger and darker."

"Hatred, you mean?"

"I've been trying to avoid that conclusion, but yes. There was something else as well. The way he jumped when she said 'murder' almost seemed as if he was giving a guilty start. As though he *could* quite cheerfully murder her, and perhaps had even contemplated doing it."

"Oh, Peter, surely you're being fanciful?" she remonstrated. "Just because crime authors write about murder all the time doesn't mean they actually go around doing it – and certainly not to each other."

"Oh, I don't know," Metcalfe said cheerily as he came into the living room with a bottle of beer, "don't they say 'write about what you know'? Perhaps all crime writers have to commit a few murders, yes and get away with them too, as a sort of apprenticeship before they're allowed to join the Association."

"Idiot," Willis said calmly as she moved up the sofa to make room for him.

"Perhaps the guilty start," she went on, gazing at Metcalfe with mild disapproval as he drank out of the bottle, "was simply because he was conspiring against her with you behind her back and got caught out. What could be more natural?"

"Yes, I suppose so," Collins murmured vaguely. "I hope she doesn't think that, by the way. I have absolutely no wish to get involved in this beastly affair."

"Why is it such a big deal?" Metcalfe asked, carefully putting his beer bottle down on a coaster with a wary glance at Willis. "It's just some writers' thing, isn't it? A bit like the Rotary or a golf club. Hardly something worth killing over, I'd have thought."

"Of course, Bob, of course," Collins concurred. "It's just that within a closed community these things can get blown out of all proportion. In this case, I think what's happened is that this Durham woman has lorded it over everyone else for so long that it's been like having the lid of a pressure cooker screwed down ever more tightly, so that when the inevitable explosion happens it's likely to be much worse than it need have been."

"Has she really been so awful?" Willis enquired. "Strange, I always thought of her as a nice person, but I suppose that's just the part of me talking that's a fan of Inspector Bergmann."

"As are we all, of course. As to being awful, I don't know

because I wasn't there, but I did detect a really unpleasant atmosphere all day."

"Perhaps that's just the natural feeling of writers being bitchy to each other," Metcalfe ventured with a grin.

"About each other, possibly," Collins corrected him. "I didn't detect any open unpleasantness. Actually most of the ordinary writers I met today were very supportive of each other – it's a tough old job, you know. But there certainly seem to be two rival factions, one for Durham and one against her, and I spoke to a lot of people who think the game's up and that she should resign rather than risk being humiliated – as she would see it anyway – in an election."

"Would she really be so very upset?" Metcalfe persisted. "It's only a job title, after all."

"I don't really know the woman," Collins replied. "I only met her today for the first time, after all. But I get the impression that she really does believe that she has some sort of natural right to speak for the whole profession. Apparently a few years back she tried to get the committee to appoint her Chair for life, but she couldn't quite get it through, and her power base has slipped a bit since then so she's never tried again."

He took a ruminative sip of gin and tonic and then went on.

"The other thing to understand is that she doesn't handle dissent very well, at least not from what I hear. She sees anyone who disagrees with her as a traitor trying to stab her in the back. So I think any sort of dialogue to persuade her to step down would probably be doomed to failure."

"Ah, well," Metcalfe suggested cheerfully, "perhaps someone really will murder her then, and you'll be on hand to solve the crime."

"Indeed," Collins replied, playing along. "I shall have to be sure to wear my Lord Peter Wimsey Prince of Wales check."

"Although," he added dubiously, "perhaps that might not be such a good idea. Nobody there seems to take their appearance very seriously – apart from that Tom Smythe chap, of course."

"Who's he?" Willis asked. "The name's familiar, but I can't quite place him."

"I'm glad you asked that. I had no idea either. Then the *grande dame* weighed in and mentioned Lewes in Sussex, and that rang a bell. Wasn't there some awful television series a while back set in Lewes, with some police inspector or other investigating bumped off antiques dealers, and grappling with over-sexed provincial housewives?"

"Inspector Naesby, that must be," Metcalfe informed him. "No worse than any of them, I suppose, but not exactly true to life. I mean, what are the odds of a different occupant of a small place like Lewes getting bumped off each week?"

He finished his beer.

"Furthermore," he said thoughtfully, "speaking as a police inspector I have to say that I have never yet been assaulted in the course of my duties by an over-sexed housewife. I live in hope, of course."

"Perhaps just a jacket with an open shirt, Peter darling?" Willis proffered, ignoring Metcalfe's observation.

"With a cravat, you mean? Yes, possibly, but I'm not sure. I'm afraid I've already made a bit of an ass of myself on that front?"

"What do you mean?" Willis asked worriedly.

"Well, I saw that some homeless chap had wandered in off the street, so I went and reported him to security, but when they came to throw him out it turned out he was actually quite a well-known Scottish crime writer. All a bit embarrassing as you can imagine, particularly as when he told me his name he guessed I'd never heard of him."

"Oh, Peter," Willis said as she and Metcalfe subsided into giggles, "you are priceless. Who was he?"

"Some chap called Chris Campbell, apparently."

"Oh, Peter, surely you know who he is? He wrote the books they turned into that series with a Glaswegian detective. We tried to watch it on DVD a while back, don't you remember?"

"Ah, yes, I think so."

"Why did you say 'tried'?" Metcalfe asked, intrigued.

"Well, we couldn't understand a word anyone was saying," Collins explained. "Really, I do think these Scottish series should come with subtitles, don't you?"

"Did you suggest that to him?" Metcalfe asked mischievously.

"No," Collins replied slowly. "As a matter of fact the conversation didn't really develop very much. I suppose you can see things from his point of view, though. After all, I had just tried to have him thrown out of the hotel."

"Oh, my Lord," Willis ejaculated weakly, having started laughing again, "but he must have said *something*, Peter."

"Not really. He just looked me up and down very strangely and then he said 'what are you doing here?'. So obviously I started telling him about my book, but he wandered off in the middle, while I was still talking. Rather rude, I thought, but there you are."

Willis tried to wipe her eyes as carefully as possible so as not to disturb any make-up.

"Oh dear, Peter, you are a pet," she said as she recovered.

"There's a Gala dinner on Saturday evening, you know," he reminded her. "You are coming with me, aren't you?"

"Yes, of course, it's in my diary."

"It says 'dress optional'," Collins said wonderingly. "What on earth do you think that means?"

"I would imagine that it means what it says," Willis replied, "but it is rather odd, I grant you. I should wear a dark suit if I were you. That's probably safest."

"Now," she went on briskly, "I'm glad you're both here because there's something I want you both to advise me on."

She crossed the room and sat down in an armchair, facing them both.

"These last few months," she began, "while we were all trying to sort ourselves out, well it brought it home to me how I didn't really have anyone I could talk to about things."

"Another woman, I mean of course," she added quickly

as they both started to look offended. "As you know, I ended up talking to Caroline Collinson and I felt really guilty about unloading all my troubles on her, awkward too. After all, I hardly know her."

"I think I know what's coming," Metcalfe observed quietly. "We've talked about this before."

"Yes, we have," she nodded, "but I've never been able to come to any real decision."

"You're talking about your mother, I take it?" Collins commented.

He knew that Willis had been adopted as a child as indeed, by a huge coincidence, had Metcalfe. He often wondered whether the resulting emotional confusion they had both felt had been part of the attraction they felt for each other. Neither had ever made any effort to contact their natural mothers. Metcalfe had gone no further than discovering that his lived in Peterborough. In respect of hers, Willis had discovered both her location (London) and her name (Susan Weedon).

"Yes. I was quite close to asking to meet her once upon a time, when I was at university. I even carried her name around with me for months, as though having it in my handbag would somehow help me to decide. In the end I chose not to, as you both know, but these last few months have made me wonder if I did the right thing."

She gazed at them both nervously. They shifted uneasily. Metcalfe wished he had another beer to hand. At least it would have given him something to toy with. Instead, he found himself self-consciously clasping his hands in his lap.

"I really don't see that you can ask us to advise you on this, my darling," Collins said gently at last. "Surely it's a decision that only you can make. Of course Bob may feel differently, but at least he has some context to work with, being in the same position."

"Not really in the same position," Metcalfe said awkwardly. "I always had a perfectly good relationship with my adoptive mother, even though her own marriage broke up while I was with her. I've never felt the need to establish contact with my real mother, but then I do see that the mother daughter relationship is a special one, and I can understand the feeling that you need another woman to talk to about things."

"But aren't you curious about why she felt the need to give you up, give you away to strangers?" Willis asked.

"No, not really," he said carefully. "I've always assumed that she must have had her reasons. Maybe she just believed that other people could give me a better life, a better upbringing if you like, than she could. If so, she was almost certainly right. As I said, I've no complaints at all about how things turned out."

"Nor do I," she countered quickly. "Please don't think that. My parents are lovely. They're warm and they're genuine and sincere, and they love me. But I could never have this conversation – the sort of conversation I needed to have with Caroline – with my mother. It would simply be beyond her comprehension. She's a very open, straightforward woman. She simply wouldn't be able to get her head around the concept of a woman being in love with two different men at the same time."

They both sat, listening.

"In fact, if you must know, it was largely for their sake that I decided not to make contact with my real mother," she went on. "I thought they'd feel hurt that I wanted to find her after everything they'd done for me. I realise now I was wrong about that. I'm sure they'd have been very understanding. They always have been, about everything."

There was another silence in which the ticking of the grandfather clock in the hall suddenly sounded very loud. Collins cleared his throat softly.

"How do you know," he enquired cautiously, "that your real mother would be able to help you? You say you couldn't have this conversation with a woman you've known for years and who brought you up, so what makes you think that things might be different with someone who would be a total stranger to you?"

"I know, I know," Willis muttered, suddenly looking very young and very troubled.

"I know she's your mother, and I'm sure there might be some sort of natural emotional bond because of that," Collins persisted, "but there again, there might not. Have you considered that? She might not be as you imagine her at all. Not a more approachable version of the nice middle class woman who brought you up, but something else entirely.

You might just be idealising your vision of her because of who she is: your mother."

Metcalfe gazed at her anxiously.

"I have to agree with Peter, darling," he ventured at last. "You do risk upsetting yourself, you know."

"But equally," Collins cut in quickly, "nobody can make this decision for you, Karen. If you feel an emotional need to do this, then weigh that very carefully because none of us can fight our emotions indefinitely. And Bob and I will support you whatever you decide."

"Absolutely," Metcalfe confirmed.

"But one last point you should consider," Collins said, "is that you need to be very honest with yourself, Karen. To what extent do you want to do this because you're feeling some sort of emotional void which you think your mother could fill, and to what extent because you're just curious about why she gave you up for adoption?"

"I do wish you could tell me what I should do," she said in a lost little voice.

"I think you should put your feet up on the sofa for a few minutes," Collins said briskly as he stood up, "while Bob gets the Serrano ham and some fresh bread from the kitchen, and I open a bottle of Puligny Montrachet."

CHAPTER 4

The next day found Peter Collins deep in conversation with Ann Durham n the speakers' room as they waited for his panel, which she was chairing.

"I hear you're actually involved with the police, Mr Collins?" she queried languidly as a woman, whom the softly rounded Fiona had earlier pointed out to him as Ann Durham's agent, handed her client a cup of something fragrantly steaming and a saucer of lemon slices, one of which the distinguished crimewriter added to the brew with a cocktail stick.

"It's Dr Collins, actually," Peter said diffidently, "and yes, but not really. I've been consulted as a psychologist once or twice, that's all."

"A profiler, why how thrilling!" Ms Durham marvelled and then, as though struck by a sudden thought, "and what a great idea for a crime series, to see how a profiler interacts with the police."

The trimly elegant lady with a saucer of lemon slices bent forward and whispered discreetly in her ear. Quite inconsequentially, Collins remembered Fiona telling him that Ann Durham's party was a large one, consisting not just of her agent but also of her daughter, and the daughter's boyfriend.

"There again, perhaps not," she went on. "Darling Angela tells me it's already been done. You must forgive me, Dr Collins; I read very little modern crime fiction. Oh, Angela Hughes, my agent, by the way. Angela, this is Mr Collins, oh, Dr Collins I should say."

"Peter, please," Collins said, standing to shake hands and noticing that she had a round, doll-like face and very dark eyes. "May I take that for you?"

He carefully relieved her of the saucer of lemon and returned it to the refreshment table.

"I'm really so glad to get a chance to meet you, Miss Durham," he ventured as he came back. "I've always been a huge fan of your work. Why, it reads almost like serious fiction and you capture the scene and the era so perfectly."

"Thank you, Peter," she acknowledged graciously, nonetheless conveying the unmistakable impression of someone who has occasion to collect many compliments a day. "And you must call me Ann, of course."

"Vienna between the wars has always been a special interest of mine," he informed her. "One of the many things I admire about your work is the way you manage to populate the books with real life characters: Zweig, Polgar, Altenburg ... In fact, speaking of real life characters, didn't you yourself have Sigmund Freud being consulted by Inspector Bergmann on a series of sex murders?"

"Do you know, I believe I did," she replied. "Dear me, what a long time ago it all seems."

"But how did you do it?" Peter asked her. "All that detail?

And the way you have historical events like the Anschluss playing out as the backdrop to your stories. You must have had to do an immense amount of research."

"Ah yes, but you do, you see," she said. "If you're going to convince a reader to suspend their disbelief then you owe it to them to get all the little details right. If you don't, then they will sense it somehow, and you risk losing them."

"Yes, that's what Sayers said, isn't it?" Collins said eagerly.

Ann Durham looked for a moment as though she was contemplating suggesting that Dorothy L. Sayers might have garnered the idea from her, rather than the other way round. If so, she resisted the temptation.

"Yes, indeed. I believe she said something very similar," she acknowledged, and sank her heavily rouged lips towards the surface of her tisane.

"But the really amazing thing is just how quickly you must have been able to do your research," Collins continued. "Let's see, you published – what? Six in seven years? Why, it takes most writers at least a year just to write the book itself, judging by what I've heard here at the convention so far. Yet you managed not only to write the book, but do all the research as well."

"Well, yes, it was a lot of hard work – late nights and weekends, you know – but I hope I've never been afraid of hard work," Ann Durham replied.

"Actually," she went on after another sip of her drink, "it wasn't as difficult as you think. You see, I grew up around Swiss Cottage and Belsize Park and a lot of my parents' neighbours had actually lived through Vienna in the twenties and thirties. They were the lucky ones, of course, the ones who got out in time. There used to be a café on the Finchley Road – the Cosmo I think it was – which was like a Viennese café home from home. I used to have cakes in there with my mother and listen to all the stories. I'd make a mental note of things and then go to the library later and look them up."

"Remarkable," Collins said. "Now tell me, Ann, why did you never write any more? It must be twenty years or more since the last one was published."

"Probably precisely because they were such hard work," she replied with a smile. "Oh, I don't know, why does one suddenly not feel able to continue with a series? I just felt written out, somehow. I actually took a complete break for a couple of years, although by then the TV series was starting, of course."

"I suppose a lot of people thought they had come to a natural conclusion anyway," Collins proffered. "Someone committing suicide by throwing himself out of window must have been a tough act to follow, in narrative terms."

"It did have an air of finality about it, yes," Ann Durham said drily.

"Well, personally I was disappointed," Collins confessed. "I would have been very interested to see how Bergmann got on under the Nazis, particularly in view of that intriguing hint towards the end that he himself might be Jewish."

"Well, as I said, it was a long time ago – why hello, Miss Marple."

Collins looked up, startled, and rose to his feet to greet a woman who was indeed the epitome of Miss Marple, looking demure but slightly scatty in a long tweed skirt and sensible shoes.

"Peter, this is Gillian, who as I'm sure you know has played the part of Miss Marple on television for ... well, I'm not sure exactly, but many years anyway."

"May I fetch you some tea?" Collins asked at once.

The apparition settled herself neatly into an armchair, her handbag clutched on her knees.

"Thank you," she said calmly in an instantly recognisable voice. "Tea would be most pleasant; with milk but no sugar, please."

As Collins crossed back to the refreshment table he became conscious of a sudden waft of perfume as Angela Hughes arrived beside him as smoothly and serenely as if she were moving on wheels.

"Did you recognise her?" she asked.

"Yes, of course, though I don't really watch the programmes that much."

"Since you've never met her before," she said, "I thought I'd better mark your card. She's highly eccentric. You know those melodramas about actors who play a role so often that they become it? Well, that's her. She insists on being referred to only as Miss Marple. I believe she may even have changed her name by deed poll to Jane Marple, but her agent's rather coy on the subject."

"Do you know," Collins said thoughtfully, "until I came

to this convention I used to think that I was eccentric, but now I'm not so sure."

Angela Hughes laughed softly but warmly and as she passed him the milk her hand brushed his; just for a split second she seemed to gaze deeply into his eyes. As she left him to go back to the seated group he felt momentarily rather confused; he wondered if it was the perfume.

"Miss Marple is on our panel," Ann Durham explained as he joined them and handed Miss Marple her tea.

"Excellent," he answered, wondering exactly how he might continue the conversation.

Should he treat her as though she actually *was* Miss Marple? Angela had given no clear indication on the point.

"Of course, Christie was something of an expert on poisons," he ventured, hoping that Miss Marple would not be offended by such an informal reference to her creator.

"Oh, my dear boy," Miss Marple said warmly, "of course she was. Why I once actually handled her copy of 'Martindale' – the drugs book, you know – and pretty battered it was too. She obviously used it a lot."

"What's your favourite one – poison I mean?" asked Collins.

"I'm really not sure that it is appropriate to talk about having a favourite poison," Miss Marple admonished him gently but firmly. "They're dreadful things."

"You must forgive we writers, Miss Marple," Ann Durham said gaily. "we can be very irreverent about such things. I happen to know that Peter here has identified many poisons which Dame Agatha used over the years. He's probably just intrigued to know what you thought of them."

"Yes, that's it of course," Collins said gratefully. "The most common one is probably cyanide, I think. Ngaio Marsh uses it as well."

"And I just happen to have some!" Ann Durham declared triumphantly.

"Or, at least, Angela has some to give me," she went on less dramatically as they both stared at her.

Angela Hughes carefully extracted a very small bottle of clear liquid from her handbag and passed it to her.

"Isn't it exciting?" Ann Durham enthused as she very gingerly removed the top of the bottle. "I've written about it so often, but I've never actually come across it in the flesh, as it were. I thought it would be great fun actually to produce it at the panel; like an exhibit in court, you know."

"But where did you get it?" Collins asked in amazement. "And isn't it terribly dangerous carrying it around like that?"

"No, not really," Angela Hughes said in a brisk, no nonsense sort of way, "not unless you're planning to swallow some, that is, and I really wouldn't recommend that. A few drops would be fatal almost instantly. It's what they used in suicide pills during the War."

Very delicately, Ann Durham finished removing the tightly twisted cap. She held out the unopened bottle and Collins caught at once the unmistakeable smell of almonds which he had read about so often. Miss Marple, who must have smelt it too, recoiled in disgust and shook her head vigorously.

"Put it away, do," she enjoined. "It isn't the sort of thing to be playing around with. Really, Ann, I am surprised at you."

Ann Durham raised the bottle to her own nose and frowned slightly. Then she shrugged and obeyed Miss Marple's strictures. Safely fastened once more, the bottle was placed carefully beside her papers.

"Two minutes, Miss Durham," someone called from the door.

She glanced at her watch in irritation.

"Where has that wretched man got to?" she tutted.

Collins knew that she must be referring to Tom Smythe, whom he noted from the convention brochure was also due to take part on the poisons panel. He glanced around the room and just as he did so Smythe came hurrying into the room.

"I'm so sorry, everyone," he said rather breathlessly. "I got caught up talking to some fans and I didn't realise how late it was getting."

He glanced nervously at Ann Durham. It seemed to Collins that there was almost something pleading about his expression. It's almost as if he's frightened of her, he thought. I wonder what that's all about?

Ann Durham gathered her papers and her bottle of liquid death and rose majestically to her feet.

"Well, now that we're all here," she said, with a significant glance of disapproval at Smythe, "perhaps we should go through."

Collins stood back to allow the women to go ahead, but Angela Hughes smiled and shook her head, squeezing his arm gently.

"You're very kind, but please go ahead. I'm in the audience so I'm going in through that door over there."

She nodded towards a double door on the other side of the first floor lobby which was propped open. Next to it a middle aged man with a pink and orange scarf looped around his neck with stylish nonchalance was signing books for a queue which seemed to consist almost entirely of women of a certain age. Collins recognised him dimly as a writer from an earlier session.

Angela Hughes walked away from him across the open area and there was something about the trim elegance of her carriage in her heels and close-fitting trouser suit that reminded him of Karen Willis. As if sensing his eyes upon her, she suddenly glanced back at him, grinned, and pointed towards the others, who were by now well ahead of him and already entering the room through the single door reserved for speakers.

He felt himself blushing slightly and hurried after them. He realised as he did so that she had never answered his query as to where she had come by the bottle of cyanide. It really was a very odd thing for an elegant professional woman suddenly to produce from the handbag. Where on earth had she procured it? You could hardly just walk into a chemist's shop and ask for it.

A helper was just about to close the speakers' door, but

he was just in time to slide through with an apologetic smile. The others were already seated but he saw there was an empty chair with his name placed in front of it and he hurried to take his place.

"Hello, everybody," Ann Durham said suddenly, her amplified voice booming slightly harshly in the crowded room and generating a quick squeal of feedback.

She frowned imperiously at the sound engineer and he hastened to make the necessary adjustment.

"Now," she continued, her voice sounding more normal, "for the next hour or so we're going to be talking poison."

The room was suddenly hushed as everyone sat up straight with that look of intense concentration that is to be found only in a group of crime fiction readers anticipating a stimulating session on toxicology.

CHAPTER 5

"You're going to be late, aren't you?" Caroline Collison asked her husband.

"I've nothing much to be late for," he replied. "I did all my paperwork yesterday and I don't have any committee meetings or anything like that. SIOs are deliberately kept clear of routine admin work, you know."

"So you're ready to spring into action at the drop of a hat, you mean? The phone call in the middle of the night, and the Rover waiting in the street with its blue light flashing?"

"Hm, that's all a bit John Creasey, isn't it?"

"Actually I was thinking of Commander Gideon," she said. "Wasn't that J.J. Marric?"

"Marric and Creasey were one and the same," Collison explained, finding himself in the highly unusual position of being able to correct his wife about anything. "He used quite a few different pseudonyms I think."

"So you're just hanging around waiting for someone to stumble across a body somewhere in North West London, are you?" she asked, ignoring the rectification.

"Something like that, yes."

"A pity you can't be like one of those fictional detectives who attract murders wherever they go," she observed. "Why,

Miss Marple only had to pop out to a local flower show for the locals to start stabbing or poisoning each other."

"Sadly real life is rather more prosaic," he lamented. "Though perhaps Peter could develop the knack. After all, he does drift in and out of that Lord Peter Wimsey persona of his. Would it really be too much to ask that he provide the occasional body, rather than just a lot of Wimseyesque dialogue? I don't think so."

Caroline perched carefully on a kitchen stool. Her pregnancy, though still hardly noticeable externally, had reached a stage at which she had to think about when and how she moved.

"So life at Hampstead nick is not exactly popping with excitement, then?"

"Got it in one," Collison admitted. "I know it sounds a rotten thing to say, but I've got so used to being in and out of the Incident Room all day that a nick without a murder enquiry is starting to feel like ... well, a school with no pupils, perhaps, or a theatre without an audience."

"But surely that gives you lots of peace and quiet to get on with your paper, doesn't it? You did tell the ACC you had nearly finished it, you know."

"I told him I had nearly finished the research," Collinson said, the emphasis on the last word coming close to correcting her again. "I'm sure the ACC understands that actually writing the damn thing is a different business altogether."

"And so an ideal one to get started on while you have a quiet and largely empty police station to work in, surely?"

"Oh yes, I suppose so," he sighed. "I really don't know what's wrong with me, darling. I just feel really jaded somehow."

"I'm beginning to wonder," she said with mock solemnity, "whether an SIO without a murder to solve is rather like an alcoholic with an empty bottle."

"God, I hope not," Collison laughed. "But I see what you mean. Here I am positively twitching for some poor sod to get killed just because it would give me something to do."

"If you want something to do, there's always that back fence that needs mending," she pointed out.

"Do you know, you're right," Collison said. "I really should be going to work. Just think what a bad example it sets, sitting around here all day."

"Fine," she said, taking away his tea mug. "Then I'll see you this evening."

Karen Willis was waiting to see the Senior Clerk at the Family Division of the High Court in that fairy tale concoction of a building, the Royal Courts of Justice in the Strand. At least, that's what it said on the door of the room she was sitting outside. There was a double rank of chairs, one on either side of the wide corridor, which suggested that sometimes long queues formed, but just now there was only one other supplicant in waiting. With his bright tie and his pile of cardboard folders, he had the look of a solicitor's outdoor clerk, a species she had encountered frequently in the criminal courts, whose only interests usually turned out to be football, the location of the nearest pub and her legs. She sighed and crossed her legs; as if confirming her Sherlockian powers of observation and deduction, he gazed at them with unashamed admiration.

Without warning the door opened and a middle aged man whose tie was as subdued as the young man's was loud shepherded an unhappy looking woman down the corridor.

"Take the staircase to the left," he told her. "That's the quickest way back to the main entrance."

She scuttled away without any acknowledgement of these directions. He turned and caught sight of Willis, who was rising hesitantly from her chair. A brief expression of astonished delight, quickly suppressed, flashed across his face.

"Karen Willis?" he asked. "Do come in, please. I'm very sorry to have kept you. I'm afraid that lady overran her appointment dreadfully."

She felt his eyes upon her as he followed her into the room, and smiled slightly. As she quickly took in the bare room, paper-strewn desk and two severe upright chairs, her heart went out to someone who had to spend their entire working life in such conditions; it smacked of mental cruelty. She wondered how many times the poor man would ever encounter an attractive woman, elegantly dressed, in the course of a year in this office; not very often, surely. She was glad she had worn heels, though they were by no means her highest for someone had warned her of the labyrinth of stairways and corridors that made up what lawyers referred to as "the RCJ". After all, she was here to ask a favour, and if she could bring a brief ray of sunshine to the unbearably drab abode of he who had the power to grant it, then so be it.

"Do sit down, please," he said.

He went around to his side of the desk and sat down in his turn. He gazed at her legs while pretending not to, and failed in the attempt.

"Now," he said, taking a file from the top of a pile and opening it, "you're here to apply to see your adoption records."

"Yes, I am," she said. "I must admit that it was a bit of a shock to find out that I didn't have an automatic right to see them. After all, I already have my mother's name and address from my birth certificate."

"Had you been adopted in Scotland, you would have done," he said. "I'm not quite sure why things are different there – it's a different legal system, you know."

"Yes, I do know."

"Quite. Well, the birth certificate is a different matter. It's a matter of public record. But do bear in mind that it will only show the mother's name at the time, and that she may in any event have given a false one; lots of people do, unfortunately. Not so many today when things are a bit different, but even twenty-five years ago there could still be a bit of a stigma about having a child out of wedlock. So a lot of women, if they'd already decided to give the baby up for adoption, used to make it difficult for anyone to trace them afterwards."

"I see."

"But down here," he went on, "things are different. If you want to see your adoption records you have to apply to the court and someone – me in this case – has to decide whether to grant your request."

"To tell you the truth," he said, leaning towards her and glancing surreptitiously at her thighs, "I wish it were otherwise. Not very fair, is it, to expect some court official to play God and decide who should get a peek and who shouldn't?"

"No, it isn't," she replied sympathetically. "It must be awful for you."

"It is," he concurred, leaning back again.

"Aren't there any guidelines to help you?"

"There are, yes, but they're not always much good. Where it's a case like yours, of a child wishing to contact their natural mother we always veer towards granting the request unless there's some good reason not to."

"Such as?"

"Such as the mother having registered with the Adoption Register stating that she does not wish to be contacted."

"And has she done that?" Willis asked, feeling the quick butterfly of momentary panic.

"No, don't worry, she hasn't."

"There is something else, though," he said as she relaxed. "To be honest I'm not quite sure how to proceed."

"What is it?" she asked, suddenly nervous again.

He reflected for a moment and then appeared to come to a decision.

"I've read your file, of course. I had to in preparation for this meeting. Why don't I tell you what's in it, and we'll see if you can help make the decision for me?"

"All right."

She brushed the hair back from her face and sat forward expectantly, her hands clasped in her lap.

"As you would expect, there are copies of the forms which your adoptive parents signed when they took you on, and also of the one your natural mother signed giving you up. I don't think they would tell you anything you don't know already. The details your mother gives on the form are the same as she used for the birth certificate."

"I see."

"There is also a lot of background material on your adoptive parents. Obviously a lot of work is done before people are approved as suitable for adopting children. I must confess that I always find this aspect of things rather difficult. After all, strictly speaking it's nothing to do with the adoptee and could be seen as an invasion of privacy, but there you are. You have the legal right to see it all if you wish."

"I don't," she decided straightaway. "All I'm interested in is anything about my mother."

"Good," he said with a nod, "I do appreciate that. Now then, that leaves us with only one item, which is the Social Services report on your mother. Again, I'm minded to let you have a copy of this but I wanted to make sure first that you really do want to see it regardless of anything it might contain."

"Why, what's in it?"

"Well, it's difficult to answer that question without giving the game away, as it were. Let's just say that it doesn't paint a very pretty picture."

She thought for a moment, but only for a moment.

"I came here to get the truth," she replied determinedly. "So, what does it say?"

"You must read it for yourself of course," he said awkwardly, "but in brief in the considered opinion of the case officers your mother was a drug addict and almost certainly a prostitute. The one was necessary to fund the other, I suppose. A sad story."

"So there's no clue to my father's identity?"

"None at all, I'm afraid. The case officers asked, of course, but she said it had been a casual encounter and that she didn't know his name. Usually in cases like this that's a cover story, I'm afraid. More often than not the poor girl simply doesn't know which man it was."

"And there's been no contact since my adoption? She's never got in touch to try to trace me or contact me?"

"No. I'm sorry."

"And no indication of where I might be able to find her, then?" she asked glumly.

"No."

There was silence for a few moments.

"I hate to be a Jonah," the clerk said gently, "but given what we know of your mother's condition twenty-five years ago, it's quite possible that she's died and so whatever you do you're going to come up against a brick wall sooner or later. Drug addicts don't have much of a life expectancy, I'm afraid."

"Yes."

She thought again.

"I will take a copy of that report, if I may," she said.

"Certainly," the clerk said briskly.

He stood up, putting the report back into the file and tucking it under his arm.

"Usually you'd have to wait for it to be posted to you, but perhaps I could show you to the general office upstairs?" he suggested. "That way I could copy it while you wait and you can take it away with you?"

"That would be very kind," she acknowledged, with a smile that was intended to dazzle, and did.

He opened the door to his office. The young man with the files started to stand up expectantly.

"Oh yes, Mr ... er, ... yes," the clerk said, pausing for a moment. "You must forgive me but there is something urgent I have to attend to in the General Office. You won't mind waiting for a few minutes, I'm sure."

Without waiting for an answer he moved off, sweeping Willis along with him, her heels echoing loudly on the stone floor. At the end of the corridor they came to a narrow and steep staircase winding upwards in a clockwise direction. Her companion seemed to hang back at this point. She smiled at him again as he turned towards her.

"Shall I go first?" she asked politely.

"Oh, yes please," he said.

CHAPTER 6

"You're looking very smart," a friendly female voice murmured to Peter Collins as he stood idly on one side of the main hotel lobby.

Looking round, he discovered that it was Angela Hughes, her hair pinned neatly back as usual, though the waft of perfume, which he seemed to recognise on some subconscious level, should have been enough to identify her.

"Er, yes," he concurred uncertainly, "I wasn't really sure what to make of 'dress optional' on the dinner invitation."

"Neither was I," she said with a smile. "Do you think I'll do?"

She was wearing a dark blue evening trouser suit with a short bolero jacket, and as she twirled around playfully for his inspection the swell of her buttocks against the tight material was almost painfully attractive.

"You look wonderful," he said simply.

"Thank you," she replied, though the smile which accompanied her words seemed to lack something of its former brilliance.

"Do you have a minute?" she asked, moving close. "There's something I really wanted to ask your advice about."

"I'm waiting for someone," he informed her self-consciously.

Why did he suddenly feel awkward to be talking to her about another woman?

"Your wife?"

"No," he said quickly, perhaps too quickly. "Just my girlfriend. I'm not married."

"Can you slip away for a few minutes?"

"Not really," he said. "I told her I'd meet her here, so if I wander off she won't know where to find me."

"Don't you have your phone switched on?"

"I don't really have a mobile phone. Well, I mean I do, Karen made me get one, but it spends most of its time shut away in my chest of drawers switched off."

"Karen – she's your girlfriend, is she?"

"Er, yes."

Angela Hughes sighed, though whether it was with exasperation at meeting a man with no mobile phone or with irritation at the mention of another woman was unclear.

"We could talk here if you like," Collins suggested. "While I'm waiting."

Now it was Angela's turn to look uncomfortable.

"It's rather confidential," she said hesitantly, looking around to see who might be within earshot.

Then, as if resolving to make the best of a bad job, she took his arm, pushed him up against the wall, and stood very close indeed.

"It's Ann," she said quietly but intensely. "I think she's being blackmailed."

"Really? Are you sure?" was all Collins could think of uttering.

"Pretty sure, yes. There's something in her past that someone's found out about, and I think they're threatening to go public unless she does what they want. She's in a dreadful state, poor dear."

"Well," Collins said, thinking fast. "Why doesn't she just go to the police?"

She shook her head sadly.

"It's not as simple as that. This is something really serious. Not criminal necessarily, but pretty bad. Certainly not something she'd want to be made public as part of a police investigation."

"I'm sure they'd be very discreet," Collins protested.

She shook her head again, more determinedly this time.

"She doesn't want the police involved," she said emphatically. "I'm sure of that, or I'd go to them myself."

She glanced around again, nervously.

"Are you sure we can't go somewhere and speak privately, just for a few minutes?" she pleaded. "I really don't feel comfortable discussing this out here."

"Well, if you don't mind waiting for my – for Karen, we could discuss it with her. She's a police officer, actually."

"Good grief, no!" she hissed. "I told you: the police can't be involved. I only spoke to you because I thought you might be able to give me some advice in confidence. Poor Ann is at her wit's ends."

"I'd be happy to try," Collins assured her hurriedly, "and of course I'll keep it confidential if that's what you want, but it's difficult to know what to say without ... hello, here's Karen."

Like Peter Collins, Karen Willis had puzzled over the correct interpretation of 'dress optional'. She had eventually settled upon a strapless 1950s cocktail dress from her vintage collection. This left her shoulders completely bare and, perhaps partly because it had probably been designed for a shorter woman, ended significantly above the knee. The various people populating the lobby spontaneously fell silent and gazed at her as she crossed the floor towards him.

"Karen, darling, this is Angela Hughes," he said as she approached.

As Angela Hughes let go of Collins's arm with apparent reluctance, she gave what might charitably be described as a smile, but actually resembled a rather cold grimace. It was a look to which Willis had become accustomed.

"Hello," Willis said brightly, "aren't you Ann Durham's agent? Peter's told me all about you, haven't you, dear?"

"So glad you could come," the other woman replied.

Willis doubted that somehow. She had observed with some amusement just how close the two had been standing. Really, she thought, Peter is such a dear. How often he manages to bring out all a woman's maternal instincts, yet he never seems to notice a thing.

Now Fiona arrived and stood beside Collins. She too seemed less than overjoyed to meet Willis.

"Oh, I say, if you're all ready, would you mind if I took you through into the dining room? You're all on the top table, you see, and I'd like to get you seated. Don't worry, you can have a good chat in there while the others find their places."

As they followed her through the bar area towards an open double door, Willis noted with surprise that 'dress optional' had in many cases been interpreted as jeans, tee-shirt and trainers. As she pushed past one young man, who was sporting a backpack which he was presumably proposing to wear all the way into the dining room, she was assailed by a sudden unpleasant odour. Resolving to try to hold her breath until they were safely in the other room, she began to view more sympathetically Collins's confusion over the Scottish crime writer a few days previously. Then mercifully they found themselves in clearer air, albeit hemmed in by many tables, and she was finally able to breathe out and then inhale again.

Fiona led them steadily across the room. At times it was a tight fit as some of the table seemed very close together, and here and there things became completely obstructed as some earlybirds were already gathering and standing around their places, chatting in desultory fashion. So once or twice they had to reverse course and make a detour. They could see all too clearly why Fiona had wanted to get them seated well in advance. In ten minutes or so it might be almost impossible to make one's way across the room short of burrowing beneath the white table cloths and making the journey on one's hands and knees.

The 'top table' was distinguishable from the others in the room only in that it was set rather apart from the others, in front and to one side of them. Beside it there was another door, and Collins wondered briefly why Fiona had not made use of this to bring them to their places directly, but then spotted the 'Service Door: staff only' sign.

Having escorted them to the table, Fiona vanished back into the growing throng. Miss Marple and Tom Smythe were already present, standing together talking, and Collins introduced both to Willis. Wandering around the table and gazing idly at the name cards he saw that the other three attendees would be Ann Durham, Gina Durham, the daughter of whom he had heard but was yet to meet, and a Barry Carver, who was presumably Gina's boyfriend.

As the Durham party approached the table, Collins inspected with interest the young woman who must be Ann Durham's daughter. There was a resemblance sure enough, but it was much slighter than he might have supposed. Gina Durham was small and dark, and gave him an intense gaze as they were introduced.

"Oh, and Gina's boyfriend, Barry," Ann Durham said, seemingly almost as an afterthought.

There was some initial awkwardness. Collins was already aware of a coolness between Smythe and Durham but fancied that there was a distance also between her and Barry Carver;

either that, or the young man was just naturally reserved. He stood quietly next to Gina and seemed disinclined to say very much at all. Collins resolved to speak to the young couple.

"Were you at the poisons session?" he asked them.

"I was, yes," Gina said pleasantly. "You were on it with Mum, weren't you? I thought I recognised your face."

"How about you?" Collins asked Carver, since no spontaneous reply seemed to be forthcoming.

"No, I had something else to do," he replied.

"Something more interesting than poisons?" Collins enquired with mock surprise.

"Yes," came the curt reply.

"You must forgive him, Peter," Gina cut in easily. "This really isn't his sort of thing. Oh, gosh, I say, isn't that Tom Smythe? I hope he's not sitting anywhere near Mum, or things could get very frosty during dinner."

"I shouldn't worry about that," Collins reassured her with a smile. "Karen and I can separate them if they start trying to stab each other with their forks."

He looked around for Willis, seeking to draw her into the conversation, but she was deep in discussion with Ann Durham and Miss Marple, leaving Tom Smythe and Angela Hughes chatting a little awkwardly to one side.

"So do you write too?" Collins asked Gina.

"Oh no, nothing like that," she answered. "To tell the truth I don't really do anything at the moment. I just graduated from Uni and I'm taking a little break while I think about what I'd like to do. I'm thinking about teaching, but Mum's not too keen. She'd like me to go into PR or something like that, but I'm not sure it's my sort of thing."

"Now, what do you do?" she asked. "I know you write, or you wouldn't have been on Mum's panel, but –"

At this point there was a commotion behind them and the unmistakeable sound of breaking glass. Turning, they saw that a jug of water had been knocked off the table and now lay upended on the carpet tiled floor in a large puddle. Looking around for the broken glass – for the jug was still whole – Collins saw that two or three glasses had also been part of whatever accident had occurred. Curiously, he glanced at the table and saw that whoever's glasses they had been, Ann Durham had obviously not been affected for she had one in her hand.

"Oh dear," she said with a pout, as a waitress materialised from across the room with a fresh jug and placed it on the table while a space cleared quickly and with some embarrassment around the broken glass and the puddle on the floor.

"That was clumsy of you, Tom," she called out archly.

"It wasn't me," he protested, "or at least, I don't think so. Somebody knocked into me as they went past."

Ann Durham gave a little sneer of disbelief. It was not a very attractive sight, but what was about to happen was infinitely more unpleasant. She raised her glass to her lips and drank. She promptly gasped, dropped the glass, raised her hand to her throat, and choked violently and hoarsely. She gave a croaking little cry as she staggered one or two paces backwards. Then she crumpled at the knees and collapsed on the floor. She made one desperate little attempt to rise, kicked out once, and then lay still.

Collins and Angela Hughes were the first ones there. As they knelt beside her, Willis was already pulling her phone out of her handbag in the background.

"Oh, can you smell that?" Angela Hughes asked, clutching Collins's hand in both of hers. "Why surely it's ...?"

"Yes, it's cyanide alright," Collins concurred.

It was hard to do otherwise; the smell of almonds was unmistakeable.

"Oh, the poor, stupid woman," Angela Hughes cried. "Oh, Ann, my darling, why didn't you wait for me to sort things out? You know I always do. Oh God, oh Ann ...!"

It was as if Collins was viewing events through a haze of unreality. He rose dumbly to his feet, raising a distraught Angela Hughes with him. He glanced around desperately for Willis; still speaking urgently into her phone, she moved across to them.

"Wait a moment," she said into the phone, and raised her eyebrows at Collins.

"It smells like cyanide," he said feeling that he was being rather stupid and choosing his words with care as if he was drunk. "You remember I told you that Ann had some. Angela thinks its suicide. She told me earlier that Ann was being blackmailed."

Angela Hughes gave a little wail and clung to him, but the time for respecting confidences had passed, he thought.

"Full SOCO crew," Willis said authoritatively to the third party at the end of the line. "And lots of uniform, please. This is a big scene to secure. And please inform Mr Collison immediately."

Willis grabbed the two nearest waiters and a character in a dark suit and staff badge who looked bewildered and vaguely managerial.

"I'm a police officer and this is a crime scene," she said crisply. "Go to the door over there. Until the police arrive you make sure that nobody leaves and nobody comes in. OK? Go."

"Now then," she went on, turning to Angela Hughes. "You think it was suicide? She had some cyanide in her possession, I understand?"

"Yes, in her handbag. She must have poured some of it into her glass of water."

Willis squatted down next to Ann Durham, her dress rising dangerously high as she did so. From her bag she extracted a pair of plastic gloves and put them on. Very carefully she opened the handbag which lay next to the corpse. She extracted a hotel room key, a lipstick, a phone, and a small pad with attached pen. Then she shook her head and replaced them.

"It was in a small bottle," Collins volunteered.

"There's nothing here," Willis said calmly.

Still squatting, with her stocking tops openly on display, she scanned the floor around and beneath the table.

"There's nothing," she said again, rising to her feet in a

single lithe movement.

Angela Hughes looked even more deeply shocked than before.

"Oh, but Peter ...," she said, but then faltered and started to sob quietly and hopelessly.

"Yes," said Collins feeling ridiculously theatrical, "then I'm afraid it's murder."

He and Willis gazed at each other in mounting disbelief.

"Harriet," he murmured so that only she could hear, "we must stop stumblin' across bodies like this. It's in danger of becoming a habit."

CHAPTER 7

By the time Simon Collison arrived at the hotel, a substantial police presence was beginning to establish itself. The crew of the local patrol car which had been the first to respond to Willis's appeal for assistance had been released from door duty, and sent back about its business. Their place had been taken by a steadily growing contingent from Hampstead police station.

The scene inside the ballroom was bizarre. Shocked diners sat stiffly in their places around the room, as if on a luxury cruise ship which had just been hijacked by terrorists. At the front, a small group of people were perched on chairs some way away from the crumpled body of Ann Durham, by which stood Detective Inspector Tom Bellamy. Collison noted his presence with relief. He had an excellent reputation as a Scene of Crime Officer, and they had worked together before.

He registered Willis and Collins standing next to the small circle of seated figures, who apart from their glum expressions might have been taken to be indulging in some rather dull Victorian parlour game. Before he had a chance to speak to them, Bellamy approached him.

"Good evening, sir."

"Evening, Tom. What on earth is going on here?"

"I've only just arrived myself, guv, but Karen Willis was here when it happened. So was Dr Collins, who knew the deceased, at least slightly. Apparently she drank some water which we're pretty certain had been laced with cyanide. You can still smell the stuff now. She died almost at once, which is of course what you'd expect."

Collison glanced at Willis as she approached in turn. Collins hung back awkwardly, unwilling to join what was clearly an official police discussion. Collison beckoned him over.

"What do we know?" Collison asked Willis.

"The deceased is a lady called Ann Durham, guv. That's Ann Durham the crime writer, of course. There was a bit of a shemozzle at the table while we were standing around chatting before taking our seats for dinner. A water jug got knocked over, and a couple of glasses. That may or may not be connected to what happened immediately afterwards."

"Which was?"

"The victim drank from a glass of water which was in her hand. Immediately she started choking, and then ... just fell down dead."

"I knelt down beside her," Collins cut in. "So did Angela Hughes – that's the lady over there in the blue trouser suit, she's Ann's agent – Angela was pretty distraught, as you might expect. We both smelt almonds immediately. It was clear that Ann was dead, so I pulled Angela up so that she didn't touch anything. We were all in shock, I think."

"Miss Hughes thought the deceased had committed suicide," Willis commented. "Apparently Ann Durham was being blackmailed and she had been carrying a bottle of cyanide around with her earlier during the conference, so she put two and two together and came up with Ann Durham having killed herself. But there was no cyanide bottle in her bag – I checked – nor on the floor anywhere around the table; I checked that too."

Collison and Bellamy stared at her in amazement.

"She was carrying a bottle of cyanide?" Collison echoed. "Why on earth would she be doing that? And where the hell did she get it from?"

"Yes, as a prop apparently, and we don't know," answered Willis succinctly.

Collison groped for something to say.

"Recommendations, Tom?"

"From the SOCO point of view I'd say that as far as the crime scene is concerned, it may have been compromised already, given the spilled water and everything, but Willis has done a good job in getting people away from the immediate area, so I'd like to clear the room to see what my lads can do."

Collison pondered this.

"In terms of clearing the room, guv," Karen proffered. "I was going to suggest that we hang onto the folk who were on the victim's table – they're the ones I've kept apart over there – and let the others go home after giving us their name, contact details and table number. There must be about two hundred people in here and we just don't have the resources to take that many statements here and now."

"Sounds sensible," Collison said after a moment's thought. "Where's Bob, incidentally?"

"He's on the way, but don't worry I can handle things until he gets here."

"Alright then. Do as you suggest. Find a separate room to hold the ones you've isolated. Tell uniform to let the others go table by table once they're happy they've got all their details."

Willis moved off to give instructions to the uniform contingent, looking more incongruous than ever in her cocktail dress and heels.

Collison saw Timothy Evans and Priya Desai enter the room. They were both members of the detective team at Hampstead who had worked with him on his last case.

"Evening, both," he said. "Listen, we need to shift that group of people over there to a separate room. You know the drill; they're not to talk to anyone on the way, and look out for them trying to dispose of anything, particularly something that looks as if it might be a small bottle."

"There's the green room," Collins suggested. "That's a sort of sitting room just off the first floor lobby, where the speakers can go between sessions."

"Excellent. All right, you two. Go with Dr Collins and keep your eyes peeled. Peter, you'll have to stay there too once you get there, I'm afraid. You're a witness, perhaps our principal witness."

"Yes, of course," Collins said.

"Before you go, tell me this. Who is that woman over there, the older one? She looks strangely familiar."

"That's Miss Marple," Collins replied archly.

"You mean the actress who plays her? Yes, of course, no wonder I recognise her. What's her real name, though?"

"It really is Miss Marple, at least so far as anyone knows. She's apparently become so obsessed with the character that she won't answer to anything else. Angela says it's rumoured that she may actually have changed her name officially."

"You mean by deed poll?"

"Yes, that's right."

"Strewth!" said Collison, and then "is this all really happening, Peter? Tell me it's all just a dream."

"I know what you mean," Collins concurred, "I said something similar to Karen at the time. It all has a sort of surreal quality about it, doesn't it?"

"OK," Collison said, having gathered his wits, "you go with the others, Peter, like I said, and we'll start organising people to take statements from you all. I'll be with you as soon as I've spoken to the doctor."

For he had noticed Brian Williams enter the room, hesitate as he looked around, and then make his way towards Tom Bellamy. More reassurance. Brian was an excellent pathologist and, like Bellamy, he had worked with Collison before.

As he approached them Williams was already kneeling beside the body, pressing a gloved finger into the neck.

74

"No pulse," he said formally to Bellamy. "Life extinct."

"Dr Williams pronounces life extinct at 2058," Bellamy intoned for the benefit of his tape recorder.

Williams stood up.

"Evening," he greeted Collison. "You're SIO, I take it, Simon?"

"I am, yes. What can you tell me?"

"Nothing formally until I've examined the body. But I could feel it was still warm as I tried to find a pulse, so informally I'd guess she's been dead no more than an hour or so."

"That fits. Can you guess at a cause of death?"

"Of course I can. Either somebody's tipped a large amount of almond essence all over her or she's taken cyanide. If so, death would have been pretty much instantaneous. But that's unofficial, of course, until we've had a chance to run some toxicology analysis."

He gave Collison a sideways glance and an arch smile.

"And I understand from the posters outside that this is a crime writers' convention? Really, Simon, it's almost as though somebody has stage managed this for you. Cyanide is very Golden Age, isn't it?"

"It crops up quite a bit, yes."

The doctor's eyes roamed across the sad, small group that was being shepherded out of the room by Evans and Desai.

"I say! Isn't that –?"

"Yes," Collison said rather sourly. "It is."

He glanced at Bellamy.

"Is there anything you need me for here, Tom?"

"No, sir. We'll get on with photos and then, if Brian's happy, we'll shift the body. But I would appreciate some uniform to help with a fingertip search of the floor. My lads will do the bit around here, because we'd like to take some glass and carpet samples, but I'd like to be quite sure that nobody's disposed of anything under any of the other tables.

"Good thinking. Yes, ask Karen. She's in charge until Bob gets here. OK, if you don't need me then I'll go and see the witnesses."

He stood for a few moments and surveyed the crime scene, the body sprawled inelegantly on the floor, the water stain on the carpet, the upturned jug and the glass fragments. Of course there would be the photos to look at later, but nothing could substitute for this first impression in the immediate aftermath of events. There was a freshness about it, already fading, which would hopefully record it at some highly subjective level and might later spark a connection on some sub-conscious, almost random basis.

He turned away and made his way to the green room. The six witnesses were sitting around awkwardly, their faces pinched and drawn. Only Miss Marple seemed relatively unaffected. She had fished some knitting out of her bag, and the clacking of her needles could be clearly heard in the silence. Barry Carver sat close to Gina Durham, holding her hand in her lap. The others sat rigidly, waiting.

"I'm very sorry to have to inconvenience you like this, ladies and gentlemen," Collison announced. "I'm Detective Superintendent Collison and I will be leading this investigation. We'll try not to keep you any longer than absolutely necessary."

As he spoke, Willis came into the room, closely followed by Metcalfe.

"These officers," he went on, gesturing not just to them but also at Desai and Evans, "will be taking you away one by one to give your statements about exactly what you saw and heard. I'm afraid I will also have to to ask you to submit to a search by a uniformed officer once you've given your statement. I deeply regret the necessity for this, but I'm sure you'll appreciate that we are looking for whatever it was that contained the poison before it found its way into Miss Durham's glass."

There was a murmur of protest, which seemed to emanate particularly from Barry Carver, but Collison ignored this and pressed on.

"So far as your statements are concerned, I'd like you to focus please on the moment that the deceased drank from her glass before collapsing. Please tell the officers exactly where you were in relation to her, but also as much as you can remember about where everybody else was standing. It might be helpful if you could draw a simple diagram on a piece of paper to illustrate this."

He noticed with approval that the four detectives were jotting down notes to themselves as he spoke.

"I'd also like you to tell them exactly what was your relationship to the deceased and anything you know about her background."

"Most importantly, of course," he said with a tight little smile, "anything you can think of that may have caused someone to want to kill her."

Gina Durham gave a convulsive sob at this point, and Barry Carver glared at Collison.

"Really, can't this wait?" he demanded. "You can see that Gina's in no state to answer questions."

"No, I'm afraid it can't," Collison replied, unmoved. "It's most important that we record everyone's recollections while they're still fresh. We will also be asking everyone to let us take their fingerprints, by the way; standard procedure you understand. But we can certainly try to bring Miss Durham's ordeal to an end as quickly as possible. Sergeant, will you take Miss Durham away and take her statement straightaway, please?"

Willis stepped forward.

"Let's go and find somewhere quiet, shall we?" she suggested.

Gina Durham nodded dumbly and followed her from the room.

"And why don't you go with DC Desai, sir?" Collison proposed before Barry Carver could say anything else. "That way you'll both be finished as soon as possible, and you'll be on hand to look after Miss Durham. And you, sir, why don't you go with DC Evans?"

Desai and Evans left the room with Carver and Smythe respectively.

"Let me brief Inspector Metcalfe here for a moment, if you'll excuse me, ladies," Collison said, addressing Angela Hughes and Miss Marple, "and then we can deal with you as well."

"I'm happy to wait," a still tearful Angela Hughes murmured, glancing rather helplessly at Collins.

As Collison spoke quietly but urgently in the doorway, Miss Marple knitted on, but as if on autopilot, her eyes darting keenly around the room.

"Dr Collins," she said suddenly. "I wonder if you'd be so kind as to make some tea? I'm sure dear Angela would like some. And put two sugars in it."

"I don't take sugar," she said.

"You will today," Miss Marple replied firmly. "Sweet tea is quite the best thing for shock. Other than smelling salts of course, but I tend to keep those as a last resort for people who are downright hysterical. Not that I can imagine you ever being hysterical, Angela. You are far too sensible."

Angela Hughes gave Collins a lopsided little grin, as if to signal that she would submit graciously, and he jumped up and busied himself with the kettle.

"Once you've got your tea, Miss Hughes, perhaps I could ask you to go with DI Metcalfe here?" Collison asked her.

She gazed at him, and then at Metcalfe, and managed a watery smile.

"Is he going to search me?" she enquired, with a laboured effort at mischief.

"No, of course not," Collison replied stolidly. "A WPC will do that once you've given your statement."

She glanced now at Collins as he stirred two sugars into her tea as bidden, and then down at her trousers, seeming to realise for the first time that they were creased from when she had been kneeling beside Ann Durham.

"Oh well," she said, trying to smooth down the material, "little did I realise when I put this outfit on that I'd end up being searched by a policewoman."

"Thank you, Peter," she went on as he handed her a mug. "And now, I'm entirely at your disposal, Inspector."

As they left the room, Collison sat down beside Miss Marple to gather his thoughts.

"A nasty business, Superintendent," she observed.

"Yes," he agreed simply, and then, on a sudden whim, "any ideas?"

"Nothing specific at the moment," she observed, "but things will probably become much clearer after the second murder."

"Second murder? What on earth are talking about? What makes you think there's going to be a second murder?"

She stopped knitting and gazed at him over her glasses in pure astonishment.

"Oh, but there always is," she said simply.

CHAPTER 8

Without being asked, Collins made Collison a mug of tea, which he accepted gratefully.

"As soon as one of my team has finished what they are doing, Miss Marple, I'll ask them to take your statement formally," Collison explained. "But perhaps while we're chatting informally, you might just give me your recollection of what happened?"

She sighed deeply and put her knitting down in her lap.

"It all happened so quickly," she observed, "but let me do my best to remember."

She steepled her fingers and narrowed her eyes in concentration. Having seen this effect on television so often, Collison felt that he was sitting opposite an old friend.

"We were all standing around the table talking while we waited for some sort of announcement that we should take our places," she began. "Rather a nasty modern habit, I'm afraid. Why we couldn't just sit down straightaway I really don't know."

Collison nodded in what he hoped was a sympathetic fashion.

"I was speaking to poor Ann, and that woman police officer who just left the room. Not that I knew she was a police officer then, you understand. She wasn't exactly in uniform, was she? So, yes, I suppose I – and of course Karen, is that her name? – must have been the last person to speak to her."

"What were you talking about?"

"I've been thinking very hard about that, but it really was just some idle chit-chat, you know, about the sessions of the convention I'd attended, that sort of thing. And she was telling the young lady how very much she liked Dr Collins here, and admired his book."

"How did she seem?"

Miss Marple paused.

"I should say that although I've met Ann various times over the years, I don't know her really well," she said judiciously, "so I may not be the best person to gauge such things, but I got the impression that she definitely had something on her mind, perhaps more than one thing. She seemed distracted, somehow. Of course there was the whole business of the election – everybody knew about that – but whether it was just that or something else, I really couldn't say. Certainly I wondered why they had put her and Tom on the same table; I remember thinking that it was going to make for a very strained atmosphere at dinner."

"She took it personally then, the fact that Tom Smythe was talking of standing against her?"

"Oh yes," she said firmly. "But then she would, you see. It was her way. She really did think that she was some sort of protector, or patroness, of the Association and she reacted to news of the election rather as if it was some sort of stab in the back – a betrayal, if you will."

"Were you aware of anything else that might have been troubling her?"

"No, but then I wouldn't. I don't think she was the sort of person to confide in others. But Angela would probably know, if anybody."

"Not her daughter, not Gina?"

Miss Marple shook her head.

"Oh no. Ann always tried to protect Gina from anything that had to do with the real world. I think theirs was a difficult relationship because of it. Gina resented her mother treating her like a little girl, while Ann tried to control what Gina did with her life – too much so, in my opinion."

Collison jotted down a few notes.

"Now tell me exactly what you can remember about what happened," he enjoined her. "The slightest detail may be important."

"But I don't have to tell you that, of course," he went on quickly as the beginnings of a frown formed on her features.

She smiled magnanimously.

"As I said, the three of us were talking, but only for a very few minutes. Out of the corner of my eye, as it were, I could see Dr Collins here talking to Gina and her boyfriend. I'm not sure where the others were, because I would have had my back to them. Then suddenly there was a loud shriek from behind me – it was a woman's voice, so I assume it was Angela – and when I turned round I saw that someone had knocked a jug of water off the table together with a couple of glasses."

"But you didn't actually *see* anyone knock it off the table?"

"Quite right, Superintendent," she said approvingly. "I should of course be more precise. I saw the jug and glasses lying on the floor and I assumed that somebody had just knocked them off the table."

"A reasonable assumption, though," Collison said with a grin. "Now, when you turned around, who was closest to the jug?"

"I think probably Tom Smythe," she said after a moment's thought. "Certainly Ann said something straightaway about how clumsy he'd been, and *she* may well have seen what happened, because she would have been able to see over my shoulder; she was facing me, and she's taller than I am."

"And then what happened?"

"He said straightaway that someone had barged into him, but whether he meant that it hadn't been him who upset the water but this other person, or whether that other person had knocked him into the table, I really don't know. The only other person I can remember being near him was Angela, but I think she was just standing still. We never got a chance to take things any further, because as I looked back at Ann she was drinking from a glass of water, and you know what happened next."

There was a pause while Collison digested this.

"May I interrupt?" Collins asked diffidently.

"Any contribution would be welcome," Collison replied.

"Well, I've just been thinking of 'Sparkling Cyanide'. Not one of yours, of course, Miss Marple. It was Colonel Race wasn't it?"

"It was indeed – in the novel, that is. But I seem to remember that it was adapted from a short story, which originally featured dear Hercule."

"You're right of course," Collins acknowledged. "I'd forgotten that. But isn't there a point in the story at which the murderer dresses up as a waiter so that he can put cyanide in someone's drink unobserved? You see, I've just remembered that there was a waiter standing very close to Tom Smythe. We mustn't overlook him just because we'd expect to see a waiter by a dinner table. You know, like Chesterton's postman."

"Stop!" Collison appealed, his head reeling. "What are you talking about, Peter?"

"In 'Sparkling Cyanide' Christie has her murderer disguise himself as a waiter, as I said," Collins explained. "But G.K. Chesterton used the same device in 'The Invisible Man'. He has his killer dress up as a postman so nobody takes any notice of him when he visits the property and they don't think to mention him later because they expected to see him there, whereas they're trying to think of anything out of the ordinary which happened."

"Of course 'Sparkling Cyanide' offers another tantalising possibility as well," Miss Marple said reflectively, "particularly in the light of the glasses that were swept off the table. If

Ann simply picked up off the table a glass of water which had already been poured, then it's entirely possible that it wasn't meant for her at all, but for someone else entirely."

Both men stared at her blankly.

"Oh dear," Collison said in a very heartfelt way. "Oh bloody dear."

"Oh dear indeed," Miss Marple agreed calmly. "So it seems to me that there are three main possibilities here. Number one, suicide. Number two, somebody intentionally murdered poor Ann. Number three, somebody intended to murder somebody else who was to sit at that table, but killed Ann by accident."

"Surely we can rule out suicide?" Collison queried.

She looked at him over her glasses again, but this time rather severely.

"It really does pay to keep an open mind in investigations such as this, Superintendent," she admonished him. "I don't see that we can rule out suicide at all. Just because you haven't found the cyanide container yet doesn't mean that she didn't have an accomplice who somehow spirited it away from the scene. Come to that, the glass might have been poisoned outside the room before she came in, in which case the bottle never had to be there in the first place."

"We'll be searching her room, of course," Collison said defensively.

"There again of course," Collins interjected thoughtfully, "even if we do find the bottle in her room, it doesn't necessarily mean that it was suicide. Somebody could have planted it there to make it look as if it was suicide, but in reality to cover up a murder."

"True," Miss Marple concurred, nodding her head in avian fashion, "but it would be interesting, nonetheless. The poison itself is key, I think. Where did she get it? How did it get into the glass? And just where is it now? If it really has vanished into thin air, then that clearly points to murder."

Collison, who was beginning to regret having started this conversation, glanced involuntarily at his watch.

"You're getting tired of listening to an eccentric old woman and hoping that one of your colleagues will return and take me away," she observed shrewdly.

"I'm sorry," he said in embarrassment. "It's just that it's getting late and there's still so much to do. Search her room for one thing, and find out about this waiter for another. It's always the same at the beginning of an enquiry; you always feel that you don't have enough people. Later, if things are going slowly you often feel that you have too many."

Miss Marple took a dainty sip of tea.

"You may be wondering," she went on, ignoring his remarks, "why I'm laying such stress on the possibility of suicide. It must seem rather unlikely to you that someone should choose to end their life by taking cyanide in public at a social event."

"Frankly, yes it does."

"Then it's as well that we've had a chance to chat," she said. "You see, you won't have any idea of what crime-writers are really *like*, as people I mean. In my experience they are both highly eccentric and highly egotistical. Tom and Ann are good examples of what I mean. If somebody like that had already taken the decision to kill themselves, then the chance to do it in a hugely melodramatic fashion – by taking cyanide at a crime convention, for example – might well prove irresistible."

Seeing that Collison looked dubious, she tried again.

"Look at dear Agatha Christie's disappearance when her husband left her for another woman. All very stage-managed, wasn't it? Don't you think she enjoyed being looked for by police forces all over the country when she was really just taking tea and reading library books in a hotel in Harrogate?"

"Really, do you think so?" Collins asked, intrigued. "I've always assumed that she was just suffering from depression."

Miss Marple gave what might, if emanating from a less ladylike source, be described as a sniff of derision.

"Well, whatever the case," she said loftily, "I'm sure it didn't do her book sales any harm for her to be featured on the front page of just about every newspaper in the world. Nor her sense of self-worth, either."

"In which case," Collins interjected, "the disappearance of the poison bottle might have been part of the stage management, designed to throw suspicion of murder onto one or more people whom she didn't like."

"Of whom there were many," Miss Marple said drily. "Tom Smythe and that young man for a start."

"Really?" Collison asked. "How do you know that?"

"In the case of Tom, she made little secret of it. In the beginning it was just a sort of lofty disdain for someone she felt was an inferior writer – unfairly in my opinion, but there you are – but more recently I fear it had turned into a very active antipathy. She was positively incandescent about the whole election business."

"And the young man, the daughter's boyfriend?"

"Nothing I could put my finger on. Certainly nothing you could rely upon as evidence. It's just that in those last few minutes, while we were standing around the table waiting to sit down for dinner, I saw her give him a look of what I can only describe as real hatred. It really was quite shocking. It was just for a second, but I'm quite certain of what I saw."

"Who might be able to tell us more about that?" Collison asked.

"The young man himself, I suppose – and Gina, of course. But if you want the full story I should ask dear Angela. She and Ann were very close, you know. This is all going to be a dreadful ordeal for her. If Ann ever confided in anyone about anything – and I'm not sure she ever really trusted anyone – it would have been Angela."

"There's something else, you know," Collins mused. "Something that's only just occurred to me. If she wasn't intending to kill herself then why would she, a crime-writer, have drunk from a glass that must have been positively reeking of almonds? Particularly as she had sniffed from a bottle of cyanide just a few hours previously, and so would have known exactly what it smelt like even if she'd only read about it before."

"Are you quite sure about that?" Collison asked incredulously.

"Absolutely certain. In fact she was sitting right here in this room in front of both of us when she did it. Miss Marple here was understandably quite severe with her for playing about with something so dangerous."

"Quite so," Miss Marple said, nodding once more. "What an interesting thought, my dear boy. Well, well, Superintendent; one more thing to consider."

With a feeling of relief, out of the corner of his eye Collison saw Evans re-enter the room.

"All done, Timothy?" he queried.

"Yessir," he replied woodenly. Collison noted with approval that he was obviously conscious of the need not to divulge any unnecessary information in the presence of other witnesses.

"Then would you please take care of Miss Marple here?"

"Of course, sir. Would you like to come this way please, madam? Perhaps I could carry your bag for you?"

"Thank you, no," Miss Marple said with dignity, "but if you could bring my tea, that would be very kind."

The two men stood as she left the room.

"You know, Peter," Collison observed ruefully, "until I started talking to you and that wretched woman I thought this case was really quite bizarre. Now I'm beginning to realise that it may actually be damned ridiculous."

CHAPTER 9

Collison got no sleep that night, popping home at about seven for a shower, a shave and a change of clothes. Soon after eight he was already in the newly re-opened Incident Room at Hampstead police station, which was put into hibernation when no major crime was being investigated. Metcalfe was already there, talking to the IT engineers who would be activating phones with dedicated numbers and making sure that new members of the team could log into the computer system as they arrived. Collison waved to him to carry on and went over to the big windows which overlooked Rosslyn Hill at the front of the building. He had that slightly itchy feeling he always experienced when he went without sleep, and he dragged a notebook out of his pocket, looking at the various comments and questions he had scribbled down since he had first arrived at the hotel the previous evening.

The door opened and Karen Willis entered, carrying three cups of coffee in a cardboard tray. How did she manage to look so immaculate, he wondered, for he knew that she too had gone without sleep. Come to that, how had she known that he had already arrived, for surely otherwise she would only have bought two coffees. He gave up.

"This really is most unfair," he said, forestalling her greeting. "Neither of us had any sleep last night, yet I look as if I didn't, whereas you don't."

She smiled and proffered the tray, his cup pointing towards him. He noticed that the cocktail dress had given way to a rather severe tweed skirt suit, which also had a distinctly 1950s look to it.

"Skinny latte with an extra shot, guv. That's right, isn't it?"

"You know it is," he replied, "and thank you."

She turned away to give Metcalfe his coffee but he seemed to have wound up his technical conversation and was moving towards them, so she stayed by the window instead.

"Morning, guv," Metcalfe said, gratefully accepting a coffee. "Get any sleep?"

"I did not. I was at the hotel until gone six. How are we doing?"

"I have the usual request in for extra bods," Metcalfe reported, "and as usual I assume they'll arrive in dribs and drabs over the next few days."

"It's probably also reasonable to assume," Willis said mischievously, "that they will be those who can be most easily spared from their existing duties."

Collison grunted; he knew she was right.

"Well, as usual, Bob, we'd better make sure that anything really important is assigned to one of our little inner circle."

"Right you are, guv. We've got Desai and Evans anyway. Luckily they were both on call last night, and they were awaiting reassignment to a new enquiry."

"Well, now they've got it," Collison observed grimly.

"Before we go any further, guv," Metcalfe said, "I have a rather strange request to relay to you."

"Yes?"

"Well, one of the organisers of the convention came up to me just before I left and asked if we'd mind if they went ahead with the last two days of the event. To be honest, I was stunned, but I said I'd ask you."

"Wow!" Collison exclaimed. "I'm stunned too, Bob, but I suppose if they really want to then we can't properly object. SOCO have released the crime scene, haven't they?"

"They say they need it until ten, just to make sure they haven't missed anything."

"Fine, then say they can kick off again at ten, as soon as SOCO take the crime scene tape down."

"The hotel will be under siege by the media by then," Willis commented. "Without wanting to sound cynical, that's probably why they want to go ahead. It's probably going to be the best PR opportunity any of them are ever likely to have."

"True," Collison agreed. "Actually it's probably for the best anyway. It means that if we need to re-interview any of the key witnesses then we know where to find them."

Desai arrived. Like Willis, she looked as if she had enjoyed a full eight hours' sleep. Collison wondered if perhaps it was make-up that made the difference.

Timothy Evans drifted into the room a few minutes

later to represent the opposite end of the spectrum. He had clearly come straight from the hotel, for he was unshaven.

"Sorry to be scruffy, sir," he apologised, feeling Collison's gaze upon him. "I've been up all night."

"So have we all," Desai interjected tartly.

"Yeah, but some of us don't need to shave," Evans replied with a grin, "well, not so often anyway."

"That's enough, you two," Collison chided them good-naturedly. "We may as well start, because it's just the five of us at the moment. Bob, why don't you start us off?"

As Metcalfe went to the board, the others found the nearest chairs and sat down.

"Let's start with what we know," Metcalfe said.

He pointed to a photo of Ann Durham which he had already fixed to the board.

"Yesterday evening at or about 1950 this lady, the crime writer Ann Durham, died suddenly while about to sit down for a gala dinner. Although we don't have official confirmation yet, we are assuming for present purposes that she died from cyanide poisoning. By coincidence she was earlier seen carrying a bottle of potassium cyanide; that bottle is currently unaccounted for."

"The other occupants of the table were, in no particular order, another writer called Tom Smythe, an actress who insists on being addressed as Miss Marple, the deceased's agent Angela Hughes, the deceased's daughter Gina, Gina's boyfriend Barry Carver, and finally DS Willis and Peter Collins."

"Murder is starting to follow you and Peter around, Karen," Collison observed. "I shall have to be more careful in your company."

"I know," she acknowledged. "That's what Peter said too."

"Statements were taken last night from all seven of these witnesses," Metcalfe went on. "While they haven't been typed up yet, I've been through them and the general conclusion is a big zero. Nobody can even remember her picking the glass up from the table, although there was a bit of a commotion when a jug of water and a couple of glasses were knocked onto the floor, and that would obviously have been a bit of a distraction."

"Hmm, was it meant to be, I wonder?" Collison asked.

"If it was," Willis said, "then the closest people to it seem to have been Tom Smythe and Angela Hughes. Yet they both claim they weren't responsible, though Smythe did admit that he could have done it without realising, as somebody bumped into him."

"The waiter, perhaps," Collison said. "Let's not forget about him. People may have overlooked him because they expected to see him there. If we're going to treat anyone who was in the immediate vicinity as a suspect, then we should include him."

"I've asked the hotel's management for a list of waiters who were working the room last night," Metcalfe reported, "but without a good description it's going to be difficult to identify him."

"If necessary the kitchen will have to organise an identity parade," Collison decided. "At least Hughes and Smythe should be able to recognise him even if nobody else can."

"He may not have been a permanent employee," Willis pointed out. "Many of these places use a lot of casual labour: students, migrant workers, that sort of thing."

"Good point," Collison acknowledged, "but they're still obliged to keep records. Priya, why don't you go back there today, get all their details, and arrange for them all to be brought in for a parade. If we can't get them all together at the same time then if necessary we can do them individually, or in small groups."

"Let me give you my other thoughts," he went on, "and after that everyone feel free to chip in with your own."

He stood up and started writing on the board.

"The cyanide: where is it now, how did she get it, and when was it added to her glass? The glass: where was it when the poison was added? Was it actually intended for her use at all?"

"You mean, she may not have been the intended victim?" Willis asked doubtfully.

"It's a possibility and we need to eliminate it," Collison replied. "For the time being, I'm working on the basis that there are three broad areas of possibility: one, Durham was deliberately murdered; two, Durham chose a particularly theatrical way to commit suicide, perhaps aided and abetted by an accomplice; three, our killer intended to murder someone else but got Durham by mistake."

"Doesn't the fact that the poison bottle can't be found point to it being murder, sir?" Evans enquired.

"Probably, but let's not get ahead of ourselves. All we know is that the bottle wasn't on her person or in her bag. Nor was it in her hotel room when we searched it last night. Nor was it on any of the other people who were at the table; we searched them all – except Karen, of course. Nor was it anywhere in the room; uniform did a fingertip search under SOCO's supervision."

Collison looked at his jottings again and then looked around the team.

"First priority, let's get everything from last night typed up and in the system. Then I want to re-interview the daughter and her boyfriend. Bob, can you arrange for them to meet us at the hotel this afternoon? I understand that they entered the room together with the deceased. It's important that they try to remember whether she was already holding the glass and, if not, when and where she first picked it up. I want to re-interview Smythe, as well. I'm not happy that he's telling the whole story about how that jug got knocked over."

"There's quite a lot he's not telling the whole truth about, guv," Willis said. "I glanced at the notes of what he said last night and there's no mention of this whole election business. We know that he and Durham were at each other's throats about that."

"Agreed," Collison said, "but you're surely not suggesting that a crime writers' election might be a motive for murder?"

"I'm not suggesting anything, guv, though they're a strange lot according to Peter. But isn't it weird that he never even mentioned it?"

"It is strange," Collison agreed, "and it is important – if only because it might bear on the suicide angle as well."

"Bob," he asked, "the Hughes woman apparently told Peter earlier in the evening that she thought Durham was being blackmailed. Did she mention anything about that when you interviewed her?"

"Yes, she did. She said that somebody was threatening to reveal something about her past, something that would be very damaging to her, and that's why she was convinced that the deceased had committed suicide – that she couldn't bear the thought of having to live with the shame."

"What was it?"

"Something to do with some of her early books. Apparently those Austrian ones, the ones that keep getting shown on the telly, you know, the ones Peter likes-"

"Not just Peter," Collison murmured. "I'm a big fan myself."

"Well then prepare yourself for a shock. She didn't write them."

Collison gazed at him in astonishment.

"But how is that possible?"

"Apparently it was all quite legal. They were written by man called …"

He consulted his notes.

"… Max Goldstein. He got out of Vienna just in time, but

they couldn't bring any money with them so he and his wife were pretty much penniless when they pitched up in London. Goldstein earned a bit of money teaching German, and he carried on writing the Bergmann books which he began in Vienna. But he couldn't get them published, though he tried for ten years or so. Apparently one of the problems was that he wrote in German, and his English wasn't good enough to translate them, so he was effectively asking publishers to pay to have them translated sight unseen."

"By about 1960 Goldstein had given up on them, but his son Thomas – they'd changed their name to Gold by this time, by the way – came across them when his father died in the early 1980s and stated trying to translate them. He finished the first one and then got introduced to Durham, who was about 20 at the time. I think Angela said that their parents used to meet from time to time in a café back in the old days somewhere around Swiss Cottage."

"Durham introduced Thomas Gold to a publisher she knew, who looked at the first book and liked it. But Thomas needed money really badly. He was a strange sort of man. The only work he could get was as a lab assistant in a local school. He was in debt and his mother was sick – she died shortly afterwards apparently – and the publisher wanted to try just one book to begin with, and wouldn't pay an advance. So a deal was struck. Thomas would translate all his father's books, but he got his mother, who was his father's sole beneficiary, to sign over all the rights to Durham. She gave Thomas a lump sum, which is what he wanted. Then the publisher brought them out in her name, with everyone involved being sworn to secrecy. Apparently she wanted to be a famous writer, and saw this as her big chance. Poor Thomas never even got credit as translator, of course."

"Good grief!" Collison exclaimed. "How have they kept that quiet all this time?"

"More to the point," Willis interjected, "what's suddenly changed?"

"Thomas has a daughter, who has only recently found out about all this. She's livid that when the various television series were made Durham never offered Thomas any of the proceeds. She says that when her father got his mother to sign over the rights he thought they were only signing away the book rights, not the screen rights as well, but it seems pretty clear that the document said 'all rights' and so that's that. Thomas is apparently an honourable man and has always kept his side of the bargain, but the daughter is trying to shame Durham into shelling out, and is now threatening to sell the story to the newspapers."

"We need to interview them both," Collison said crisply. "Find them, Bob."

"You know, it's interesting." Willis said. "Peter has always been curious about those books. He could never understand why she suddenly stopped and then went onto other things, or why they were so different from what she turned out later. To be honest, I don't think he liked her other books very much."

"It certainly gives a boost to the suicide story, doesn't

it?" Desai observed. "You can imagine a victim murdering a blackmailer, but not the other way round. It wouldn't make sense."

"The agent certainly thought so," Willis said. "While I was dialling up the nick she was beside herself, shouting at Durham, asking her why she'd done it, that sort of thing."

"Poor girl," Metcalfe said sympathetically.

Willis gave him a very odd look.

Did you say 'girl'?" she demanded. "She must be thirty-five if she's a day. Don't tell me you've fallen for her too? Peter's been gushing about her ever since he met her."

"Just a figure of speech," Metcalfe said defensively, as Collison looked on, amused.

"She's just a flirt, you know," Willis told him. "Some women are like that around men. They get very close and gaze into your eyes. I've seen her do it with Peter."

"If I had a whistle I'd blow it at this point," Collison said briskly. "Come on, we've all got work to do."

CHAPTER 10

Tom Smythe entered the room and looked around curiously. It had been provided by the hotel for the use of the police and was evidently used normally as a meeting room, so that Collison and Metcalfe were sitting on one side of a long table.

"Do come in, Mr Smythe," said Collison, rising to greet him. "I'm sorry about doing this here, but I thought you'd find it more convenient. I understand you're chairing a panel later, so it will save you from having to walk backwards and forwards between here and the police station."

Smythe simply nodded and sat down.

"I'm not sure what you want to talk to me about," he said uncertainly, looking from one to another. "I gave a full statement to that young officer last night."

"Well now, that's a matter of opinion," Collison said with a smile. "You see, we're not so sure it was that full. In fact, we've asked to see you again so that we can talk about what you *didn't* divulge to DC Evans last night."

Smythe tried to summon up an indignant glare, but it didn't really work.

"Such as?" he demanded.

Collison looked down at Smythe's statement.

"Such as the fact that there was bad feeling between you and the deceased," he said.

"Who told you that?" Smythe asked, still quite belligerently.

"Never mind who told us," Collison replied evenly. "That's our business. I'm asking you if it is true."

"Well," Smythe blustered, "I suppose it all depends on what you mean by bad feeling ..."

He stopped and looked from one to the other again. They gazed back at him impassively.

"Then why don't you describe your relationship with the deceased in your own words," Collison suggested. "All you said to DC Evans is that you were 'longstanding friends and professional associates' and that you were 'deeply shocked by her death'. I'm prepared to take the last two of those statements on trust for the moment, but in the light of what certain other people have told us, I must query the first. I have it on good authority that you were anything but friends."

Smythe shrugged.

"Ann was a difficult person to be friends with. In fact, she was just a very difficult person full stop. Certainly I thought we were friends, but perhaps she took a different view, I don't know."

"Was there any particular reason why she might have taken a different view?" Collison asked.

"Not that I can think of off-hand, no."

"Oh dear, Mr Smythe, why are you making this so

difficult for everyone? Surely it's common knowledge that you were about to contest an election with her?"

"I was thinking of doing so, certainly. I hadn't actually decided one way or the other."

"But she believed you were about to do so, didn't she?"

"I believe she did, yes, but as I said, I hadn't actually decided. Nominations weren't due for another couple of weeks."

"Why don't you just tell us the facts, Mr Smythe," Collison pleaded, "and leave us to draw our own conclusions. Tell me the background to this election business."

"Well, we haven't actually had a proper election, a contested election that is, for many years, not since Ann took over, in fact. I'm afraid she just sort of assumed ownership of the Association and treated it as if it was her own little personal fiefdom for her to do with as she wished. At the same time she was terribly condescending, almost as if she was doing everybody a favour by acting as Chairman."

"What sort of Chairman was she?"

"Terrible. She was a complete dictator. The concept of discussion, of compromise, of working with a committee were all alien to her. She simply couldn't handle disagreement. She would just stare at you and repeat what she wanted, but this time more slowly and more loudly, as if you were a child who wouldn't do as you were told."

"But if that was the case," Metcalfe asked, "how did she survive as Chairman for so long? Why didn't anyone tried to unseat her before now?"

Smythe shrugged again.

"Lots of reasons. She had enormous prestige because of her Bergmann books; a lot of the ordinary members absolutely idolised her. So we knew that even if we did force an election then she might well be re-elected, and she'd then be more strongly entrenched than ever. It was easier just to resign from the committee and leave her to it, which most people did sooner or later because she was impossible to work with. That left her with a loyal little coterie of yes-men who would basically do whatever she proposed."

"So what had changed recently?"

Both I and Chris – Chris Campbell that is – had started to sense a certain stiffening of resistance on the committee. In fact, it was this very convention that was the catalyst, in a way."

"Explain," prompted Metcalfe.

"Well, it had always been a bone of contention. You see, she didn't really have to worry about readers. People would buy her books just because they'd been on television, and she'd already made a fortune from all the screen rights anyway. So her idea of a fun convention was just swanning around among a group of admiring fellow writers and giving some media interviews. It was different for the rest of us, though."

"How so?"

"For us, readers *do* matter. In fact, they're about *all* that bloody well matter. If we're going to shell out our hard-earned cash on a few nights in a hotel, we want to see some benefit in return. And that means meeting readers, and lots of them, and selling as many books as possible. She could never see that. She hated having to mix with readers; in fact I don't think she really liked people in general."

"And you said this a catalyst for some sort of resistance movement – how?" Collison asked.

"Well, there'd been quite a bit of moaning about this for a few years now and attendance had really started to drop off. Then we had a stroke of luck. The committee meeting that was due to consider the arrangements for the next convention – this one – happened to be one that she couldn't attend. What she didn't know was that the usual hotel in Bristol was going to be closed for refurbishment, and so it couldn't be a matter of just rubber stamping her yearly proposal for more of the same. Or so Chris and I argued, anyway. We said that if we were going to have to change venues anyway then this would be a great opportunity to re-examine the whole concept of the event and reach out to members of the public in a big population area such as London."

"How did that go down?" Collison asked.

"There were a lot of unhappy people. They knew what Ann wanted and her mob tried to get the discussion postponed until the next meeting, but we pointed out that to get a different hotel booked we needed to move quickly. Chris proposed this place and we managed to get it voted through because a few of her folk weakened and defected. Then we quickly put out a press release the same evening announcing that in future the convention would be here, and openly marketed to the public so that it was too late for her to get things changed when she heard about it."

"And what did she do when she found out?" Metcalfe asked.

"She went completely ape-shit, as you might expect," Smythe said with a lopsided grin. "Took it very badly indeed, took it personally. Started accusing people of 'treachery' and 'betrayal' and things like that. Chris suggested rather mischievously that if she disagreed so fundamentally with the committee's decision then she should resign in protest, which was of course just throwing petrol on the fire. That's how the idea of an election took hold, I think. People started to realise that there could be an alternative future for the Association without Ann."

"For what it's worth," he went on, "we were right and she was wrong, not that she would ever have admitted that. Attendance this year is nearly six times what it was last year in Bristol and about three quarters are ordinary readers who've walked in off the street. Most of the writers are pretty happy about that."

"So that's where the bad feeling came from?" Collison asked.

"On her part, yes, I'm afraid so. Like I said, she took it all very personally. I would have been very happy just to carry on and have a normal professional relationship with her, but I'm not sure she was capable of doing that."

"There now," Collison said lightly, "that wasn't so difficult, was it? If you'd told us all this last night, Mr Smythe, we wouldn't had had to drag you back this afternoon. Now, I wonder if you'd like to tell us everything you can remember about the time leading up to the moment when Miss Durham took a drink from her glass?"

"I did tell everything I knew about this last night."

"Please try again, Mr Smythe. You'd be amazed how often people suddenly remember something which they'd overlooked before. Let me help you. Did you see Ann Durham enter the room?"

"No, I didn't see her until she arrived at the table. I'd be surprised if anyone could have seen her enter the room, actually, even if they had been looking in the right direction, because it was getting very full."

"All right, good. Now, do you remember if, when first you saw her, she already had the glass in her hand or did she pick it up off the table?"

Smythe frowned hard in concentration. "I think she already had the glass in her hand, but I can't be certain. Definitely I didn't see her pick it up, but then I was talking to Angela, so I wasn't necessarily concentrating on anyone else."

"All right," Collison said, "let's try something else, shall we? Tell me exactly what you can remember about the jug being knocked over."

"I've tried thinking about this very hard," Smythe said slowly. "All I can remember is someone barging into me. I really can't be certain who it was because there was a sudden press of people around me; I think they were waiters

108

gathering round to put things on the table – the starters, perhaps? – and it was one of those situations where you just feel yourself stumble. I can remember knocking into the table, but whether it was me that knocked the jug onto the floor I really don't know. It was behind me, you see; I had my back to it."

"So there was more than one waiter by the table?" Metcalfe asked quickly.

"Oh yes, of course," Smythe said in a puzzled tone of voice. "As soon as the jug had fallen onto the floor there were at least a couple of waiters there picking it up and trying to mop up the water and clear away the broken glasses, though I only watched that happening for a few seconds of course until I realised something was wrong with Ann."

"So they must have been near the table when it happened, you mean?"

"Yes, exactly. They could hardly have emerged from thin air, could they?"

"Would you be able to recognise any of them again?" Metcalfe pressed him.

"Oh, maybe, I don't know. I'm not sure I would remember any of their faces. By the way, I'm saying 'waiters', and they were all wearing trousers, but I'm pretty sure I remember at least one of them being a girl."

"Think ahead a few moments," Collison urged him. "You've just seen Ann Durham fall to the floor and you've realised that there is something wrong with her. Perhaps by this time Peter Collins and Angela Durham are already kneeling beside her. Do you remember seeing anything of that group of waiters again?"

Again, Smythe thought hard.

"Yes, I can remember looking around the room trying to work out what the hell was going on, and by then the waiters had moved away from the jug. Then almost at once that very attractive lady in the black dress who turned out to be a police officer grabbed two of them. I heard her send them out to guard the door and stop anyone coming in or out."

"Can you remember anything about those particular two waiters?"

"I think they were a man and a woman," he said slowly, "and perhaps the woman had short blondish hair, but that's all."

"It's something, anyway," Collison reassured him. "Something we didn't know before. Every little bit of new information is helpful, even though it may not be obvious at the time."

"On a completely separate point," Metcalfe asked casually. "Were you aware that the deceased was in the habit of carrying cyanide around with her?"

"No, I most certainly was not. You could have knocked me down with a feather when she produced it in the poisons session and started waving it around. Incidentally, I'm not sure it's right to say that she 'was in the habit of carrying cyanide'. Certainly I'd never seen her with any before, and I've seen her in action at lots of conventions. I think it was just some silly stunt that she pulled for this one."

"So you have no idea what she had acquired it for?"

"Absolutely not. Like I said, I've never seen her with any before."

"And you have no idea where or when she acquired it?"

"None whatsoever," Smythe said emphatically. "But then, I would have thought that it shouldn't be difficult for you chaps to find out. After all, it's not exactly an everyday item, is it?"

"Hopefully that will indeed be the case," Collison said. "Now, is there anything else you'd like to tell us, Mr Smythe?"

"Perhaps I might point out one thing which, as a crime writer, I think should be highly relevant to your enquiry?" Smythe queried.

"By all means," Collison agreed. "We're always grateful for assistance from any quarter."

"Well, surely it must be obvious that while it's just possible that dear Ann was so mightily incensed about all this to want to murder me, I had no motive whatever for murdering her?"

"Unless of course it was in self-defence?" Collison suggested.

"Self-defence? What on earth do you mean?"

"Well, you see, a thought has just occurred to me," Collison said with a smile. "Given the ill-will which you now admit the deceased bore towards you, didn't it worry you just a little bit when you saw her with a bottle of cyanide?"

"You mean –?"

"I'm being fanciful, of course, but didn't it occur to you even for a moment that she might have been intending to slip some in your drink at some stage?"

Smythe's features tightened visibly beneath his facial bronzer. Then suddenly he smiled.

"You know, Superintendent, I make a pretty good living out of writing this sort of dialogue. It comes as quite a shock to find myself actually taking part in it."

"Then what would you think comes next?" Collison asked, intrigued.

"I would imagine that you're about to thank me for my co-operation and ask me to keep myself available should you wish to interview me again."

"Not bad," Collison nodded in approval. "That will do nicely."

CHAPTER 11

At much the same time, Willis and Evans were calling at a block of flats in that sprawling area of North London known to its residents as Finchley, a term which covers anywhere from the outskirts of Hampstead Garden Suburb in the south to the edge of Barnet in the north. The apartment building was just yards from the North Circular Road and Evans's attention was diverted by the statue of a naked lady holding a sword aloft which stood poised on the apex of the junction.

"It's called 'La Délivrance' or something like that," Willis commented, following his eyes. "It was made for the French after the First World War but some press baron – Rothermere I think – saw it, fell in love with it, bought it and brought it over here."

"But why here? Why Finchley?" Evans asked.

"Not sure. I think his mother was in a home somewhere around here, and he said that he wanted to see it when he drove out this way to see her."

"How do you know all this stuff, Sarge?" Evans marvelled.

"Oh, I read about it somewhere. It's amazing how much stuff gets squirrelled away, isn't it?"

Evans looked from the statue to Willis, paused

appreciatively, and then cast his contemplative gaze back to the statue.

"Have you ever-?"

"No," she said sharply. "Now let's get on with this, shall we? What number is it?"

"46," came the response as Evans consulted his notes.

Willis jammed her finger on the button.

"Mr Gold? It's Detective Sergeant Willis from Hampstead CID. We spoke on the phone."

"Third floor," said a disembodied voice, as the door buzzed open.

Willis looked dubiously at the heavily scratched door of the dilapidated lift. It was of a type which she had not seen for some time, having a trellis-like sliding inner door which was manually operated. A handwritten note adjured users to be sure to close it properly behind them.

"I think we'll take the stairs," she decided.

Their footsteps reverberated around the building as they did so, Willis's heels ringing out like hammer blows. As they reached the third floor a man was holding the door of his flat open, peering nervously around it. Willis guessed that he was in his sixties, although it was hard to be sure; he looked tired and worn.

"Please come in," he said.

The flat had a musty air, which might have been partly to do with the fact that it was overfull with old furniture. With difficulty they worked their way around a large sofa and some occasional tables and perched themselves in two armchairs which felt rough and coarse to the touch. Willis cursed inwardly and tried to sit very still. The last thing she needed was a ladder in her stockings; unusually, she wasn't carrying a spare pack.

"I've just been reading about Ann Durham," he said, nodding to a newspaper which lay on yet another table. "What a shocking business. Do you know what happened? They said something about cyanide on the radio this morning."

"That's what we're trying to establish, sir," Willis answered. "We were hoping that we might speak with you – and your daughter."

"Sonia's not here, she stayed with a friend last night. But I called her after we spoke and she's on her way now."

"Fine," Willis replied. "Well, to save time, would you mind if we started with you on your own?"

"Certainly. I'm eager to help in any way I can."

"Thank you, sir. Now to begin with, I wonder if you can confirm a rather startling story we've been told by somebody else …"

"You mean Angela Hughes, I assume?" he cut in. "She telephoned me this morning to tell me what had happened, and to warn me that the story was likely to break. She said she thought Ann had killed herself, by the way. Is that true?"

"I can't comment on that, I'm afraid," Willis replied. "But, for the record, can you confirm that Ann Durham was not the author of the Bergmann novels?"

Gold sighed heavily.

"No, that's right, she wasn't. Oh dear, I knew this would all have to come out one day, but I'm still not really prepared for it. I hope people won't think too badly of me."

"For the record, sir, we really do need you to tell us who *did* write them."

"Of course, I'm sorry. It was my father, Max Goldstein – he changed his name later – who wrote them. They were in German and he couldn't get them published. I came across them after he died and showed them to Ann, as I thought she might be able to help. I translated one, and she showed it to a publisher, but he wasn't prepared to take a chance on a whole series by an unknown novelist. The best he would offer was to publish the first one and see how it went."

"And that wasn't good enough for you?" Willis enquired.

"No, it wasn't. Not at all. I was in desperate need of money, you see. I had a gambling problem when I was younger and I'd got myself into serious debt. Added to that my mother was ill and I wanted her to be properly cared for. That's why when Ann suggested what she did I accepted at once. It seemed like the answer to my prayers; it *was* the answer to my prayers."

"What did she suggest?"

"She offered me a lump sum for the rights to all the books, plus a translating fee for each one as I did it. Like I said, I accepted straightaway."

"Did you know that she intended to publish them under her own name?"

"Not at first, no. But I didn't have a problem with it

when she told me. I'm sure my father would have been very upset had he still been alive, but they didn't really mean anything to me. They were just some old manuscripts which were lying around gathering dust."

"What about your mother? Didn't she have to sign over the rights as your father's executor, or beneficiary, or whatever?"

"Both, actually, just to be on the safe side. And to tell the truth …,"

He broke off, embarrassed.

"You didn't tell her?" Willis proffered grimly.

"Not explicitly, no. I just told her that I was going to translate them and Ann was going to have them published. Mutti remembered Ann from when she used to see her in some café or other as a little girl, so that was alright."

"Did she ever find out the truth?"

"No. As it happened, she passed away just before the first one was published. It was very sudden, actually. She just went downhill very quickly over the course of a week or so."

"What was the cause of death?" Willis asked curiously.

"I think the death certificate said 'renal failure'. She had blood in her urine, you see. But she was in a bad way overall. She had bad stomach pains, and pretty chronic diarrhoea. I think her body was just generally giving up and closing down. The doctor said it was possible she had some sort of intestinal infection as well – you know, gastro-enteritis, that sort of thing. But it was her kidneys packing up which killed her, he said. Just old age, basically."

"Did Ann Durham visit at all, in the period leading up to your mother's death?" Willis asked.

"Oh yes, she was marvellous. She came to visit her a lot after the publishing deal was signed. She used to bring her little packets of expensive stomach powder from some fancy private doctor she knew. At first they seemed to suit Mutti very well, but when she got really ill they didn't really do any good."

There was a pause. Evans and Willis looked at each other. Willis glanced meaningfully at his notebook.

"Did her hair fall out, by any chance?" Willis asked at length.

"Yes, it did actually. That last couple of weeks almost all her hair came out. She was very upset at first – she'd always taken great care of her appearance – but by the end she was too ill even to notice."

"I see. Well, let's fast forward to the present, shall we? We understand that your daughter was threatening to expose this whole story. What's that all about?"

Thomas Gold stared hard at the grubby wallpaper as if gathering his thoughts.

"My daughter is not always an easy person to deal with," he said finally. "She has very decided views about things. She goes out with other young people at weekends holding placards and demonstrating about things. Capitalism. Globalism. Climate change. I think she gets it from her mother – she could be very difficult too."

"Where is your wife?" Willis asked.

"I haven't the slightest idea," he replied simply. "She left me ten years ago. At the time she said she was going to Israel to live on a kibbutz. I assume she did so, because Sonia used to get postcards from Israel for a while. Then they stopped."

"So tell me what Sonia has been up to," Willis said.

He sighed again.

"I had a phone call from Ann a few weeks ago, saying Sonia had been to see her and 'started shouting and screaming' in Ann's words. She claimed that Sonia seemed mentally unbalanced. She was frightened; I'd never heard Ann sound frightened before, but she definitely was."

"Frightened of what?"

"Of Sonia going to the press with the story, which is apparently what she'd been threatening to do. Ann said 'can't you see that it's in nobody's interests to have the story come out' and of course I agreed with her. But she was assuming that I could control me daughter, and I can't; nobody could."

As if on cue there was the sound of a key in the door and a very thin young woman came into the room. She had very black hair, very white skin, and was wearing heavy black mascara and deep purple lipstick. She glared suspiciously at the two detectives.

"What do you want with my father?" she demanded.

"Miss Gold, I assume? I'm Detective Sergeant Willis, and this is Detective Constable Evans."

"Ms Gold," the woman replied, making a buzzing noise on the 'Ms' by way of emphasis, and staring with evident disapproval at Willis's heels and stockings.

"Why don't you sit down, Ms Gold?" Willis countered calmly. "We'd like to ask you a few questions."

"Do you have a search warrant?" Sonia Gold asked belligerently. "You can't just come barging into people's homes, you know. This isn't a police state."

"We're not here to conduct a search," Willis explained with exaggerated politeness. "We're here to ask some questions, and your father invited us in. Now, why don't you sit down and we can carry on?"

The woman turned her glare to her father.

"You don't have to do this, you know," she told him. "You don't have to tell the filth anything at all."

He gazed at her helplessly.

"Please, Sonia," he said plaintively, "sit down. The lady just wants to ask a few questions about poor Ann Durham."

Sonia stood defiantly for a moment or two but then sat down with a theatrical sigh.

"I heard the old cow topped herself anyroad, if that's what you want to talk about," she threw out.

"Sonia!" her father protested desperately.

"How do you know that?" Wills enquired, ignoring Gold's feeble chastisement.

"It was the telly this morning, wasn't it? Said she took poison at that hotel. Must have been right after I saw her."

Again Willis and Evans exchanged glances.

"You were at the hotel yesterday evening?" Willis queried.

"Yeah, what of it?"

"I think you'd better tell us what happened."

"No. Why should I? It's none of your business."

Willis set herself to remaining calm and imagining what Collison would say in a situation like this.

"It's important that we eliminate you from our enquiries," she said carefully, "but we can't do that unless you tell us what happened."

"Eliminate me? What, you mean like I'm a suspect or something?"

"Anyone who had any contact with the deceased in the hour or so before her death is a suspect until we can eliminate them. As I understand it, you're saying you're one of those people. Therefore we need to eliminate you."

"I'm not saying nothing," Sonia Gold said defiantly. As if to make her point, she stood up and folded her arms across her chest.

"Now, get out," she said, pointing to the door.

Her eyes were staring and she was breathing quickly. She seemed to be controlling her temper only with difficulty.

"Mr Gold, is it your wish that we should leave?" Willis asked.

Again he gazed at his daughter helplessly.

"Perhaps it would be for the best," he said sadly. "I apologise for my daughter's behaviour."

At this, she snapped.

"Apologise? Don't you dare apologise for me, you pathetic little creep! That vile bitch stole your money and you didn't even have the nerve to do anything about it. Call yourself a man? Call yourself a father?"

Thomas Gold seemed to crumple completely under the weight of this tirade. It was if he had been transformed mysteriously from a man wearing a cardigan into a cardigan wearing a man.

Willis and Evans stood up to take their leave.

"Ms Gold," Willis said carefully as she slipped her bag onto her shoulder, "we need to ask you some questions whether you like it or not. You can either answer them here voluntarily now, or we can bring you to the police station later, if necessary against your will."

"What, you going to arrest me then, are you?" shouted Sonia, who was by now trembling visibly with rage.

"If that's what it takes, yes," Wills replied. "But first I'm inviting you to co-operate in helping us to eliminate you from this enquiry so we won't need to trouble you any further."

All the other three occupants of the room gazed silently at Sonia Gold.

"Piss off!" she hissed.

CHAPTER 12

"Charming!" Collison commented wryly at the next morning's briefing as Willis finished her report on Sonia Gold's outburst.

Metcalfe looked across at him. He was only part of the way through his 'to do' list.

"Shall we discuss that now, guv, or carry on with the list?" he asked.

"Carry on, please, Bob, then we'll circle back to it."

"Right-ho. The waiters: Priya, where are we on this, please?"

"I couldn't get the hotel moving fast enough yesterday. Sorry – I was most insistent."

Everyone smiled. They had all seen Desai being insistent before; it was not a pleasant experience for anyone on the receiving end.

"They said that it was difficult to get people together just like that," she continued. "Only some of them are permanent employees. The rest come through an agency and work shifts. But finally I got the hotel and the agency working together to contact everyone who was on duty at the dinner and bring them in. It wasn't easy. The agency is grumbling about who's going to pay for it all."

"Shouldn't be a problem," Collison observed, making a note. "I'll ask the DCS to authorise it."

"Provisionally it's set up for this afternoon," she said, "but I'll keep chasing."

"I think we need to bring together everyone who was a guest on that table," Collison said thoughtfully. "We can let them go down the line one at a time."

"Agreed," Metcalfe said, making a note of his own. "In that case, guv, why don't we re-interview the daughter and boyfriend then as well?"

"You think we need to?"

Metcalfe nodded.

"Can't do any harm. We got bugger all out of them last night."

"OK, I agree. Did you have anything else?"

"That's all I had on my list, guv. Except to comment that we're still no closer to finding out where the deceased got the poison from. We need to think about what we can do on that. Angela can't help. She says Durham sourced it herself from God knows where, and suddenly gave it to her for safe keeping. She slipped it into her handbag, where it stayed until Peter saw her take it out when Durham asked for it. What we don't know is ..."

"... its provenance," Collison finished the sentence for him, rolling the word exaggeratedly. "Yes, quite."

He got up and crossed over to the board, turning to address the team, which had by now swollen to include some new members whom he neither knew nor recognised. He would have to address that, he thought.

"Let's try running through the cast of characters and see if that can focus our thinking at all," he suggested.

He pointed at the list of names and went through them one by one.

"Peter Collins. Karen Willis. I think we can safely ignore them."

There was the predictable slight smile around the room.

"Angela Hughes appears to have no motive, and neither does our Miss Marple. Anyone think differently?"

"On the basis of what we know at the moment," Willis pointed out. "That doesn't mean we shouldn't still be digging for a possible connection."

"Agreed. Alright, Karen, why don't you think about some further questions we should be asking? I was going to propose that we re-interview Angela Hughes anyway. She's our best source of information on Ann Durham. Why don't we do her last, after we've spoken to the others? That way we can hopefully cross-check everything with her."

Willis started to suggest that this time Angela Hughes be interviewed by a female officer, but stopped herself.

"The daughter, Gina, and her boyfriend Barry Carver. I've been through their statements. Neither was terribly helpful. Any thoughts, anyone?"

"I'd like to know a lot more about the family's financial arrangements, guv," Metcalfe said. "The deceased was obviously supporting Gina, but we need more detail. Does she have money of her own? What happens on the mother's death? That sort of thing."

"Also, I remember the family group entering the room together," Willis proffered, "or, at least, they all approached the table together. So we need to press these two on whether Durham was already carrying that glass. If she was, that obviously makes the absence of the cyanide bottle in the room less relevant."

"For my part," Collison said, "I'd also like to know a lot more about Barry Carver. Remember Miss Marple's impression of extreme bad feeling between him and the deceased."

"If we're going to investigate impressions, guv, don't forget what Peter thought about the relationship between Durham and Smythe."

"Yes, I was just coming to him," Collison said, rubbing his finger down to the next name. "Tom Smythe. Well, at least we got a much fuller story out of him, but, as he helpfully pointed out, I'm not sure it takes us much further. There's plenty of reason why she might have wanted to murder him, at least if she felt as strongly about things as people seem to think she did, but no reason that I can see why he might have wanted to kill her."

"Two things he said so however take us further," he went on, moving his finger down to the next item which read 'waiters?'. "First, he alerted us to the fact that there could in fact have been multiple waiters clustering around the table, hence the ID parade. Second, he thought that Durham might have carried the glass to the table with her, although he did say that he couldn't be certain about that."

"So far as the waiters are concerned," he went on, rubbing his finger ruminatively from side to side, "I don't see there's much we can do until we have some individuals identified. Hm ..."

He then finished with the last name, freshly written on the board that morning.

"Sonia Gold. By all accounts an obstreperous young woman with a grudge against the accused. She admits to having been with her shortly before she died, but won't tell us why, when or where. I don't know about you lot, but if the poison could have been administered before Durham entered the room then she's a clear suspect."

Nods of assent rippled round the room.

"Timothy," Collison said decisively. "I'm authorising PNC searches against Gina Durham, Barry Carver, Tom Smythe and Sonia Gold. Let's see what we know about them."

"What about Angela Hughes, guv?" Willis prompted, as Evans bent forward and began tapping on his keyboard.

Collison and Metcalfe looked at each other dubiously.

"You really think it's justified?" Collison queried. "We have to be careful these days, you know."

"There's something about her, guv. Something I just can't put my finger on."

"Copper's nose, eh? Alright then, Angela Hughes too."

"I'll take her," Willis called across to Evans, "and Priya, you take Tom Smythe."

Desai was finished first.

"Smythe has a drink driving conviction from ten years back," she announced.

"Naughty, yes, but not exactly murderous," Collison quipped.

Willis finished next, looking ill at ease.

"There's nothing on Hughes," she admitted.

Metcalfe grinned at her and she smiled weakly in return.

"But I think I've hit the jackpot, sir," Evans announced, beaming.

"The daughter and the boyfriend are clean, but the Gold girl has quite a history. Two arrests at demos recently – once released under caution and once convicted of threatening behaviour under the Public Order Act. One count of criminal damage – chucking a brick through a window. That was when she was 14, and she was placed in care as a result – the father said he couldn't control her. Then arson when she was 15."

"Don't tell me," Collison said disbelievingly, "that she set fire to the care home?"

"Got it in one, guv. She was given a custodial sentence, released when she was 16. She's on probation at the moment, on the POA charge, and she's already missed two appointments with her probation officer."

"Contact them and get them in," Collison said at once. "The probation officer, I mean. I think Miss Gold may have given us a way of pulling her in against her will, bless her."

"She'll go ape-shit if you call her 'Miss', guv," Evans told him, grinning broadly. "I thought she was going to clock the DS when she did it. I was getting ready to ride to the rescue."

"Thank you, Timothy, but I think I'd have been able to handle it," Willis said coolly. "And I think she'll go ape-shit anyway. She no sooner saw me than her lip started curling. She obviously just loses it at the sight of the police."

"Actually, Sarge, I'm not sure it had anything to do with you being with the force," Evans said mischievously.

"Well, whatever the case," Willis replied, colouring slightly, "she clearly has a huge anger management issue. We sensed that when we met her, and her record confirms it. Arson, criminal damage, threatening behaviour: they're all offences which can be symptomatic of venting excess anger. Incidentally, the first two can also be indications of a psychopathic personality when they occur in teenagers, but I don't think that's the case here. Psychopaths are usually very controlled in their immediate dealings with other people, at least in public and on the surface."

"Let's not get ahead of ourselves," Metcalfe broke in. "Like the Guvnor says, let's get hold of the probation officer. Do you have the details, Timothy?"

"I'm on it, guv," Evans said, peering at the screen as he reached for the phone.

Lisa Atkins, Sonia Gold's probation officer, turned out to be quite unlike anything anybody had been expecting. Blond, pretty, and sporting a bright blue dress, she had the wholesome everyday sort of attractiveness that characterises the archetypical girl next door. As she sat and smiled gently at Collison and Metcalfe, they both found themselves wondering how a sweet young person like this could possibly deal with a character like Sonia Gold, let alone violent hardened criminals.

"So you see," Collison was summarising for her, "we urgently need to speak to Sonia about what happened when she met with Ann Durham, but she won't play ball. When two of my officers met with her yesterday she told them to piss off, if you'll pardon my French."

"That sounds pretty much like Sonia," the girl next door said with another smile. "She seems to have a very real problem with any sort of authority figure. In particular, she reacts very badly to police officers. Of course, she's been in trouble with the police a lot, so that may have something to do with it, but to be honest I'm not sure what came first, the chicken or the egg."

"Do you think she could be capable of something as serious as murder?" Metcalfe asked.

"I don't know her well enough to answer that question," Atkins replied evenly. "I haven't been able to complete my assessment process because she doesn't keep her appointments, but in theory, yes. Her criminal record shows that. My initial conversations seemed to indicate that she seems unable to control either her temper or her behaviour. That in itself makes her a dangerous person to be around. But also ..."

She hesitated.

"Go on," Metcalfe urged.

"This isn't any sort of formal psychological assessment. As I said, I haven't been able to formulate one yet. But informally and in everyday terms, she's one of these people who seems to feel they've been wronged by life somehow, who has a chip on their shoulder. I think that's part of the anger management thing. She's in an almost constant state of suppressed anger against the world in general, so it only takes a small increase in her stress levels to push her over the edge."

"So you think she could be violent?" Collison asked.

She nodded sadly.

"Yes, I do. I've seen exactly these symptoms before in serious offenders in prison. Men who had committed extremely violent acts for little apparent reason, sometimes just because someone had looked at them in the wrong way. Of course, those were typically men with very low IQs, whereas Sonia is quite an intelligent woman, but I get the same feeling from her that I did from them. I'm actually very surprised that none of the psychiatrists picked it up when she was in custody. If I'd had anything to do with it I wouldn't just have released her back into the community unsupervised."

"Would tranquilisers help?" Collison asked.

"They'd calm her down a bit, yes of course, but I'm not a great fan of controlling someone's state of mind with drugs – not unless they've got a recognisable biochemical condition. You need to get into their mind and try to find out what's causing the symptoms in the first place."

"And you can't do that because she won't keep her appointments?"

"Correct. She's always been very sporadic, but she's got worse. She's missed the last two. In fact, before you called I'd already come to the conclusion that I was going to go back to court and recommend a return to custody."

"That's fine," Collison acknowledged, "but we need to act quickly. It's very important in a homicide enquiry that you don't let the trail go cold. So, rather than waiting for your next scheduled hearing, would you be prepared to go with DI Metcalfe here today – now – and see the duty magistrate?"

"Of course. I'm happy to help in any way I can. I would venture a suggestion, though."

"What's that?"

"Well," Atkins said, "there's a very real chance that when she realises she's in danger of heading into custody she might become completely uncontrollable. It might be an idea to have a duty doctor on hand, because she may need to be sedated."

"That's good advice," Collison said uneasily, "and of course we'll follow it, but I do hope not. We need to speak to her, and we can't do that if she's sedated."

She gathered up her bag and they said their farewells.

As Metcalfe opened the car door for her she said "thank you, Inspector."

"Please call me Bob," he replied, closing the door and reflecting appreciatively that this enquiry seemed to be replete with more than its fair share of attractive women.

"Tell me," he said as she started the car, "did anyone consider the possibility of abuse at all?"

"Yes, of course, that's the first thing we think of in the case of disturbed teen behaviour. It was all investigated, but it seems there was nothing. The father is a caring, though rather weak and inoffensive character so far as I can make out – though I've only met him once. It's possible that the root cause may lie in the mother having run off suddenly like that; the daughter was only about ten so it must have affected her very badly."

"I never knew my mother," he found himself saying as he turned away. "I was adopted."

"I'm so sorry," she said sincerely.

He knew he should glance back at her, but did not. For some ridiculous reason he suddenly felt himself to be on the verge of tears, and suspected that to look at her might prove too much.

CHAPTER 13

"You're not sleuthing, are you?" Angela Hughes asked with a sad attempt at humour.

"Not sleuthin' exactly," Collins replied, "but obviously I'm keeping my eyes and ears open. You never know what you might spot that could turn out to be important."

"I'm so sorry," he added quickly, "I never asked you how you were. I didn't see you this morning."

"Thank you, I'm fine, I think. And no, I wasn't here. I had to slip into the office to handle the fall-out. I pity the PR team; their phones were ringing non-stop. Thank God I don't have to deal with that sort of thing."

"What were you doing, then?"

"Cranking up production, of course. Every bookshop in the world is going to want shelves and shelves of Ann Durham in the next few weeks, so it's extra print runs all round. Our main printer is going to lay on extra staff and run overnight. The foreign language markets are going crazy as well, particularly Germany. You know, I was just doing some calculations this morning, and it's possible that we could sell half a million copies worldwide over the next week or two."

"Well, well," Peter said, taken aback, "so it really is an ill wind that blows nobody any good."

"Yes, sadly. Of course, it remains to be seen how long it will be before the Bergmann story breaks. That could kill everything stone dead, but you never know, it might just crank up interest all over again."

"Oh, surely not?" Peter protested.

Hughes gave a grim laugh.

"The reading public is a strange animal, Peter. Why do you think bookshops lay in stock of anything which is being shown on television? You'd think that sales would plummet then, wouldn't you? After all, who would want to read something that they've already just seen on the telly? But in fact the opposite's the case."

"But wouldn't it just stimulate interest in Max Goldstein instead? 'Unknown author revealed as creator of great series stolen by the Queen of Crime', that sort of thing?"

"Yes, I've been considering that," Angela Hughes said seriously, "but do you know, I'm not sure it matters. Don't forget that Ann owned the rights to the books regardless of who wrote them, so the estate could simply re-issue them under Goldstein's name as part of a huge PR campaign, and pocket the proceeds."

"Good God," said Collins, genuinely shocked. "I can see I'm not cut out for business, Angela; I wouldn't have the stomach for anything like that."

"Please don't think that I'd feel any less comfortable about it than you," she said quickly, laying a hand on his arm, "but unfortunately there's no room for sentiment in business. Ann taught me that."

She looked at him plaintively.

"Oh, I'm sorry," he said awkwardly. "I didn't mean to imply any personal criticism. And I suppose it's good for you to have things to keep you busy."

"Yes, I think so too," she said edgily.

She could hardly have got much sleep, he thought. It showed, poor girl. She was making a huge effort to appear on top of the situation, but as a result was coming across as bright but brittle. He wondered how he might be able tactfully to suggest that perhaps she might do better to give an outlet to her distress. It was too difficult, though. He would struggle even with Karen, while he hardly knew Angela.

"And speaking of keeping busy I had a call from your girlfriend earlier. There's an identity parade here a bit later. They want me to attend."

"Yes, me too," Collins confirmed, feeling a sudden unexpected pang at her use of the word 'girlfriend', "I think the idea is to try to identify any waiters who were around the table at the time."

"Waiters?" Hughes asked sharply. "Why on earth would they want to do that? Surely they can't think any of them had anything to do with it? They'd be much better employed trying to find out what happened to that cyanide in my opinion. I'm still pretty sure it was suicide."

"Suicide, dear?" Miss Marple asked mildly as she came up to them. "Well, we'll see."

"You don't think so?" Peter enquired politely.

136

"I think it's a viable theory," she said cautiously, "which I was at pains to point out to the Superintendent because he seemed inclined too easily to dismiss it. I've seen women in the village where I live get things out of proportion when they're troubled: money problems, a difficult husband, these are not matters which would induce anyone to do something stupid, you'd think, would you? Yet they do."

Peter steered her to a seating area and they sat down.

"And if Ann, *was* troubled," she went on, "and dear Angela here says that she was, then one must remember that Ann had all the pride and ego of a crime-writer, and she might well have decided to bow out in a blaze of melodrama. Oh, yes."

She paused and gazed at them both contemplatively.

"You say it's a viable theory, and I agree," Collins ventured, "But something tells me you don't think it's the most likely one."

"I think there are two difficulties with it," she replied judiciously. "First, if she did administer the poison herself then why is it that nobody has been able to find the bottle? The police searched the area of the table. They searched all of us, so they know that none of us could have carried it away. They searched Ann's room: nothing. It seems to me that unless the police are able to find it then the suicide theory is very difficult to make good."

"And the second?" asked Angela Hughes, intrigued.

"Second, I remain convinced that there will be a second death, and that would make it clear beyond doubt that

Ann did not take her own life. Unless of course the two deaths were genuinely unrelated, which would be almost inconceivable."

Hughes looked shocked; she had not heard Miss Marple's prognostication of the previous evening.

"What on earth are you talking about?" she demanded. "A second death? What do you mean?"

Miss Marple thought deeply before answering.

"On one level, just because there always is, as I told the Superintendent last night. After all, if one is living a real life situation which has all the hallmarks of a detective story then is it really unreasonable to expect real life to observe the conventions of the detective story? We already have death by cyanide poisoning, a policeman with a public school accent, an apparently closed circle of immediate suspects ..."

"Not to mention," she continued with a coy glance at Collins, "a beautiful woman and her gentleman companion who are present when the death occurs."

"But no," she went on briskly. "I am being playful, of course. The real reason I believe a second death will occur is the absence of the poison bottle. That points very strongly to the presence of an accomplice; either to administer the poison, spirit the bottle away afterwards, or both."

"And accomplices always fall out," Collins said thoughtfully. "Or that at least is the convention, isn't it?"

"It is," nodded Miss Marple rather absently, for she had by now pulled out her knitting and was counting rows with a frown, "and not a bad one. Either one of them attempts to exploit the situation, perhaps by blackmail, or one of them loses their nerve and may crack under interrogation. In either case, they must be silenced."

"There are other possibilities," Collins pointed out with a rather donnish air. "The second victim may observe something important about the first murder, or may be in danger of realising the significance of something they have previously overlooked."

"Yes, yes," Miss Marple conceded vaguely as she plied her knitting needles, "all good possibilities."

"It is an interesting convention, of course," Collins said, turning towards Angela Hughes, who was looking rather lost and suddenly very tired. "The first murder appears insoluble, with a welter of possibilities, but when the second one occurs then the task is narrowed down considerably. It is now only a matter of discovering the connection between them, for that will be the key to unlocking the mysteries of the first."

"It is almost as if the first murder *requires* the second," he expounded, gazing gently into her eyes, eager for her to grasp the point, "to define it, to give it meaning. And of course the first murder is usually the prime mover in the chain of causation which leads to the second, so in a sense each requires the other."

"You're so wise," Angela Hughes told Collins weakly but admiringly, "you seem to understand everything, somehow."

He was about to reply when he noticed that Karen

Willis had joined the group and was observing him rather pointedly.

"Ah," he said, "hello."

"We're ready for the ID parade," she said, looking down at them as they sat. "We all need to go to the green room, please."

The ladies gathered up their bags, a process which took a few minutes for Miss Marple as she had to finish the row, make sure that her knitting was secured to its needles with a plastic clasp, and then stow it away carefully. Willis watched patiently and then shepherded them to the green room where Collison, Metcalfe and Evans were standing waiting for them. Seated, and displaying varying degrees of uneasiness, were Tom Smythe, Gina Durham and Barry Carver.

"Before we start," Collison said, "I'd like to thank everyone for their co-operation. What we've done is to organise a parade of all the waiters who may have had anything to do with the top table at the gala dinner. There are rather a lot of them, and I appreciate that it may be asking a lot of you, but we'd like you to go into the room one at a time, walk down the line, and see if there are any faces you recognise as having been anywhere near the table. If so, just stop at each familiar face and tell the officer who will be accompanying you."

He glanced around the room.

"Also, having had a chance to read your initial statements, we'll be asking some of you to let us use this opportunity to ask you some follow-up questions. Very sorry to inconvenience you but we'll get you away as quickly as we can and, as I say, we appreciate your co-operation."

Barry Carver frowned and shot an irritated glance at Gina Durham.

"Dr Collins," Collison went on quickly, "why don't you go first, just to show there's nothing to be afraid of?"

"Yes, of course," Collins said, turning to go with Evans.

They went together to the door of the ballroom, where Desai was waiting.

"Hello, Priya," he greeted her.

She gave him a brief smile; she seemed distracted. Collins guessed that the logistics involved in bringing together all the waiting staff from hotel and agency alike had been far from straightforward. He stepped into the room and then stopped. A straight line of waiters, all dressed in identical white jackets and charcoal trousers stretched away from him.

"Just walk slowly down the line, looking at people's faces," Desai urged him. "If you see anyone you think you remember, just stop and tell me."

He walked hesitantly along the line, Desai hovering at his elbow. He stopped about two thirds of the way along.

"I think this is the man I saw standing close to Tom Smythe and Angela Hughes when the jug fell," he said uncertainly.

"Before or after?" she prompted him.

"After, I think. Yes, I turned around when I heard the commotion."

"OK, let's carry on shall we?"

This however was to prove their only success. Dispirited, Collins returned to the door where he found Barry Carver waiting with Evans. This police shuttle service saw Carver being handed off to Desai and escorted into the ballroom while Collins was returned to Evans and, somewhat disconsolately, they returned to the green room.

"Any luck, sir?" Evans enquired.

"Not really. Only one."

"Better than nothing," Evans observed philosophically.

The atmosphere back among the group felt a little like a doctor's waiting room. One by one they were shuffled out of the door to go down the line in their turn, coming back a few minutes later. Finally, Willis left.

"Now then," Collison said heartily. "Re-interview time. Mr Smythe and Miss Marple, we don't need to detain you, so thank you again and goodbye for the present. Mr Carver, would you come with me, please, and Miss Durham, could you go with the Inspector. Miss Hughes, it would be doing us a huge favour if you wouldn't mind waiting until last. Please feel free to make some phone calls or whatever else you want to do."

He turned to Collins.

"Dr Collins, I needn't detain you any longer, either. Unless of course you'd like to stay and keep Miss Hughes company?"

"Yes, I would, gladly," Collins replied.

He had spoken without thinking, and he stopped and

looked at Angela Hughes. Their eyes met and she gave him a tired but grateful smile.

Desai came back into the room with some handwritten notes on a piece of paper, which she handed to Collison. He glanced at it carefully and gave it back.

"Thank you, Priya. Once you've finished here get this back to the nick and into the system, please. Arrange for us to interview these names ASAP. And please ask Timothy to join the DI, and DS Willis to join me. Team meeting tomorrow morning as usual."

CHAPTER 14

"Am I a suspect?" Barry Carver asked suspiciously as he sat down.

"Not in the sense we use the term, no," Collison said carefully. "If you were, we would have to tell you so and interview you under caution. No, we're simply anxious to ask you some more questions as a witness, and a key one at that, if I may say so. After all, you were right there when the death occurred and you were a member of the family circle, both actually in the room and figuratively speaking."

"All right then," Carver acknowledged reluctantly. "But I've already told you everything I know, when I gave a statement right after … well, you know."

"I appreciate that," Collison replied, "but there are a few new angles we wish to pursue, and anyway, we frequently find that things may suddenly come to mind which were forgotten or ignored earlier. For example, did you enter the room with Ann Durham?"

"Yeah, I did. Gina and I were just about to go in when her mother came up as well, so we all went in together."

"How did she seem – the mother, I mean? Was she at all agitated, for instance?"

"She was permanently agitated when I was around,"

Carver observed with a sudden grin, "she didn't like me at all and didn't bother to hide it."

"Why didn't she like you?" Willis asked.

"Thought I wasn't good enough for her precious daughter, of course. I can remember the first time she found me at Gina's flat. She started screaming at her – 'are you out of your mind?' – that sort of thing. She tried to send Gina away to some friends in the South of France. Thought she might meet 'a more suitable sort of boy', but Gina wouldn't go. They argued about it for weeks. I used to hear the old bag screeching down the phone at her."

"And how were things later – after the arguments died down?" Willis enquired.

Carver shrugged.

"How do you think? She just ignored me. Wouldn't speak to me. I always wondered why Gina put up with it all. I told her she should just tell her mother to sod off and go and live her own life."

"But she wouldn't?"

"Nah. I think it all had to do with a trust or something. Gina doesn't own her flat, she just gets to live there. Apparently the old bag could have had her chucked out anytime she wanted. Threatened to a couple of times if she didn't get rid of me, but Gina called her bluff. We had to pretend I wasn't actually living there, just visiting from time to time, if you know what I mean."

"Who could tell us more about these financial arrangements, do you think?" Collison asked.

Carver shrugged again.

"Gina, I guess. Or Angela Hughes; I think she took care of all the business stuff."

"So you can't recollect how Ann Durham looked when you met up with her outside the ballroom?" Willis quizzed him.

"Not really, no. To tell the truth we both used to ignore each other as much as possible."

"All right, let's leave that then," she said. "Can you remember if Ann Durham was holding a glass when you first saw her that evening?"

Carver thought deeply.

"I can't honestly say," he responded at length. "I'm sorry, I'm trying but I just don't remember."

"We don't want to press you into saying anything you're not certain about," Collison said quickly. "But perhaps we could try asking the question a different way. Do you remember the deceased picking up a glass from a table at any time, or being handed one by someone else? Or anyone pouring anything into her glass?"

Carver thought long and hard again.

"Do you know," he said slowly. "I think I do remember something. I'm not sure, but I have a vague recollection of her being handed a glass by a waiter."

"You mean taking one off a tray?"

"No, actually being handed one – and now you come to mention it, that's odd, isn't it? I mean, at that sort of do they would have glasses on trays, like you say. Why would anyone give her a special glass all of her own?"

"Can you describe the waiter?" Collison asked, ignoring the question.

Carver thought hard again.

"Was it the same one you picked out of the line-up?" Collison pressed him, looking down at his notes.

"No, I don't think it was. I can remember him being near the table – very near in fact – when it all kicked off. But this was something that happened further away, before she got to the table."

"How much further away?"

"Not much. I can remember pushing through a lot of people and then space sort of opening up as we got near the top table, and I think that's when it happened."

"So it could have been one of the waiters around the table after all?" Willis cut in. "From what you say, they would have had time to hand off the glass and still make their way over to the table."

"Yeah, I guess so, but I honestly don't remember very much about it. Actually, I'm beginning to wonder if I did really see anything at all or whether I'm just imagining it."

"Don't worry," Collison reassured him. "This is all very valuable. If nothing else it gives us something we can try to check with other witnesses."

In the other room, Metcalfe and Evans were making progress with Gina Durham.

"I don't remember Mum picking up the glass once we were in the room," she was saying, "although I wasn't paying too much attention. I was trying to stay close to Barry, and then I got talking to that nice Dr Collins; you know, the one who's written a book about poisoning."

"So she might have already had it with her when she entered the room?" Metcalfe asked.

"Yes, I suppose she might. But I didn't really notice. You see we only met up at the door of the ballroom, and even that was quite by chance. Barry and I had been in our room. It just so happened that Mum must have come down at the same time. It wasn't what I would have wanted, I can assure you. I was hoping to keep Mum and Barry apart as much as I could."

"She didn't approve, then?"

"No, it was all very silly somehow. She always called me her little princess, and I think she had some crazy idea that I'd marry an Earl or maybe an Italian Count or something like that. Mum was a terrible snob, you see. She used to get invited to a lot of high society events, the sort you see photos of people standing around at in the glossy magazines, and she liked to believe that she really belonged to that set. She was always trying to persuade me to come with her and let her introduce me to 'nice people', as she called them. She didn't like my friends; they were all a bit rough and ready for her."

"So Barry didn't measure up to her idea of a future son-in-law?" Metcalfe queried.

"God, no. At first she sort of tolerated him because she thought he was just someone I'd get over and move on but every time I tried to tell her that I was really serious about him she just went ballistic and started going on about him. How he'd ruin my life and all that sort of thing. This last time was the worst of all."

"Why was that?"

"Well, we'd decided some time ago that we wanted to get married but I'd been putting off telling her. I finally plucked up courage to tell her just about a week ago."

"And?"

"At first I thought she was going to have a heart attack. She went bright red in the face and started breathing really loudly. Then suddenly she went sort of icy calm. It was really scary. She just looked at me and said that if I married Barry I wouldn't get a penny of her money. I told her I couldn't care less, but out of curiosity I asked her what she meant. It seems she's drawn up a will leaving everything she's got to me, but she said she can change it anytime, and she would if I wouldn't dump Barry. Long story short, we had a huge row and I left. I hadn't seen her or spoken to her since then, except to say 'hello' when we met at the hotel."

"I'm surprised you still came, in the circumstances," Metcalfe observed. "Didn't you think of cancelling?"

"Yes, but we thought – I thought anyway – that if she saw me and Barry coming along to support her then it might help change her mind about him. She's like that sometimes; she really blows up about something and then the next time you see her it's all forgotten about. I think it's that she's got used to being able to scream and shout at people over the years with nobody answering her back, so it's just become her default reaction to anything which upsets her."

"Do you know anything about the bottle of cyanide she had with her earlier in the conference?" Metcalfe asked, changing the subject.

"No, absolutely not. The first I remember hearing about it was when I heard Dr Collins and Angela Hughes talking about it after Mum collapsed."

"Can you think of anyone she knows who might have supplied it? A chemistry teacher, for example, or someone who works for a company that might use the stuff?"

She shook her head decisively.

"I don't know Mum's friends that well," she explained, "but I definitely can't think of anyone like that, and quite frankly I can't imagine her mixing with someone like a teacher. Like I said, she was a frightful snob."

Metcalfe paused. Quite often when it felt like an interview was going nowhere he liked to launch the conversation suddenly down a new track, and he decided to do so now.

"What do you know about the other people who were at the table? Apart from your Mum and Barry, I mean."

"Dr Collins I'd never met before, but he seemed very nice. I didn't really get a chance to speak to his girlfriend – she's one of your colleagues, isn't she?"

Metcalfe smiled and nodded.

"Angela Hughes I've known for a long time. She spends so much time with Mum, and she's helped us with so many things over the years that she almost feels like a big sister rather than Mum's agent. She's nice; I really like her. She comes over to our place sometimes when we have people round."

"Tom Smythe?"

"Oh, I've met him quite a few times. He and Mum were always on committees together. I think once upon a time they got on quite well – I mean, not friends or anything, but a good working relationship – but that had changed recently. Mum said he'd betrayed her about something, 'stabbed her in the back' was how she put it, I think. Poor Mum, she always fell out with everyone sooner or later."

"What about Miss Marple?"

Gina smiled.

"Oh, her! She's rather a dear, isn't she? I hadn't met her before the conference, though of course it felt almost like I knew her already, having seen her on telly so many times."

"Did your mother know her well, do you think?"

She thought carefully.

"I think they certainly knew each other from attending these sort of events over the years, but I wouldn't say they were close; Mum never really had any close friends, unless you count Angela. As a matter of fact, I seem to remember that Mum had upset Miss Marple a few years back, but I can't remember the details. You'd have to ask Angela; it was she who told me."

"Hm."

Metcalfe watched Evans writing.

"And what about Barry?" he asked quietly. "What can you tell me about his background?"

She looked at him sharply.

"Why do you ask?"

"Just trying to build a picture," Metcalfe replied blandly. "What does he do, for instance?"

"Not very much," she admitted with a little laugh. "He's an actor, you see, and when you're young and just starting out it's really just a matter of going to auditions all the time and hoping for call-backs. Most actors are out of work most of the time, you know; they call it 'resting'. There's just a small number of actors who get all the jobs. I think it's very unfair that they should be on the telly all the time. I'm sure the public must get awfully bored with seeing them in everything."

"How did you meet?"

"At a party. It was a couple of years back. He was just finishing at the drama college at Swiss Cottage. One of my friends had been at school with one of his classmates and when she got invited she took me along. We hit it off at once. He wasn't like anyone else I'd ever met. He doesn't take any bullshit from anyone, but he's also incredibly sensitive."

"And does he live with you?"

"Yes, but we've tried to keep that quiet. Mum owns the flat you see, and I wouldn't put it past her to chuck us both out on the street. Oh, I mean I wouldn't *have* put it past her, of course. How silly."

She looked down suddenly as her eyes filled with tears.

"I think we've detained you quite long enough," Metcalfe said hurriedly. "Many thanks again for your assistance."

CHAPTER 15

After Gina Durham and Barry Carver had left the hotel together, Collison sent Evans back to help Desai gather material on the selected waiters. The remaining three detectives then joined Collins and Angela Hughes, who were still sitting chatting quietly and drinking tea. Hughes still looked tired, but less strained than before.

"If you feel you're up to it," Collison said, eyeing her doubtfully, "there's quite a lot of background we need you to fill in for us."

"Don't worry about me," she said steadily, "I just want to do whatever I can to help you get to the truth."

"I'm glad you feel like that," he replied as he sat down. "Karen, would you take notes, please?"

"Now then," he went on, looking at the notes he himself had made, "I wonder if you could start by telling us everything you can about Gina Durham. Who was her father, for example, and is he still alive?"

"He was a publisher," she said, "and no, he's not. He was quite a lot older than Ann, but he still died relatively young – about sixty, I think. Gina would have been about four at the time, so she has no real memories of him."

"A publisher?" Metcalfe interjected in surprise. "Not *the*

publisher, surely? The one who published the Bergmann books?"

"The very same," she replied with a sad smile. "He was desperately in love with Ann and always had been. I sometimes wonder if that clouded his judgement over the publishing deal. He would have done anything she wanted. She was very attractive, you know, when she was younger. You can see that from her old publicity photos."

"Just so I'm clear about this," Collison said, "did anyone else at his company know about the real identity of the author?"

"Not so far as I'm aware, no. The deal always was that everyone would keep the secret. David – that was his name, David Molyneux – edited the books himself, and it was his family company so nobody would ever have been able to query what he was doing even if they'd wanted to. They *were* good books, after all. It wasn't as though he was publishing stuff that didn't deserve to see the light of day."

"So the only people who were in on the secret and still alive are you and Tom Gold?"

"Yes, although I didn't know originally; I was just a little girl. Ann took me into her confidence when I became her agent. That's why it was such a tragedy when that wretched Sonia found out. Tom Gold is completely trustworthy and would have taken the secret to the grave with him, but now it's going to be all over the news."

"How did David Molyneux die?" Willis asked curiously.

"I don't know. It was well before I appeared on the

scene. I can remember Ann saying that he'd been ill for a while but then it suddenly got much worse and within a few weeks he was dead, but I don't know what it was that he had. I suppose there must be a death certificate somewhere though, mustn't there?"

"Yes, I suppose so," Willis agreed.

Collison shot her an enquiring glance but she shook her head in a 'tell you later' sort of way.

"What can you tell us about the financial arrangements between mother and daughter?" he asked, "and do you know the provisions of her will?"

"I can tell you what I know," Angela Durham replied, "but you should probably speak to her lawyer – I can give you his details."

"Thank you."

"Basically I think Ann just gave Gina money when she needed it. I know that she had a monthly allowance while she was at university, but I'm not sure how much it was. And of course she had a flat to live in which Ann provided. There was talk of setting up a trust from time to time, but Ann had already decided that she would only do that if she could retain ultimate control of the trust fund – for example if Gina married someone of whom she disapproved – and the lawyers advised that any such arrangement would be horrible from a tax point of view, so it never got done."

"Did she always have that attitude?" Collison asked curiously, "or did it start when she became aware of Barry Carver?"

"She was always very controlling, but I think, yes, it's fair to say that it got much worse after she met Barry. I think it brought it home to her that Gina was a grown-up woman now and that inevitably she'd want to settle down with a man sooner or later. Ann was desperate that it should be 'the right sort of man' as she used to say."

"And Barry didn't qualify?"

Angela Hughes laughed.

"Definitely not. Ann hated him, and I think the feeling was mutual."

"What about the will?"

"I never actually saw it. I remember it being made a few years ago. Ann said I couldn't witness it because it contained a bequest to me, but I think it left pretty much everything to Gina. As I say, you'd need to ask the lawyer. She told me that she'd named me as her literary executor – in other words I get to carry on making all decisions required in connection with the rights to her books."

"We understand that there had recently been talk of the deceased changing her will," Collison said cautiously. "Can you tell us anything about that?"

"Oh dear. Yes, I can, I'm afraid. Ann had spoken to me a couple of days before she died. She'd had an appalling row with Gina about Barry – Gina told me about it too – and she was hopping mad. Apparently she'd threatened to cut Gina out of her will unless she stopped seeing Barry, and Gina defied her, told her to do her worst and that she didn't want the money anyway. I don't think I'd ever seen Ann so upset.

Coming on top of the whole CWA election thing I think things were really getting her down in a big way; she was drinking quite heavily, for example. That's why I still tend to believe that somehow she found a way of taking her own life. She really did think she'd lost Gina for good. 'I've lost her, I've lost my baby' she kept saying – that sort of thing."

"Hm," said Collison noncommittally. "Well, we have to keep an open mind, you know. We're not ruling out anything at this stage."

"I'm sorry, I wasn't trying to interfere, I just thought –"

"Not at all," he assured her smoothly, "it's very helpful to hear the opinion of someone who knew her so well. Now, what more can you tell us about Sonia Gold?"

"Ann thought she was mad. I wouldn't go so far as that, but I do think she has massive anger management issues. She can lose control very quickly, and when she does it's very easy to believe that she could become violent. She's really very scary."

"What did she want exactly?"

"Well, that's one of the problems. It's really very difficult to tell. She seems to find it difficult to have a normal, rational discussion. You keep trying to steer the conversation round to the rights and what she thinks should happen to them, but she keeps going on and on about her family and all the hardships they've suffered."

"Couldn't you get her to appoint a lawyer, or an agent, or someone to speak for her?" Willis suggested.

"Exactly what I proposed," Angela Hughes said with

a shake of the head, "but she wouldn't hear of it. She said her family had been cheated once and she wasn't going to see them be cheated again. She hates what she calls 'the establishment' and has some sort of paranoid mistrust of anyone she thinks that includes – which seems to be just about everyone."

"What stage had the discussions reached?"

"In terms of progress, none at all. She seemed to think that we were just going to apologise and hand over a huge sum of money. She couldn't grasp the fact that there had been a fully binding contract which had been freely entered into by consenting adults, as it were, and that legally she didn't have a leg to stand on."

"Are we sure about that? Had you taken fresh legal advice?"

"Lots of it. The very best and the most expensive. She got hold of some left wing activist who had a ghastly little legal aid law practice somewhere, and he was trying to argue that the original agreement didn't cover the screen rights, but our lawyers said that it clearly did, and that he just wasn't a very good lawyer."

"And how long had all this been going on?"

"Two or three months, I suppose. At first she met with me a couple of times and, like I said, we just weren't on the same wavelength at all. Then we had our lawyers meet with her lawyer, and apparently he wasn't very much better. He just kept going on about what his client wanted, without focussing on the legal issues. Then Ann suggested that she should meet with her, and that was a disaster. Within the first ten minutes it turned into a screaming match. Sonia attacked her and Ann had to run out of her office and get her secretary to call the police. By the time they arrived, of course, she'd gone."

Collison and Willis exchanged glances.

"When you say 'attacked'," Collison said carefully. "Do you mean physically?"

"Oh yes. She started by slapping her face and pulling her hair. Then when Ann managed to get out of the room she started doing karate kicks on her, and when the secretary – Julia, her name is – tried to help, Sonia started throwing things at her, including a heavy ornament which hit her on the leg – she's still got the bruises. By the time I got there the police had arrived and they were both quite hysterical, poor dears."

"I see," Collison said heavily. "Well, it would be helpful to see the police report of course."

"Julia would be happy to give you the details; you have the office number. But you should be able to find it very easily. You see, Julia was in such a panic that she rang 999, and they log all those calls don't they?"

"They do indeed," Collison agreed, "and record them too."

"Hang on," said Angela Hughes as she fished a diary out of her handbag. "It was the 26th July, at about eleven fifteen."

"That's very helpful," Collison said as he watched Willis jot it down.

"And so," he went on, turning back to her and watching

her carefully, "I presume that's the last time anyone from your side saw Sonia Gold?"

"Oh no, at least, I don't think so."

"No?"

"No, Ann saw her on the night she died, or at least I assume she did. I never got a chance to find out."

Both detectives stared at her.

"You never mentioned this before," Collison pointed out after a pause, "though as it happens we already have information from another source that something of the type occurred."

"Oh gosh, I'm so sorry, I suppose it was because I was concentrating on what happened at the dinner and then afterwards there was so much to deal with I was just too busy to think that it might be important."

"It might be very important," Collison said with a hint of impatience. "I think you'd better tell us everything you know."

"Well, the day before Ann died Sonia phoned the office and left a message for her. She said that unless we agreed to pay her and her father half a million pounds within 48 hours then she was going to go to the newspapers. She claimed that she'd already spoke to one and they'd offered her a hundred thousand for her story."

"Is this message on tape?"

"No she left it with Julia, who wrote it down and then got in touch with Ann – she was here, of course, at the convention."

"What did she do?"

"Ann spoke to me. She asked me to arrange a meeting between her and Sonia in her room here at the hotel before dinner the next evening, which was the night she died, of course."

"And you did?"

"Yes, but only under protest as it were. I said 'you must be mad' and quite a lot else. This woman had just attacked her, don't forget; tried to kick her around the office. I was particularly upset that Ann wanted to meet with her alone and in private. To be honest, I was afraid for her. I thought it was way too dangerous."

"But she insisted?"

"Yes. For one she was absolutely icy calm. She said it was unthinkable that the truth should come out; her reputation would be ruined. She said she was prepared to do anything it took to stop that happening. I asked if that included paying the blackmail money and she said that if that was what it took, then yes. I said she was crazy, that there was nothing to stop them leaking the story anyway, and that even if they played ball this time they could come back again and again and bleed her dry."

"What was her reaction?"

"For once she didn't get angry. She just smiled and took my hands. She looked terribly tired and as she looked at me she said something like 'Angela, dear, this is the end of the line'. Oh, how stupid of me not to guess what she intended to do."

"Kill herself, you mean?"

Angela nodded tearfully.

"For the record," Collison said, suddenly feeling very tired himself, "what you should have done was to come to the police. Blackmail happens to be against the law, you know."

"I know, I know," she replied lamely, "but Ann seemed so confident she could work things out somehow."

"But you don't know whether she did or not?"

"No, I was hoping to have a word with her before dinner, but of course I never got the chance."

At this point Angela, who had been sobbing quietly under her breath for a few minutes, succumbed to a heavier bout, excusing herself between gulps. Collison nodded at Willis, who closed her notebook.

"I'm sorry," he said gently. "I know this can't be easy for you. Thank you very much."

CHAPTER 16

"So what have you decided about your mother, Karen?" Bob asked as the three of them had a belated dinner at the house that evening.

She shrugged and reached for her wine glass.

"It seems pretty pointless, doesn't it?" she replied with the glass raised, ready to drink. "She was a crackhead and almost certainly a tom. Even if she's still alive, I can't really see us having long sisterly conversations."

"I'm sorry," Peter said quietly.

"I'm sorry too," she replied as she put her glass down again. "Sorry for myself, of course, though I always knew it was a pretty slim chance. But for you too, Bob, because I'm afraid it may put you off looking for your own mother and it's important that it shouldn't – not if that's what you decide to do."

He nodded.

"Yes, I know, but to be honest I haven't really given it much more thought – and certainly not in the last few days."

There was a collective smile. An active murder investigation took over people's lives, often at the expense sooner or later of marriages, friendships and relationships. Until the last moment they had not even been sure whether they would be able to snatch this meal together.

"Are you back at the Convention tomorrow, Peter?" Karen asked.

"Yes, I thought I should. Even though I don't have any specific reason to be there I just feel somehow that I should keep a sort of watching brief. Anyway, it's the last day tomorrow."

"By the way, Angela was right about demand for Ann Durham's books taking off," Metcalfe commented. "I walked home past the bookshop and they had both windows stuffed with nothing else – the Bergmann books in one window and her later stuff in the other."

"It's an ill wind ..." Willis said sagely.

"Angela's still convinced it was suicide, presumably?" Peter asked. "That was certainly her line when I spoke to her before she was interviewed."

"Strictly speaking I suppose we shouldn't be discussing this with you," Metcalfe said half-jokingly, "but since you're involved anyway ... yes, she is."

Collins chewed and swallowed thoughtfully.

"It's a puzzle, isn't it?" he mused at length. "On the one hand the disappearance of the cyanide container strongly suggests murder, but on the other hand why on earth would a crime-writer, and one who has so recently handled cyanide herself at close quarters, willingly drink from a glass which we know from having been there positively reeked of the stuff?"

"The argument for suicide," Metcalfe contributed, "is

certainly consistent with her having been under great strain on a number of fronts. We now know for certain, for example, that she was staring down the barrel of the imminent deadline of a blackmail demand from Sonia Gold."

"Yes," Collins concurred, "and didn't Miss Marple say it would be entirely consistent with what she knew of Ann Durham's character for her to commit suicide in such a melodramatic way?"

"Opinion," Willis said dismissively, "and anyway, she wasn't saying it *was* suicide. My understanding is that she's simply reminding us not to rule it out as a possibility."

"Yes, and to be fair when I spoke to her today she was definitely moving away from the suicide idea," Collins observed, "though to be honest I'm not sure how seriously we should be taking her anyway; she's only a dotty old actress, after all."

"Did she give any reason why she felt murder was a more likely explanation?" Metcalfe asked, intrigued.

"Yes, and that's one of the main arguments for disregarding her views, I'm afraid," Collins replied, looking rather awkward. "She remains convinced there will be a second murder, apparently on the basis of nothing more tangible than the fact that there always is one in the stories in which she appears."

They had finished their main course almost together, and Metcalfe smiled broadly as he collected the plates.

"Well, that certainly *would* indicate murder, wouldn't it?" he said gravely.

Willis smiled weakly in reply as she sat slumped on her chair. She could feel the dull beginnings of a headache; clearly the strain of the last few days was beginning to tell. She could not remember ever having worked so intensely as this. The first two days of any murder enquiry were always the most important, but now they had slipped past and she could not help feeling that, despite all their hard work, they were really no farther forward.

"Is there dessert?" she called dully after Metcalfe.

"Not really," Collins answered for him, rising from his own seat, "but there is cheese, and I have a nice half bottle of Montbazillac I can open."

"That would be nice," she said automatically and then, with more animation, "actually, that would be really nice. I could just fancy that."

"Then consider it done, Harriet," he answered as he glided from the room.

"Well then," she said once they were all gathered back around the table in companionable mood with their glasses of dessert wine, "if we were to go round the table in time honoured fashion, what would our current favourite solutions be?"

"Murder," Metcalfe said straightaway, "but I'm damned if I know by whom. Nobody seems to have a proper motive – nothing worth murdering for, I mean."

"You're discounting Tom Smythe, then?" Collins asked. "I'm inclined to as well. But what about Barry Carver and Gina Durham? If Ann had succeeded in changing her will, they would both have lost out on a great deal of money."

"Gina told her mother she didn't want her money," Willis pointed out.

"In the heat of the moment, yes, but what about later in the cold light of reason?" Collins argued. "Would anyone really turn their back on a fortune, just like that? Would Barry Carver, for example? After all, they don't need to have been in cahoots. If he knew about the business of the will then he might have killed Ann on his own initiative."

"He might at that," Metcalfe agreed. "And don't forget that they came into the room together, so he might have had a good opportunity to slip the poison into her glass. You said it was very crowded in there."

"It was, and he might," Willis conceded, "but where would he have got it from? The last we know, it was in Durham's handbag at the end of the poisons session."

"But we know it wasn't when she died, because you searched it," Collins commented. "You know, it seems to me more and more that the poison is the way to solve this case. If only we could find out what happened to it between those two points in time then at least we'd have a reasonable idea of who could have administered it and who could not."

"My money would be on Sonia Gold at the moment," Willis asserted. "There's something evil about that woman."

"Something vicious and out of control, yes, from what I hear," Collins opined, "and somebody like that could very easily lose their temper and commit murder. But where's her motive? She was expecting a big pay-off from Ann any day, wasn't she? Why murder her before she could hand over the money?"

"Perhaps Ann told her she *wasn't* going to pay?"

"But I thought Angela said Ann was prepared 'to do whatever it took, including paying the half a million if necessary' or words to that effect?" Collins challenged her.

"Oh, I don't know. Perhaps Durham said it as a negotiating tactic. Or perhaps *she* lost her temper …"

"I think you're clutching at straws," Collins suggested gently. "For one thing, how could Sonia Gold have come to administer the cyanide?"

"She was in Durham's room, as far as we know," Metcalfe pointed out.

"Yes, but she didn't even know about the poison, did she? So how would she have known to take it out of Ann's handbag?"

"Perhaps Durham went into the bathroom, and Sonia rifled through her handbag and found it by chance?" Willis hazarded.

"You're not going to let this go, are you?" Collins asked with a chuckle. "Alright, I accept that it's possible, but I think it's pretty tenuous."

"What about you then, Peter?" Metcalfe asked.

Collins was silent for a few moments as he went around their glasses sharing out the last few drops.

"I still incline to suicide," he said gravely, "though I agree that we need to explain away what happened to the poison bottle. But there's something that's really troubling me.

Nothing I can explain rationally; just a strange feeling that I know something that I'm overlooking."

"Something important?" Willis asked.

"Yes, very. Something that could be the key to the whole case. It's so frustrating – like waking up trying remember something you've just been dreaming about."

"Well," said Collinson the next morning as the briefing started, "we got a lot done yesterday, and there's a lot more to do today. I'll ask DI Metcalfe to bring us up to speed."

"First up, my own report," Metcalfe said. "Lisa Atkins and I successfully got an order issued yesterday to take Sonia Gold back in front of a court for breach of the conditions of her probation order, and to take her into custody if we believed that was the only way to ensure her appearance, though judging by what Mr Collison and DS Willis found out yesterday we may have enough to feel her collar anyway."

"First order of business today will be to bring her in for interview," Collison called out. "DI Metcalfe on that, please, plus the probation officer."

"Right you are, guv," Metcalfe acknowledged. "Item two: the waiters. You'll see DC Desai's report already on the system but why don't you update us verbally, Priya?"

"Sure, guv," Desai said, getting to her feet.

"Three waiters were identified," she reported, referring to the typed copy of her report. "The first, Ben Michaels, was identified by both Dr Collins and Gina Durham as having been standing near them when the jug fell from the table.

It's therefore unlikely that he could have had anything to do with it. The second, Jose Villanueva, was identified by Angela Hughes, Mr Smythe, Miss Marple and DS Willis as having been close by when the jug fell. Dr Collins also thought he remembered the face, but couldn't be sure."

"So, just to be clear, Priya," Collison asked, "Ben Michaels was not identified by Barry Clarke, even though he was standing next to Gina Durham and Peter Collins at the time?"

"That's right, guv. Barry Clarke didn't recognise anyone, or so he said. To be honest I got the impression he had no intention of co-operating and was just going through the motions."

"Female intuition?" Evans enquired mischievously.

Desai scowled at him.

"Let's call it copper's nose, shall we?" she retorted.

"Nothing wrong with that," Metcalfe said quickly. "Go on, Priya."

Desai gave Evans a long hard look and then returned to her report.

"Our third waiter is a bit of a puzzle. Her name is Peta Lepik, and she's Estonian, here on a student visa. She's a bit of a puzzle in that both DS Willis and Miss Marple identified her as having been in the same area as Villanueva, but neither Hughes nor Smythe did, and logically they would have been closer to her."

"That is curious," Collison admitted.

"Particularly as she was a woman, and blonde," Desai

persisted. "I think that's important for two reasons. First, most of the waiters were male and/or dark-haired, so she should have stood out. Second, Tom Smythe is a middle-aged man, and they tend to notice young blonde women even if they don't notice anything else."

"He did say in his last interview," Willis interjected, "that he remembered at least one of the waiters being a girl."

"Yet he didn't ID Peta Lupik," Desai pointed out, "and, well, there's something else ..."

"Yes?" Collison prompted.

Desai looked uncharacteristically hesitant and shot another hostile glance at Evans.

"I'm not sure if I should mention this after recent comments about female intuition," she said pointedly, "but, well, I thought something happened when Smythe and the Estonian girl looked at each other. A sort of glance that flashed between them, a moment of embarrassment something like that."

"I wouldn't discount that at all, Priya," Collison reassured her. "A lot of communication is non-verbal. That doesn't make it any the less important. You mean you thought they might have known each other, and were sort of agreeing to keep it quiet?"

"Yes, sir, but – Oh God, I wish I hadn't mentioned this now ..."

"Go on," Collison urged her.

"Well, this is going to make me sound really stupid," Desai said desperately, "but I got the same sort of feeling both from Angela Hughes and from Barry Clarke."

There was an embarrassed pause, as Desai stared down at her notes and refused to meet anyone's glance. Collison struggled to find something to say.

"All useful stuff, I'm sure," he said at last. "Let's bear it in mind, but probably best not to put it in the file, eh?"

"What are we doing about interviewing the waiters, Bob?" he went on quickly.

"We have them all coming in this afternoon, guv."

"Fine. OK, let's think about what else we need to do."

He stood up and consulted his own notes.

"First, we need to contact the deceased's lawyer. Timothy, you do that this morning. Find out if he's prepared to talk without a court order. Given that his client is dead and this is a murder enquiry then hopefully the answer will be 'yes', but if not then liaise with DI Metcalfe to get an order. Either way, fix an appointment."

"Understood, sir," Evans acknowledged.

"Second, we need to check out this story of a fracas between the deceased and Sonia Gold. Priya, you do that. Find the relevant police report, get a copy of the emergency call recording, and get a statement from the secretary, Julia."

"Right away, guv."

"Third, I understand that we've drawn a blank on the cyanide. That's not good enough. It's not the sort of stuff you can get just by wandering into a chemist's shop. You others get onto that. Research businesses that have a legitimate reason to use it and find out if they've lost any recently. DS Willis will assign responsibilities."

"Fourth, I really don't want to wait any longer for forensics. Chase Brian Williams will you, Bob? I know it probably won't tell us anything new, but we need to have it anyway. It's always possible the toxicology report might give us some clue about where to look for the supplier."

"Fifth, I think we should re-interview Miss Marple. It's really just a matter of form, but Angela Hughes told us that there was some sort of trouble between her and the deceased a while back, and we need to find out as much about that as we can. After all, she was at the scene. If she had anything like a motive, we need to know about it. It may be we have to do that tomorrow, given everything else we have to do today. Any other suggestions, anyone?"

There was silence, and just as Collison was about to dismiss the meeting a uniformed constable put his head round the door. Collison looked at him quizzically.

"Beg pardon for interrupting, sir, but I have a Lisa Atkins downstairs for DI Metcalfe."

CHAPTER 17

Metcalfe checked his appearance quickly in the mirror on the stairs before he walked into the reception area. Lisa Atkins saw him at once, stood up and smiled. She was looking very colourful again, this time in a red skirt suit, a white blouse and a blue and red silk scarf. His first thought was that she looked like an air stewardess. His second thought was that he liked the effect very much.

"Hello," she greeted him. "Are you ready? Have you got the Order?"

"Yes, I have it here," he confirmed, patting his breast pocket and at the same time feeling curiously short of breath.

He moved towards the door but then paused.

"I'm not quite sure how to play this," he said suddenly.

"How do you mean? Play what?"

"Well, strictly speaking we're supposed to take a uniformed officer with us if we think there may be any trouble. It's some old common law thing about a breach of the peace. Is she likely to cut up rough, do you suppose?"

Atkins thought for a moment.

"I would think it's highly likely," she said in a considered fashion. "However I have to say, from the little I know of her, that the presence of a police uniform is likely to make things worse rather than better. Does that help, or does it just make things more difficult?"

"Not sure," he said dubiously, but then "oh, sod it, let's go. I can always call for back-up if we need it."

He opened the door for her and then led her round the corner to where his car was parked flagrantly on a yellow line.

"Aren't you afraid you'll get a ticket?" she enquired as he opened the door and she got in.

He pointed to the dashboard where an old fashioned police whistle hung from the heating control.

"It's an old copper's trick," he explained as he got in behind the driving wheel. "It's a signal that it's a police car. Doesn't always work these days, but this is Hampstead and the wardens know this is where we park, so it's usually OK. They need us to ride to the rescue when they have a motorist who gets a bit threatening, so it's in their interests to stay on good terms with us."

"Gosh," she exclaimed in mock horror, "so I've only been with you a few minutes and already you're dishing me the dirt on police corruption."

He laughed as they drove up Rosslyn Hill, which was unusually free from traffic. As they passed the bookshop on the left, he gestured to it. Both windows contained A3 publicity photos of Ann Durham, each surrounded by a sea of books.

"Amazing what getting murdered can do for your book sales, isn't it?" he asked wryly.

"Was it murder?" she asked curiously. "Golly! The telly said this morning that the police still thought it might be suicide."

"I really shouldn't talk about it," he replied awkwardly, "but you're right. Officially we do still have an open mind."

"Officially?" she echoed playfully. "That sounds even worse, Bob. Do you mean that there are things you're holding back. Or that opinions are divided …?"

"I'm sorry," he said, "I really shouldn't have got us into this. But the latter, yes. There are things which point in each direction. That's why Sonia is so important. We really need to know about what happened when she and Durham met. If you rule out the last few minutes of her life, which lots of people observed, then Sonia Gold was the last person to see Ann Durham alive – so far as we know, at least."

"I see," she said seriously. "Well, I hope you're not going to be disappointed, Bob. It could well be that the more she knows the police need her to talk, the more delight she'll take in staying shtum."

He glanced across at her in surprise.

"Staying shtum?" he asked. "What's that all about?"

"It means not saying anything."

"I know what it means. I just wondered what a nicely brought up lady was doing using London criminal slang."

"Well, I am a Londoner actually, but not a criminal; not unless you count an overdue library book, anyway. And please don't say 'you don't sound like a Londoner'. We don't all have to speak like Bob Hoskins, you know."

"I know that you mean. You might also have said Janet Street-Porter."

"Oh, you're right, isn't she just awful? You know, the first time I heard her talking on TV I thought it was a joke, a sketch from a comedy show, something like that. But then I found it wasn't a joke after all, it was real life."

"Yeah well, real life can be like that," Metcalfe observed sagely as he brought the car down through Golders Green (past my old flat, he thought inconsequentially) towards the North Circular.

"Now you're trying to be both profound and humorous at the same time."

"Am I succeeding?"

"It's a difficult trick to pull off," she replied judiciously, "but on the whole yes, I think your attempt was not wholly unsuccessful."

"Thank you."

"Though whether you can keep it up for our entire journey is, of course, a different matter entirely," she added.

They both laughed, and for some reason went on laughing together for most of the rest of their journey.

"Oh look," she said suddenly as they reached their destination and Metcalfe started looking for somewhere to park, "there's Dirty Gertie!"

"What on earth are you talking about?" he asked, bewildered.

"The statue, silly – look! I can remember my Grandfather showing it to me when I was little but I'd completely forgotten about it. Oh, it's got some posh French name or other, but the locals always called her Dirty Gertie because she hasn't got any clothes on, and back in those days that was regarded as rather risqué for a statue in the middle of a road."

"He lived around here, did he?"

"Yes, Grandpa lived in some flats just up the road there, but things got a bit much for him once Gran died and he's in a home now."

"Hm," said Metcalfe, who was not really listening as he was trying find somewhere to park.

"Can't you just stop here and use the whistle?" she asked.

"I don't think I've got much choice," he admitted grudgingly, "though I'd rather not. I don't know if it will work around here."

"Don't you have any handcuffs, or a truncheon or something, that you could leave on the seat?"

"I do have handcuffs," he said grimly, "but I think I'd rather keep them with me. Any sign of trouble from Sonia Gold and on they go."

He parked the car rather nervously on a yellow line, turned off the ignition, and then came around to open the door for her.

"Thank you," she said, and stood waiting for him to lock the doors.

"You know, Bob," she said, sounding serious suddenly, "I think you're quite a special sort of man."

"Well, thank you," he acknowledged, startled and

embarrassed at the same time, "but you're mistaken. I'm really a very ordinary person."

"I disagree," she replied at once. "I have a lot of experience of being a woman – I am one in case you hadn't noticed, by the way – and I can't remember the last time a man came round and opened the car door for me."

"Ah," he said ruefully, "well, let's just say that I was well trained."

"By your father?"

"No, I never really had a father."

"By your mother then?"

He was about to say 'no, by my girlfriend, actually' but instead found himself saying something else.

"Yes. She wasn't my real mother – I was adopted – but yes, by the lady who brought me up."

He was experiencing a very strange sensation, which he would have difficulty describing. It was almost as if someone had changed the points somewhere and switched him onto a different track. He could see a whole new route stretching out before him. At the moment the two tracks were still together, running parallel, with him gazing curiously at the one he had always taken it for granted would last out his journey. There was still time to jump back, but some deep instinct told him that this moment would soon be past, that up ahead somewhere the tracks would diverge and he would be irredeemably heading off in another direction. Over it all hovered a strong sense of unreality. It wasn't just that he couldn't understand what had happened; he was having problems grasping whether something had really happened at all.

He became aware that Lisa was looking at him with a rather lost expression.

"Well, I could say the same about you," he countered awkwardly. "How many women today would stay in the car expecting to have the door opened for them? You did. Bit risky, wasn't it? Most men would have walked off into the distance and then looked back and wondered where you'd got to."

"Perhaps I just sort of knew you weren't one of those men," she said quietly. "Or hoped, anyway."

Then there was one of those pauses when nobody quite knows what to say. Metcalfe broke it.

"Come on," he said, jerking his head towards the flats, "we've got a job to do."

They walked up the long path which ran across the extensive lawns in front of the old mansion block. For Metcalfe the sense of unreality continued. It felt as if he was sitting in a cinema watching himself on screen. Once they had got about halfway, Lisa Atkins spoke, without looking at him.

"You know, Bob," she said, staring straight ahead, "if we weren't both here on business, I would very much like to take your arm about now."

"Thank you," he said.

What the hell, he thought. It was clumsy but at least it was sincere.

Once upstairs, they rang the bell of the flat and waited. The door was opened by Thomas Gold, who seemed nervous.

"Mr Gold," Metcalfe began, "I'm Detective Inspector Metcalfe. You met two of my colleagues recently. I'm afraid we need to see your daughter, Sonia. Is she here?"

"Yes, she's in her room," Gold replied. "I'll go and fetch her for you."

The two of them lingered uncertainly by the door. They heard Gold knock briefly on the door of his daughter's room and call out that there was someone to see her. Coming back, he motioned them into the flat and they walked into the living room, Metcalfe closing the front door behind him.

There was a brief wait before Sonia Gold emerged from her room. As soon as she set eyes on Lisa Atkins a look of ferocious fury appeared on her face.

"What do you want, bitch?" she asked venomously.

"Please calm down, Miss Gold," Metcalfe said quickly. "I'm afraid we need you to come with us to answer some questions, and we would really appreciate your cooperation."

"In your dreams," she replied scornfully.

"In that case," Metcalfe said carefully, "I'm afraid we must insist. You will see here that we have a court Order allowing us to take you into custody for breach of your probation order."

He took the Order from his inside jacket pocket and attempted to hand it to her. He watched her carefully, but was quite unprepared for what came next.

Sonia Gold gave a scream which sounded like an animal

in pain. She snatched up a small but heavy ornament from the sideboard and brought it down with great strength on Lisa Atkins's head. Atkins collapsed as if poleaxed. She crumpled at the knees and fell to the floor, a deadweight. With a dreadful sense of unreality, Metcalfe saw a small pool of blood form around her head and begin spreading.

Sonia Gold stared at him wildly, then turned on her heel, ran to the front door, threw it open and disappeared down the echoing staircase. Every instinct told Metcalfe that he needed to stay with his fallen companion, but equally he knew what he had to do. Snatching up the phone, he punched 999 into the keyboard, threw the handset to a horrified Gold and, shouting at him to call an ambulance, set off in pursuit.

As he ran down the staircase, he fumbled with his radio. At the bottom, he transmitted a brief message asking for back-up, reinforcing the urgent need for an ambulance, and putting out a warning that Sonia Gold had evaded arrest and should be considered highly dangerous.

He ran outside the building and looked around. There was no sight of Sonia Gold. Cursing, he ran back into the lobby of the building. He knew that in these old mansion blocks there was usually a door leading to a service area or car park at the back. Quickly, he found it down a little half flight of steps. Taking these in a single stride, he allowed his weight and momentum to throw the door backwards, banging against the wall. He found himself in an open area, largely taken up by tightly parked cars. He ran forwards, quickly scanning the gaps between the vehicles, and dropping to his knees to check underneath them. Nothing. Then he spotted the bins lined up against the back wall. Somebody had dragged a smaller bin, which clearly did not belong there, in front of one of the large ones, creating an impromptu flight of steps which made accessible the top of the wall, which must have been a good eight feet above the ground.

Urgently, he mounted the bins himself. He could see that behind the flats was a gravelled area which led down to the main road. Of Sonia Gold, however, there was no sign. Jumping down from the bins, he ran back to the front door of the block with a growing sense of panic and futility. As he dithered on the pathway, he noticed a police car using its lights and sirens to force its way up the inside lane of the North Circular Road, clearly intending to turn left at the traffic lights and stop outside the flats. He ran to meet it and waited impatiently for it to complete its manoeuvres.

At last it pulled up in front of him. The constable in the passenger seat sprang out, the driver a second or two behind him.

"I'm Detective Inspector Metcalfe from Hampstead CID," he said breathlessly, showing his ID. "I have a fugitive on the run around here somewhere and a colleague down in a flat upstairs."

"There's an ambulance on its way, sir," one of the constables said. "I heard it on the radio as we were coming round the corner."

Metcalfe considered the situation briefly and came to a decision.

"Okay," he said curtly, "this is what we'll do. I'll go with the driver. We can go round the block a few times and see if I can spot her. You stay here, and when the ambulance arrives make sure they know to go to flat 46."

"Right you are, guv," said the constable on the passenger side of the car, stepping aside for Metcalfe to sit beside the driver.

"Blues and twos, guv?" queried the latter.

"No," he decided. "If we do spot her, no sense in scaring her off."

In the distance, he could hear a siren growing steadily closer. He had a growing sick feeling in the pit of his stomach. He could only hope that they would be in time. He thought of the pool of blood spreading out from the fallen woman and suddenly felt dizzy. He clutched at the door handle and held it tightly.

CHAPTER 18

Shortly after the morning meeting, Collison phoned Jim Morris, his immediate superior, to bring him up to date with developments as he did most days.

"You know, Simon," Morris was saying with some amusement, "if ever a case was tailor-made for you, this must be it. Cyanide, crime writers ... why, you've even got Miss Marple. I only hope that you're not enjoying it so much that you'll never want to get around to solving it."

"I can assure you that I want to solve it very much indeed," Collison replied, "it's just that the more we find out, the more confusing it seems to become. To be honest, I'm not even really sure myself whether we are looking at murder or suicide."

"Yes, I've been reading the file," Morris said. "I think you're right to identify the cyanide as the key issue. Find where that came from, and where it went to, and you will probably crack the case."

"We now think that the cyanide may well have been administered slightly earlier in the proceedings," Collison commented. "Perhaps as she was walking across the room, or perhaps even earlier. That complicates matters rather."

"I agree," Morris concurred. "So what's the order of business for today?"

"We are still waiting for the forensics report. I don't suppose for a moment that it's going to tell us anything we don't already know, but it is very irritating not having it. So we are pressing for that, but we are also pulling in Sonia Gold for questioning. Alongside that I have people working on the cyanide angle and also on disentangling the deceased's legal affairs. If there is time, I plan to interview the three waiters who were identified as having been near the scene of death; that's probably for this afternoon."

"I'll happily do whatever I can to chase the forensic report for you," Morris promised. "Other than that, it sounds as if you have things well in hand, Simon. I'll leave you to it."

"Thank you, sir. I'll keep you posted of course."

Collison put down the phone and started doodling on his pad. This sense of lack of direction in the early stages of an investigation was starting to feel familiar. He had been questioning whether the failure to see any particular path clearly had been due to any failing on his part, so it was reassuring to hear that Jim Morris, a vastly more experienced officer than himself, was unable to suggest anything which he may have missed. He started to jot down a list of the people to be interviewed. At that point there was a tap on the door. He shouted "come in" and Willis put her head around the door, looking worried.

"The Yard have picked up a message from Bob, guv. It sounds like he's hit trouble. From the sound of things Sonia

Gold has attacked Lisa Atkins and done a runner. Bob is searching the area for her in a patrol car."

"Is she badly hurt, do we know?"

"Bob was asking urgently for an ambulance so I guess so, yes. We don't have any further information at the moment."

"Okay, that sounds bad. Please ask the information room to keep me fully updated on any news of Sonia Gold, and we need to find out which hospital the probation officer has been taken to so we can get some firm indication of her condition. Get somebody onto that, will you?"

"I'll do it myself, guv," she replied. "All of the others are busy."

She left the room and Collison picked up the phone and dialled Metcalfe's mobile. He answered at once.

"Bob, it's me. What's happening? We picked up a radio message from you earlier."

"It all went pear-shaped, guv. Sonia Gold freaked out as soon as she saw the Order. She grabbed something – a statuette or something, I think – and cracked Lisa over the head with it. There was nothing I could do. It all happened so quickly."

"Is she badly hurt, do you think?"

"Yes, I'm afraid so, guv. There was blood coming out of her head. When I was in uniform I saw a kid like that once who'd been hit by a car. The ambulance guys said she had a fractured skull. She died later in hospital."

There was a silence while Collison digested this news. Then he spoke again.

"And where is Sonia Gold?"

"I wish I knew," Metcalfe replied bitterly. "She had just enough of a head start on me that I lost her. I'm quartering the area now in a squad car, but there are lots of bus stops here. She may just have jumped on the first one she saw, in which case she could be anywhere by now."

"Get back here then," Collison decided quickly. "Leave it to uniform. We have her other address on file from the other day. I'll make sure we have someone staking that out."

He rang off and immediately called DCS Morris back.

"Simon?" he asked in surprise "what's up now?"

"We have a situation, sir," Collison explained. "Sonia Gold has attacked the probation officer who was with Bob Metcalfe when he tried to bring her in. It sounds like the poor girl may be badly injured – perhaps even a fractured skull."

"Get Metcalfe back to the nick pronto," Morris said at once. "He'll need to make a full statement while everything is still fresh in his mind. If anything happens to that probation officer there will have to be a full enquiry – perhaps even if not. In the meantime, I'll brief the ACC. Keep me updated as soon as you have any news, understand?"

"Yes, sir. I've already called him back, by the way."

"Good," Morris said curtly and rang off.

Collison went downstairs to the incident room, where there was a distinct atmosphere of shock and dismay.

"Karen," he said, "get the other address we have for Sonia Gold and have someone staking it out round the clock."

"Already done, guv," she replied. "I did it before I came upstairs to see you; hope you don't mind."

"Not at all – well done. Do we have any further news of Lisa Atkins?"

"Only the first message from the ambulance," she observed. "It doesn't sound good: probable fractured skull, condition critical."

Collison cursed under his breath.

"Well at least she's still alive," he said philosophically. "Have Bob come straight up to my office as soon as he arrives, will you?"

He went back upstairs, struggling to think straight. Of all the possible courses he might have envisaged the day's activities taking, this was not one of them. As he went into his office the phone was ringing. He picked it up and a female voice said "Superintendent Collison? Will you hold for the ACC, please?"

"Simon," a familiar voice said. "Understand you're having a spot of bother. Jim Morris just briefed me. Bad business. A probation officer is pretty much one of us, you know."

"Yes I know, sir. There really isn't very much more I can tell you at the moment, though. I'm waiting for Bob Metcalfe to get back. As for the girl, first indications are that it's pretty serious. She's critical according to the first report from the paramedics."

"Bad business," the ACC said again. "A word of advice, Simon. Follow procedure on this, to the letter. Have Bob Metcalfe make a full statement as soon as he gets back to the nick. See that it comes to me as well as Jim Morris, will you?."

"Yes, sir."

There was a brief pause.

"He may need to be suspended, you know," the ACC said gently, "particularly if anything happens to the girl. It doesn't necessarily mean that he's done anything wrong, it's just a procedural step pending an investigation."

"I'd like to avoid that if at all possible, sir. He's playing a key role in an active murder enquiry. His absence would be very disruptive."

"Well, I'll do what I can of course," the ACC replied. "But if the girl dies then all bets are off, Simon. That will be a code black, just as if a police officer had been killed."

"Let's just hope that doesn't happen," Collison said quietly.

"Amen to that," the ACC said soberly. "You can phone me direct any time you need advice, Simon. In the meantime, keep me advised won't you?"

As he was saying goodbye to the ACC Bob Metcalfe knocked on the door and looked in. Collison beckoned him to enter and sit down. Metcalfe looked ashen and drawn.

"Very sorry to hear your news, Bob," he said sympathetically. "What a rotten thing to have happen."

"Have we heard anything about Lisa?" Metcalfe asked wretchedly.

"Nothing good, I'm afraid. It sounds like your suspicions

were correct. Fractured skull is what we hear, and in a critical condition."

Metcalfe shook his head wordlessly.

"Listen, Bob," Collison said urgently, "there's something I have to ask you. We knew that Sonia Gold had a tendency to be violent, so why on earth didn't you take some uniform with you to execute the Order?"

"I was going to, of course," he responded, "but Lisa thought a police uniform would act like a red rag to a bull and that it would be better not to go mob-handed."

Collison considered this.

"I see that, of course, but the fact remains that you are a police officer and Lisa is not. There is an established procedure in these matters, and you chose not to follow it. Forgive me, Bob. I'm simply anticipating the sort of questions that the DCS and the ACC are likely to ask."

"I understand that, guv, and I'm not sure there's anything I can say. I chose to ignore procedure, as you said, and it's blown up in my face. If I'd had some uniform with me they might have been able to grab that nutter before she clobbered Lisa."

"Well, never mind that now," Collison said hastily. "Go and make a full statement. I've promised the ACC that he'll have it before close of play. Make sure you specifically mention Lisa's recommendation not to take uniform with you. If I were you, I would also stress that everything happened so quickly it's doubtful whether it could have been prevented even if another officer had been present."

"Yes, guv," Metcalfe acknowledged woodenly and left the room.

Collison rang down to the incident room and asked Willis to join him.

"Karen, I'm very worried about Bob," he told her as soon as she arrived. "He's had a really bad experience and I'm pretty sure he's in shock. He's making a statement right now but as soon as he's finished I'm thinking that he should probably go home for the rest of the day. If I can spare you, I'll let you go with him."

"Thank you, guv, that's very thoughtful of you."

"That's not all," he said awkwardly. "Well ... the fact is that I may have to place Bob on suspension."

She stared at him in consternation.

"It's just a procedural thing," he explained desperately. "It doesn't mean that he's done anything wrong, but if there is to be an enquiry then it's standard practice for the officer concerned to be suspended until it's finished."

"But will there have to be an enquiry, do you think?"

"If Lisa Atkins dies, then yes definitely. It will be out of everybody's hands by then, including the ACC's."

"But if she doesn't?" she asked hopefully.

He shrugged.

"That won't be my decision, but my guess would be yes. You see, Bob just told me that he ignored procedure. He knew Sonia Gold was violent, or at least potentially violent, and yet he chose not to take a uniform officer with him. You know the rules as well as I do, or as well as Bob does come to that: "if a breach of the peace is anticipated ..." all that sort of thing."

"I see," she said tersely. "Yes, I suppose that does make a difference. But surely even if it was an error of judgement, it was the sort of thing that any of us might do."

"That's right of course, but in this case it was an error of judgement that had very serious consequences. I'm going to have to inform the ACC and after that things will be out of my hands, I'm afraid."

"I see," she said again numbly.

There was a knock on the door.

"What is it?" Collison called irritably.

Evans looked nervously into the room.

"Can it wait, Timothy?" Collison asked tersely. "I'm rather tied up right now."

"Afraid not, guv," he said apologetically. "We're needed down at the hotel."

Collison looked at him blankly.

"Needed? What do you mean?"

"The manager just called, sir. He tried DI Metcalfe and DS Willis but I ended up taking the call. Sounds like there's been another murder."

"What?" they chorused.

"That's what it sounds like anyway," he said stoutly. "That Estonian girl – the one we were going to interview this afternoon – has been found dead on the service stairs."

Collison and Willis stared at each other, scarcely able to believe what they were hearing.

"Miss Marple's second murder," Willis said in wonderment.

"So it would seem," Collison agreed. "Karen, get down there and take charge, will you? Take as many of the team as you can and secure the crime scene. I'll call SOCO and meet you there."

As Willis and Evans departed hurriedly, Collison made a couple of calls setting in motion the various specialists whose services would be required. This done, he stood up, crossed the room and opened the door. He stood for several moments with the door half open. Then, resignedly, he closed it again and turned back to his desk to call the ACC.

CHAPTER 19

By the time Collison reached the hotel there was a uniformed constable on duty restricting access to the building to those who had a legitimate reason to be there. As he entered the hotel lobby he noticed the manager, who understandably was looking more haggard and worried than ever.

"A dreadful business, Superintendent," he said, literally wringing his hands. "Shall we have to close the hotel do you think? We are almost full you know."

Collison thought for a moment.

"I don't think that will be necessary," he said after deliberation. "At least, not at the moment. Has the convention finished by the way?"

"Yes, it finished at lunchtime," the manager told him. "Most of the attendees left an hour or two ago."

"But I thought you said you were almost full," Collison queried.

"Yes. You see they checked out during the morning and we had a couple of coach parties check-in almost immediately afterwards. It was a real challenge turning the rooms around, actually."

Collison nodded and walked around behind the bank of elevators to where the service stairway began. Again, a uniformed constable was on duty. He showed his ID and pulled open the doors to be confronted immediately by crime scene tape stretched across the doorway. He ducked underneath it and went on.

As he started climbing the stairs he came almost immediately upon Peta Lepik who lay sprawled across the first landing, her head twisted to one side and one arm stretched out in front of her. The back of her head was a mess. Surrounding it for a surprising distance was a pool of dried blood, now almost black. He remembered what Metcalfe had said about Lisa Atkins and gave an involuntary shudder.

Beside the body hovered Tom Bellamy and Brian Williams. He looked at them expectantly.

"As a crime scene I'm afraid it's a bit of a disaster, guv," Bellamy said straightaway. "As you know, it's a service stairway so dozens of people go up and down it every hour. We've done a fingertip search of the flight of stairs she must have fallen down in order to end up here, but we found nothing. There are some blood splashes on the floor and walls on the next landing though, so it looks like she was clobbered up there and then fell down this whole flight. Her momentum must have been enough to carry around the bend in the stairs."

"I see," Collison said automatically. "How about you, Brian?"

"I think I've done just about everything I can here," Williams said carefully. "Cause of death appears to be this blow to the back of the head and I'm guessing that it was inflicted by some sort of blunt instrument rather than having been suffered in a fall down the stairs. Can't be sure of course, but – see here – the skull has been completely crushed. That would require considerable force."

"Time of death?"

"Body temperature suggests within the last couple of hours," Williams replied. "Obviously a full forensic report will have to wait until I can get on the slab."

"Talking of forensic reports by the way," Collison said suddenly, "when are we going to get the one on Ann Durham? We're still waiting for it you know."

"I'm sorry about that," Williams responded. "I'm afraid we're short staffed and we've been rather busy lately. But not to worry, I put it out for dispatch this morning. If it helps I can give you a quick resumé."

"Yes actually, that would be very helpful."

"Cause of death was cyanide poisoning, as you were probably assuming. A massive dose of cyanide to be precise; at least seven times a lethal dose. Nothing very remarkable other than that. The contents of the glass were gin and tonic by the way, not water. She already had quite a lot of it in her stomach as well, so she must have been drinking during the day. Alcohol absorbs through the stomach lining pretty quickly, as you know, so that probably means that she had been knocking the stuff back in the two or three hours before her death. The alcohol in her blood count was at least twice the legal amount for driving."

"Thank you. I must say that's a bit of a surprise. If it was gin and tonic that opens up other possible times and places for the cyanide to have been administered."

"Yes well, I'll leave you to wrestle with that little conundrum if I may, Simon. As I said, we are rather pressed just at the moment. Can I move the body, Tom?"

"Yes, go ahead," Bellamy confirmed. "We've got all the photos we need."

Collison stood aside as the mortuary assistants began dealing with the body.

"Show me these bloodstains," he asked Bellamy.

"Right up here," he said as he led Collison up the stairs. "You can see that there is splashing on the wall here just about at head height. That suggests they were sprayed there by the impact. On the other hand, there is comparatively little on the floor, which suggests that she fell, or was pushed, down the stairs almost immediately before she had a chance to start bleeding out."

"Any sign of a weapon?"

"No, none."

"Okay, thanks very much, Tom. I'm sure your chaps have done everything they can. Do you know where Karen Willis is by the way?"

"She said to tell you that she would be in the green room. Said you'd understand what that meant."

"Yes I do, thanks."

He headed off through the service doors on the second floor and made his way quickly to what had until very recently been the lobby of the crime writers' Convention. Already it had a somewhat desolate air. The booksellers' stalls had disappeared and what had been in use as a signing table had been covered by a white cloth and pushed back against the wall. Only a solitary signage board remained, and this too had been pushed against the wall as though discarded immediately its usefulness had passed.

Willis, Desai, and Evans were waiting in the green room which Willis had evidently decided to use as an impromptu operations centre.

"What do we have then, Karen?" he asked. "What about CCTV for a start?"

"Sadly there is no CCTV on the service stairway, guv, but there are cameras in each corridor so it may be possible to pick her up, or indeed anybody else, as they entered or left the service stairs. I've got the manager's people working on that now."

"Very good. What else?"

"She clocked off to take her lunchbreak at 1335, so we know she was alive then. Her body was discovered at 1413 – the man who found her had the good sense to check the time on his mobile phone as he was calling 999 – so we can assume that death occurred between those two times. I've asked the manager to put a message out to all members of staff asking if anybody saw her after she clocked off."

"Great, well done, Karen," Collison acknowledged. "So nobody saw or heard anything on the service stairs? That's a bit strange, isn't it? I mean, there must be people going up and down all the time. Tom Bellamy just said so."

"Yes, I was thinking that too. If the stairway really is very busy then surely that suggests that she can't have been killed much before 1413?"

"Always dangerous to leap to conclusions, of course," Collison cautioned, "but yes, that does seem a reasonable assumption."

"What do we know about her – anything?" he went on.

"I've been asking whether she had a particular friend here," Desai cut in. "So far I haven't had a chance to speak to many people obviously but what I hear is that nobody really knew her. She comes in through an agency rather than being on the permanent staff here. I have their details and was just about to go round there."

"Do that," Collison confirmed. "We need to know everything about her, Priya, and quickly."

He thought deeply for a moment as she gathered up her things and left the room.

"Since we now have Miss Marples's second murder," he commented wryly, "then we may as well use it as any good crime writer would intend us to. Do we know where our various key characters were at approximately 1400?"

"Haven't had time to do that yet, guv," Willis said apologetically, "but I agree it's an obvious step to take."

"You get onto that will you, Timothy?" Collison said. "Contact them all ASAP. I want a list of exactly where they say they were and anyone who can corroborate that; you know the form."

"I could do that more easily from the nick, guv," Evans suggested. "All our records and things are there."

"Unless you want to establish a full operations centre here?" Willis asked.

"No, I don't think so," Collison said as he pondered. "No, I really don't think it makes sense. We need to leave someone here to follow up on CCTV and arrange interviews with the staff – arrange for someone to do that, Karen – but let's keep our permanent base at the nick. Like Timothy says, all our records and systems are there."

"That's all right, guv, but I think I can manage it myself," she said. "I've already got the manager's secretary and the HR people checking work shifts and making a list of people we need to speak to. I can follow up by phone once we're back at the nick. What do you want to do about the other two waiters by the way? The two we were due to interview this afternoon before all this happened?"

"You'd better put them off until tomorrow," he decided. "We just don't have enough bodies to deal with everything we need to today. Ask them to come to the nick and we can get somebody from the team to take their statements. In the light of what's just happened I suspect we've lost the only one who might have been able to tell us something, dammit."

"Seems that way, doesn't it?" she agreed quietly.

"And talking of Miss Marple, guv," she continued. "Do you want to go ahead with her interview? She's here now. I believe she stayed behind after the convention specially to see you."

"Dammit," he said again crossly. "Yes I should see her really, shouldn't I? Now we really are running out of bodies. I must ask the DCS for some more people."

As he was considering how best to proceed, his mobile buzzed and, looking at it, he saw that it was Metcalfe calling.

"Guv, I finished that statement," Metcalfe said. "What should I do now?"

Collison thought quickly.

"It's all a bit of a mess here, Bob. Too many things to do and too few people to do them. Miss Marple is here for re-interview, for instance. Do you feel up to doing that?"

"Sure. We just want to find out about whatever happened between her and Ann Durham, right?"

"Yes, but also find out, just as a matter of form you understand, where she was at about 1400 today."

"Right you are, guv. I'll be right over. I've sent you the statement as an email attachment, by the way."

"Great, I'll read it later," Collison said awkwardly.

As he rang off he realised that Willis was looking at him strangely.

"Can I give you a lift back to the nick, Karen?" he asked.

"Thank you, guv, that would be great. I came over with some of the uniform guys."

Once they were out of the hotel and walking towards the car Collison glanced sideways at her.

"What was it you wanted to say back there?"

"Well if you must know I was a bit taken aback," she replied frankly. "Back at the nick you gave me the impression that you were going to suspend Bob, but then I hear you asking him to come over here to take Miss Marple's statement. Does that mean you've changed your mind?"

"No," he said, choosing his words carefully, "it means I'd like a little time to decide what to do for the best, and in the meantime it makes sense for Bob to continue to be involved. For one thing, I'm sure he'd like to keep busy rather than have time to brood on what happened earlier. For another, it's the pragmatic thing to do anyway; I don't want to keep Miss Marple hanging around unnecessarily and we don't have anybody else to take that statement."

"Incidentally, there was something I meant to remind you of," she said as they reach the car and got in.

"What's that?" he asked as he reached for his safety belt.

"Well you remember from my report on that first meeting I had with Sonia Gold that the description her father gave of the way his mother died sounded awfully like arsenic poisoning? When we were interviewing Angela Hughes it suddenly struck me that the publisher chap's death might have been suspicious too."

"You mean that Ann Durham might have been a murderer herself? Perhaps even a double murderer?"

"I know it sounds a bit fanciful," she admitted, "but just think: there was only ever a very limited number of people who knew about the Bergmann deal. Originally just four and then later five, when Angela Hughes was added. Well, both the mother and the publisher were part of that group.

What if Ann Durham suddenly reckoned, for whatever reason, that she couldn't trust them anymore?"

"I do remember the arsenic question, as it happens," Collison replied. "Believe it or not I even have it jotted down in my notes somewhere as something we need to pursue. It just got lost in the noise somewhere. But you're raising an interesting point, Karen. Make a note to raise it at the meeting tomorrow morning."

"Like I say, it may be just fanciful speculation," she said, "but it does raise an intriguing possibility. Suppose Thomas Gold found out somehow that his mother's death was not as natural as he thought at the time. Wouldn't that give him a motive to kill his mother's murderer?"

Collison whistled softly as they waited to turn left at the traffic lights at the end of Englands Lane.

"It might indeed," he agreed. "But here's another thought for you. Suppose that Thomas Gold told his daughter...?"

CHAPTER 20

Detective Chief Superintendent Jim Murray had ambivalent feelings towards the man seated in front of him. On the one hand, he and Detective Chief Inspector Tom Allen had been friends and close colleagues for many years, and there was much in the latter's background to command both respect and sympathy. On the other hand, Allen was a man in whom natural awkwardness discouraged a close relationship, and in whom frequent irritation could sometimes spill over into truculence.

"I've just been reading your report on that prison murder, Tom," he began. "It's a good piece of work. Even though we'll never find out who did it, it's clear that you did everything you could. It was a hopeless exercise from the first to expect prisoners to grass on each other."

"Well, let's hope the brass see it like that anyway," Allen responded. "Like it or not, closing an unsolved case is a failure, and I don't like it."

"None of us like it," Murray said briefly, "but there comes a time when we have to stop spending time and resources on a case we know we're never going to solve."

As if symbolically, he pushed his bound copy of the report to one side, leaned forward and clasped his hands together.

"Now then," he went on. "Enough of that. I've got something else for you if you want it."

"What do you mean, if I want it? Why shouldn't I want it?"

Murray drew a deep breath and then continued.

"It means working with Simon Collison," he began, gazing carefully at Allen to see his reaction.

"I don't understand," Allen replied. "He's an SIO. I'm an SIO. So how come we could both be leading the same enquiry?"

"It's complicated," Murray said, "and before I go on there's something I must tell you. I'm afraid Bob Metcalfe is being suspended."

"What?"

"He's being suspended pending a disciplinary hearing for possible dereliction of duty," Murray explained apologetically.

"Is this Collison's doing?" Allen demanded angrily. "I know he's a stickler for procedure, but that's ridiculous, whatever Bob is supposed to have done. He's one of the best coppers I've ever worked with."

"Shut up, calm down, and listen," Murray snapped. "Yes it is Collison's doing, but only in the sense that he's the one who has to do it. For the record, he's very upset about it; much more upset than you could possibly imagine, in fact. Bob went to take into custody a very disturbed girl, whose history he knew, and despite being aware that she had severe anger management problems he decided not to take a uniformed officer with him. Things went wrong – badly wrong. A probation officer has been seriously injured; she's probably going to die."

He paused to allow these words to sink in.

"Dear God," Allen said soberly. "Poor Bob."

"Poor Bob indeed," Murray agreed. "Things don't look too good for him right now. The ACC has already briefed the Commissioner. If she dies then the probation service will be duty-bound to make a complaint, if only to be able to show that they have done everything in their power to investigate what happened."

"She may not die," Allen offered hopefully.

"She may or she may not," Murray replied. "I'm sure a lawyer would argue that the outcome doesn't really matter either way. The breach of duty would still be the same regardless. Anyway, we don't have time to worry about that. I'm much more concerned about an ongoing investigation which has suddenly lost its DI. What I'm asking you is a big favour, because you're obviously way too senior and way too experienced for the role, but it's not fair to ask Simon to fly solo on what is now a double murder enquiry, nor is it fair to ask another DI to come in cold and pick up everything Bob was doing – anyway, we don't have anyone suitable who would be immediately available. You are, and you're knowledgeable enough that you probably could do the impossible; hit the ground running, that is."

"I don't think I owe Simon Collison any favours," Allen

said sourly. "The last two cases I worked on he took away from me."

"Now you know that's not true, Tom," Murray chided him gently. "The first one was taken away by the ACC because he felt you needed a break; frankly, I think he was right. Nothing personal, you were just knackered, that's all. The second one was taken away because Collison believed that it was connected with his existing investigation. The ACC agreed with him, and, again, frankly so did I."

Alan looked mulishly at him and said nothing. Murray sighed; he had known this would not be easy, and his instincts had not played him false.

"All right, I can understand you being reluctant to work with Collison-"

"*For* Collison, not *with* Collison," Allen cut in. "I'd be under him, wouldn't I? His number two. His bagman."

"Yes, you would," Murray agreed reluctantly, "but it's a big case, Tom, and it's not unknown for a Superintendent to have a DCI underneath him."

"I'd rather have another assignment, please," Allen said evenly.

"There isn't another assignment right now," Murray informed him. "Not as an SIO anyway. Now why don't you consider this, Tom? Have you thought how Bob must be feeling right now? Oh yes, he'll be feeling stupid about what he's done, and doubtless very worried about the girl too, but worst of all he'll be feeling guilty for leaving the rest of the team in the lurch. He knows just as well as you and

I know that it's the DI who runs the nuts and bolts of an investigation. He assigns responsibilities. He make sure that all the notes and records are full, complete, and filed in the right places. It's him that people bring leads and suggestions to. Remove the DI in the middle of an investigation and the whole process could simply fall apart."

Allen thought for a moment.

"There's Willis," he proffered. "She's good."

"Yes, she's very good," Murray agreed, "but she's not ready to step up yet. This is only her second case as a DS for goodness sake. No, it has to be you, Tom. Think of it as a favour to Bob if you like. With you stepping in he won't have to feel that he's let everybody down."

The other man still appeared unconvinced. Murray sighed again.

"I could make it an order," he said gently. "I'm the District Commander and at the end of the day I have full discretion how an investigation gets handled, and how it gets staffed."

His words hung between them as Allen gazed at him in dismay.

"And would you?"

"Yes, Tom, I'm afraid I would. At the end of the day only one thing matters, and that's nicking villains. We can't allow personal feelings to get in the way. Simon Collison needs our help and I'm going to see that he gets it, one way or the other."

"And it looks like I don't have any choice," Allen said gloomily.

"Now you listen to me, Tom," Murray said earnestly. "We've known each other a long time – I was your DCI, remember? – and I'm going to give you some advice for your own good. First off, I think you've misjudged Simon. I did too, I put my hand up to that. I believed what I heard about him, that he was arrogant and inexperienced and a bad copper who'd been over-promoted. But then I got to know him and I realised that he was basically a good bloke trying to do his best. It's not his fault that he's been fast-tracked so that he hasn't spent as much time in the job as we have. It's not his fault that he's always very concerned about doing the right thing, and that this sometimes comes across as being a bit pompous. The fact is that he's a very intelligent man and he's in the process of building a very good track record. But never mind that, let me put something else to you."

Allen gave a grunt, which Murray chose to take as acquiescence.

"Very well, whatever you may think of Collison personally – and I think you're wrong, mind – remember this: he's the protégé, or whatever you want to call it, of the ACC and quite possibly even of the Commissioner himself. They've already tried to promote him to DCS once but he managed to persuade them to leave him in place to do proper police work. They'll try again very soon, and this time it may be impossible for him to say no; the ACC could order him to take on a new role just as I can order you. I happen to know that the ACC won't be content until he's at least a Commander. Just think about what that means."

"And what does it mean, then?"

"It means that he will be a very good person to have as a friend, and a very bad one to have as an enemy, you stupid bugger. Now stop being a plonker and give your brain a chance. This is a wonderful opportunity for you to make your peace with Simon Collison and do him a favour at the same time. Get stuck into the investigation. Be respectful and nice as pie to Simon. Get a result, or rather see that he gets a result."

"And that would make you happy, would it, Jim?"

"Yes it would," Murray said heavily. "More to the point, it would make the ACC happy and that's something you should be very concerned about right now."

"What do you mean?" Allen asked in surprise. "I'm not in trouble am I?"

"No, you're not in trouble as such," Murray conceded, "but your annual review is due. It's in that file of things to do that my secretary puts on my desk every morning and I ignore for as long as I can. I was just looking at it the other day. You are aware, I suppose, that as at the end of this year you have enough time in to take early retirement?"

"I was, yes, but it's irrelevant. I have no plans to retire."

Murray sighed yet again.

"I really didn't think I was going to need to spell this out to you, Tom, but you might not be given a choice."

"Eh?"

"The Met's stated policy now is to fast track officers with university degrees; the more relevant the degree, the faster the process. That's why people like Willis and Collison are moving up the ranks so quickly."

"Well? I don't see how that affects me. I don't have a degree."

"My point exactly. How do you think they're going to clear the way for these bright young things? By getting rid of time served middle ranking officers, that's how. There must be a list somewhere in the ACC's office of DIs and DCIs who are never going to get promoted any further. Well, I wouldn't mind betting that that's exactly the same list from which they're going to select candidates for forced early retirement. If we were bankers instead of police officers, they'd call it redundancy. Call it what you like though, it amounts to the same thing. One day you'll be an active DCI; the next day you'll be sitting at home watching daytime TV. So get smart, Tom. If you want to carry on nicking villains instead of growing roses then earn yourself some brownie points."

Allen sat quietly for a few moments, allowing this to sink in.

"You know, Jim," he said eventually, "I'm not at all sure that I want to be part of this new police force. It seems to be becoming like everything I became a copper to avoid in the first place. Politics, committees, job appraisals, political correctness..."

Murray nodded sympathetically.

"You think I don't feel the same? Do you have any idea just how many committees I have to sit on? Or how much paperwork I have to deal with every week? And it can only get worse if I get promoted."

"So don't get promoted then. DCS is a perfectly good rank, isn't it? Why put yourself up for Commander?"

"Because it's a merry-go-round, that's why, or a rollercoaster perhaps. You either stay on or you get off, and the only way you can stay on is by staying ahead. If I was to let it be known that I wasn't interested in promotion then I'm sure the ACC could find a place on that list for me."

"Particularly as he is looking for a DCS slot for Simon Collison," Allen pointed out shrewdly. "And this one – your job I mean – would be a straightforward line promotion for him."

Murray shrugged.

"If it wasn't Simon snapping at my heels – not that he is, mind you – it would be someone else," he said simply. "I guess that like you I have a decision to make, Tom. For my part I confess that I stopped enjoying the job some time ago, but I'm not ready to start growing roses any time soon."

"You stopped enjoying it? I never guessed. When?"

Murray hesitated and then suddenly grinned.

" To be honest," he said, "about the time I got promoted from DCI. Solving cases is what turned me on, not supervising efficiency studies, or sitting on policy committees. Collison's brighter than us you see, Tom. He's worked that out for himself in advance without having to wait and find it out by experience. Even though as a Superintendent he's not supposed to be an SIO, he's hanging on by his fingernails, resisting all the ACC's attempts to move him into the deskbound world of a Chief Police Officer…"

They sat briefly in silence together, but now it was a more companionable silence.

"If you please, sir," Allen said with heavy irony, "I would very much like to volunteer to join Superintendent Collison's team in any capacity in which you think I may be able to be of assistance."

CHAPTER 21

The mood in the house in Frognal was sombre that evening. Collins and Willis waited in near silence for Metcalfe to return from the nick, where they knew he was meeting with Collison. The tension was palpable and a sense of sad foreboding hung heavily in the air. Collins made them both a gin and tonic, and then another, but it was not until he was on the verge of suggesting a third that they heard Metcalfe's key in the latch. They sat awkwardly in the living room, waiting for him to come in. He did so, his face bearing the expression of a man who was composed, but only at the expense of having had to make a deliberate effort to be so.

He nodded stiffly and sat down, nodding again but this time gratefully at Collins when he raised the gin bottle in invitation.

"Bob, darling," Willis implored him, unable to wait any longer, "do tell us what's happened."

"I've been suspended," he replied briefly and then, as if feeling that some further explanation was necessary, "suspended pending an enquiry, that is. Apparently it's a procedural requirement."

"Well it is, Bob," she said soothingly. "You know it is. The guvnor really didn't have any choice."

"No, I'm sure that's right," he agreed calmly, "particularly as I expect he's got the ACC and God knows who else on his back. Apparently they're expecting the probation service to make a formal complaint."

"Can they do that?" Collins asked as he handed him his drink. "The probation service I mean."

"I suppose so," Metcalfe shrugged. "I must confess that I haven't checked the disciplinary procedures recently."

"Oh, Bob," Willis said helplessly as she sat next to him on the sofa and grabbed his hand. "How awful for you."

"Oh, I expect things will sort themselves out," came the rejoinder with a poor attempt at a smile, "they usually do, don't they?"

"I know this is not my business," Collins interjected with an air of faint embarrassment, "but don't you think you should get some advice, Bob? Proper advice I mean; somebody professional. Somebody who knows the regulations, or at least can bone up on them."

"The guvnor has already suggested that actually. He suggested his old university friend, Adrian Partington. He was junior counsel on our first case together – do you remember? He said he'd already spoken to him, and that he'd be very happy to talk to me informally in the first instance."

"Well, that's good advice," Willis said warmly. "You're going to take it, of course?"

"I suppose so, yes."

There was a pause while Collins and Willis looked at

each other in quiet concern and Metcalfe took a few sips at his drink and looked at nothing in particular.

"I still can't quite believe that any of this is really happening," he said at length. "I know this sounds incredibly corny, but I feel as if I'm in the middle of a bad dream and that sooner or later I'll wake up. Silly, isn't it?"

"Not silly at all, old man," Collins assured him. "You're in shock, that's all. A sense of unreality is one of the most common symptoms. It's –"

He was about to launch into a fuller explanation, but desisted as Willis shook her head subtly but definitely.

"Now," Willis asked brightly, "what about something to eat?"

Metcalfe shook his head silently.

"I really don't feel like anything. You two go ahead."

"Now that really won't do, you know," Collins adjured him, shaking his head in turn. "You must eat, Bob, particularly if you're in shock. Awfully important to keep your blood sugar level in whack."

"What about some comfort food?" Willis suggested. "We could phone out for pizza if you like."

"Yes, all right then," came the response, but entirely lacking Metcalfe's usual enthusiasm when pizza was mentioned.

"That's better," Collins said approvingly as Willis went out of the room to phone through their usual order. "Now then, what would be a good pizza wine do you think? A nice Sangiovese perhaps?"

Metcalfe smiled wanly and flapped his hand as if to say "whatever you think".

Now it was Collins who bustled from the room in search of a bottle and corkscrew. As he passed Willis in the hallway he reached out and squeezed her hand. She kissed him sadly on the lips and hurried back into the living room.

"Did Collison say how long all this was expected to last?" she enquired as she sat down next to him again and slipped her arm around his shoulders.

"No, he didn't, and I didn't think to ask. Do you think I should have done?"

Now it was her turn to shrug.

"I don't suppose it would have mattered very much if you had," she replied. "Thinking about it, he probably doesn't have any idea himself. They'll probably need to wait and see what happens to Lisa."

"I'm no lawyer," Collins said as he came back into the room and busied himself with opening the bottle of wine, "but is that actually relevant?"

"How do you mean?" Metcalfe queried.

"Well, whatever they're going to suggest in relation to your conduct, surely it hinges on the decision which you took, doesn't it? Either the decision was right or wrong. The outcome – what happened in practice – is a completely different matter."

"You might be right as a matter of pure logic," Metcalfe commented as Collins handed round the glasses of red wine, "but I'm sure the mind of the average policeman doesn't work like that."

Metcalfe took a quick sip of his, glanced at his watch, and set the glass down on the table again.

"I think I'll just slip upstairs and get changed before the pizza arrives," he said.

Collins and Willis gazed at each other as they heard him go upstairs.

"Oh dear," Collins said helplessly, "what on earth can we do to help?"

"Not a lot, I fear," Willis replied.

She hesitated but then went on.

"Actually I think it could be rather worse than we think," she said nervously.

"How do you mean, old thing?"

"He told me that when he saw Lisa lying there on the floor of that flat bleeding from her head wound, it reminded him of something that happened when he was just starting out, when he attended an accident. Apparently there was a young girl with a fractured skull – she died later – and he remembered that she had a pool of blood around her head the same way Lisa did."

"You're right," Collins concurred, "that could indeed be serious. It sounds like the association between the two images may have released emotions that he kept bottled up at the time."

"You mean that he might effectively be suffering two lots of shock at the same time?"

"Something like that, yes. There was quite a bit written about it back in the 50s, about people who had seemed perfectly well-adjusted suddenly going into delayed shock about things which had happened years before during the war, but it was pretty much all swept under the carpet. There was a lot of stigma attached to any sort of mental health issues back then."

"So what should we do?" she asked plaintively.

"Well, he should seek treatment obviously," Collins replied, "but all we can do is make the suggestion. Whether he actually follows through on it is up to him."

"I wonder whether we should tell Collison...?"

Collins shrugged.

"I only wish I knew. Isn't that really a matter of police procedure?"

Willis thought hard.

"Well, you're supposed to disclose any health issue which may affect your ability to discharge your duties," she began.

"But surely that's a personal obligation, not one that can – or indeed perhaps should – be assumed by a colleague," Collins objected, "and anyway he doesn't have any duties to discharge at the moment; he's been suspended."

Willis threw a cushion on the floor in frustration.

"If only I knew what to do for the best," she moaned.

At that moment the doorbell rang. Shouting "Bob – pizza!" up the stairs as she did so, Willis crossed the hallway and opened the front door. To her surprise she found herself face to face not with a proffered armful of pizza, but with a rather breathless young woman who seemed highly nervous.

"Oh gosh, hello," the apparition faltered, "oh, I say, you're that policewoman aren't you?"

Willis nodded in reply, concentrating as she did so. The woman seemed familiar but she could not quite place her. Suddenly it dawned on her.

"You were at the crime convention, weren't you?" she said suddenly.

Relief flooded across the visitor's face.

"Yes, I'm Fiona. I was hoping that Dr Collins might be in. He did say that I might call..."

"Yes of course," Willis replied, trying hard to conceal her curiosity. "Please do come in."

She shepherded Fiona into the living room. Collins, who was busy with plates and cutlery, looked up in surprise and then suddenly said "oh damn!" rather viciously to himself.

"I'm terribly sorry," he said as Metcalfe came into the room, also looking enquiringly at their guest. "The fact is I completely forgot you were coming."

"Oh," Fiona said crestfallen, "well I suppose I could always come back another time..."

"Don't be silly," Willis admonished her briskly, "you must stay of course. Do sit down. We've got pizza arriving any minute and we always dramatically over-order so there'll be plenty for four. Peter, why don't you be a dear and get another glass?"

"Yes of course," he said at once and then, while heading towards the kitchen, "but it's really you she's come to see."

Before further explanation could be forthcoming the doorbell rang again. This time it really was the pizza.

"Now then," Collins said once they were all comfortably settled around the table with pizza on their plates and wine in their glasses, "I really must apologise for all this confusion. Fiona rang me this afternoon to tell me something about the case, but of course I said that I was nothing to do with the investigation officially and so she should speak to someone on the team. Since it sounded urgent, I suggested that she pop round this evening. It's just that with everything that's been going on, I'm afraid I forgot about it."

"No problem at all," Willis assured him and then, to Fiona, "have you remembered something you didn't tell us before?"

Fiona nodded, her mouth full of pizza, and went somewhat red in the face.

"Yes," she confirmed after swallowing, "and I suddenly realised that it might just be jolly important."

The three of them gazed at her expectantly.

"You see, it was on that last afternoon," she began. "The last afternoon that Ann Durham was alive, I mean, the afternoon before she died. I suddenly remembered something that happened."

She looked at them uncertainly.

"Go on," Willis urged her.

"Well, Ann Durham was in the green room with Tom

Smythe and they were having a dreadful row. I didn't hear it start, so I don't really know what it was about, but I heard Tom say very distinctly "if you do anything like that, Ann, I will kill you. I really will, I will kill you." I can't think why I didn't remember it before. Maybe I did, but just didn't think it was important."

"Did he sound as if he meant it?" Willis asked. "Was he shouting, for example?"

"No he wasn't shouting at all. In fact he was talking very quietly but very intensely. Did he sound as if he meant it? Well of course I didn't think so at the time. Maybe that's why it slipped my mind."

"Might anybody else have heard him, do you think?" Metcalfe ventured suddenly.

"Well yes, and actually that's why it suddenly occurred to me that it might be so important. You see there was a waiter – a waitress I should say, I suppose – clearing away some tea things. It didn't register at the time but I suddenly remembered today who she was. It was that Estonian girl who got murdered on the stairs."

There was a silence while the other three looked at each other.

"Are you sure she overheard?" Willis demanded. "After all, you said he was speaking very quietly."

Fiona nodded vehemently.

"Yes, yes I'm sure she did. You see she suddenly looked at them in a very startled way. Tom saw that she had noticed – I'm sure he did. He suddenly looked very embarrassed and clammed up on the spot. There was one of those awkward sort of pauses while she cleared the things away onto her tray and left the room."

"What happened then?" Collins asked curiously.

"I don't know. I wasn't in the room, you see, I was just passing. I didn't want them to think I was eavesdropping so I just carried on where I was going."

"Which was where?" Willis asked.

"I think it was my turn to sit on the book table to help with sales – yes, I'm sure it was."

"But that's on the same floor as the green room," Collins pointed out, "and quite a short distance away. Are you sure that you couldn't hear anything else – anything that happened afterwards?"

"No, nothing I'm afraid. There was quite a bit of background noise, and anyway he had been talking very quietly. I think the only reason I heard what he was saying in the first place was that there was one of those sudden lulls and I just happened to be in the right place at the right time."

"Are you quite sure about this, Fiona?" Willis pressed her. "You do realise that what you're saying could have serious implications?

Fiona nodded again.

"Oh yes, I'm quite sure," she confirmed, suddenly tearful. "Oh, isn't it dreadful? Do you really think that poor girl might have been murdered just because of something she overheard?"

"We can't know that," Willis said calmly. "It's just

conjecture. Anyway, saying that you'd like to kill someone and actually doing something about it are two very different things."

"So what you want me to do?" Fiona asked uncertainly.

"I'll need you to come into the police station tomorrow and get this down in a formal statement for you to sign," Willis informed her. "It may be that Superintendent Collison will want to see you as well."

"Oh dear," Fiona said nervously.

"Don't worry," Collins said, reaching across and patting her arm, "you've done absolutely the right thing in coming to see us, and I'm sure that tomorrow won't really be such an ordeal after all."

He picked up his glass and saw that it was empty.

"And now," he said briskly, "I propose another bottle of Sangiovese."

CHAPTER 22

"Good morning everybody," Collison greeted the team. "Before we begin this morning I have an announcement to make. DI Metcalfe will be unavailable for some time, but I'm very grateful indeed to DCI Allen who has very kindly agreed to step into his shoes at incredibly short notice. Most of you will know DCI Allen, of course. Tom, welcome."

"Thank you, guv," Allen said as he stood up and walked to join Collison at the front of the room.

"Now I've been up all night reading the file," he continued with a bleak smile, "and I think I'm up to speed, but please forgive me if I have to ask people to fill in the gaps as we go along."

He consulted some notes which he had jotted down in advance.

"First up," he said, "I've put a statement on file which the DI Metcalfe took from – and I still can't quite believe this – Miss Marple. You'll see that it doesn't take us very much further. She says there was no serious dispute between her and the deceased, just what she described as 'a professional difference of opinion' when Ann Durham was rather critical in a television interview of one of the episodes in which she appeared."

"That's a bit strange," Collison mused. "I had the impression from Angela Hughes that it was a bit more serious than that. Perhaps we should make a note to follow up on that, Tom."

"Yes, I agree," he said calmly. "Now I have a list here of assignments for today and I would also like to review exactly where we are with some outstanding issues, but first does anybody have anything else by way of a new update?"

"Yes, guv, I do," Willis piped up and then, as everybody gazed at her expectantly, "one of the volunteers at the crime convention came to see me last night, saying she had some new evidence which had only just come to mind. Apparently she overheard Tom Smythe making death threats to the deceased in the presence of our second victim."

There was an immediate hubbub through which Collison struggled to make himself heard.

"And why on earth has she suddenly remembered this now?" he demanded.

Willis shrugged.

"She says that she only twigged yesterday that the waitress was the second victim, and that as soon as she realised that she knew it could be important. I've got her coming in to make a formal statement and I did tell her that you might want to see her yourself."

"I certainly do," Collison said determinedly. "I'll sit in with you."

"Okay, so that's a new item for my to do list," Allen commented wryly. "Now, as I said, I thought it might be useful to review where we've made progress and where we still have work to do. To start with, let's look at the key characters who were there when Ann Durham died."

He stood by the board and ran his finger down the list of names as he spoke.

"Karen Willis and Peter Collins. I'm assuming we can safely eliminate them from our enquiries."

A dutiful chuckle ran around the room.

"Tom Smythe. An interesting character, and even more interesting in the light of what we've just heard. There must be a suspicion that he was actually responsible for the diversion which occurred at the table, perhaps while either he or an accomplice were adding the cyanide to the gin and tonic. Problems: one, nobody saw him doing that, and it would be a difficult thing to pull off – not impossible, mind you, but difficult; two, he doesn't appear to have any motive for wanting to kill the deceased, although in the light of this new evidence it may simply be that we haven't been able to uncover one."

He looked around the room quizzically but nobody had anything to add.

"Angela Hughes. No obvious motive, although we're still waiting to find out exactly where she stands financially with respect to the deceased, particularly so far as any will is concerned. She was physically close to the deceased when she died but, again, nobody saw her tip anything into the drink, or indeed handle the glass in any way."

"Miss Marple." He rolled his eyes theatrically. "What can

I say? From reading the file she seems to be a harmless old eccentric, but why was she so sure that there was going to be a second murder? Does she know something that she isn't telling us?"

"Gina Durham and her boyfriend, Barry Carver. More promising in terms of motive. They stood to lose out big time if the deceased changed her will. I'm assuming that there would have been a great deal of money involved. Again, no sign of either of them having tampered with the drink, but it seems we're not sure when or where that happened anyway. I think we need to look some more at this pair, both jointly and individually."

Collison nodded in agreement.

"Sonia Gold, who seems to be something of a screaming psychopath, especially where Ann Durham was concerned. If we ignore the events in the dining room itself, she may well have been the last person to have an opportunity to administer the poison. Problems: one, blackmailers do not normally murder their victims – it's usually the other way round; two, for someone with anger management issues poison is a strange weapon to choose – it's much too premeditated. They normally just pick up the nearest heavy object and batter someone around the head with it – exactly as she did in fact with the probation officer. What's her name?"

"Lisa Atkins," Willis prompted him sadly.

"Sonia Gold seems to be our prime suspect at the moment," Collison commented, "and she's not helping her cause by having gone on the run. I'm sure we'll get her soon, though. Both addresses are under observation and we're watching out for her to use her bank card or her Oyster card."

"On that, guv," Evans interjected, "we now know that she jumped on a bus outside the block of flats. It was an 82 heading south, presumably just the first bus that pulled in as she ran out of the building. The driver thinks she may have got off outside Selfridge's, but he's not sure. The trail goes cold there anyway. She hasn't used the Oyster card since."

"So it looks like she's moving around central London on foot, then," Desai observed, "but you can't do that forever without being spotted."

"And in the meantime, we will just have to be patient," Collison said, realising too late that he was stating the obvious.

"And then there's the question of the second murder," Allen reminded everyone. "Where are we with finding out more about our victim, and where the people with just mentioned were at the time she died?"

"Tom Smythe, Angela Hughes, and Miss Marple were all still at the convention," Willis replied, checking her notes. "Gina Durham and Barry Carver had checked out about an hour earlier. We're checking CCTV to see if we can spot exactly when they left the hotel, and whether either of them might have sneaked back later. As for Sonia Gold, we've no idea – it's one of the things we want to ask her."

"Exactly where do the first three say they were at the

time?" Allen persisted. "In the session itself, listening to the speakers?"

"Yes, but the way these things work there are people going in and out at the back of the room all the time," Willis explained, "so I'm not sure just how good an alibi that might be."

"I remember seeing a CCTV camera in that big open area outside where the sessions take place," Desai chipped in. "You know, where they have the big tables for selling books. Why don't we get hold of the film for that, and check exactly who came in and out of the room?"

"Great idea," Collison said at once. "Let's make that a priority, please, Tom."

Allen nodded and added it to his list. Suddenly the phone on Willis's desk chirped. She grabbed it up, listened for a moment, said "right" and put it down again.

"It's Fiona, guv," she informed Collison. "The girl from the convention. She's here, downstairs."

"Right, then let's you and I go and see her," he said at once. "Tom, I'll have to leave you here to carry on, I'm afraid."

Though clearly nervous, Fiona duly repeated for Collison's benefit everything which she had told the Three Musketeers the previous evening.

"But how is it that you only remember this yesterday?" he pressed her. "It really does seem most remarkable that it should have completely slipped your mind."

"Yes I know, I'm so sorry," came the flustered reply. "It

was just a matter of a couple of seconds, you see, and I was so busy with lots of things to do. It was only yesterday that it suddenly occurred to me that the waitress in the room was that poor girl who died on the stairs. That's when I realised how important it might be."

"Hm," Collison said noncommittally, and then, "on a completely different topic, can you tell me where you were when the body on the stairs was discovered?"

"Yes, I know exactly," she said at once. "I was on the book table, and I had been for the last couple of hours because the girl who was supposed to relieve me – another Fiona, actually – never turned up. I was jolly annoyed about it as it happens because I had other things to do."

"So would you have been in a position to see people going in and out of the conference session?" He asked curiously.

"Yes, I suppose so. But I would have been serving people some of the time and so I might not have noticed everybody. And sometimes there might have been people between me and the door – you know, blocking my line of sight."

"Do you remember either Tom Smythe, Angela Hughes or Miss Marple going in or out? Or Ann Durham's daughter or her boyfriend?"

Fiona thought carefully.

"Angela Hughes definitely. She's difficult to miss, isn't she? Always so elegant. Tom Smythe ... yes, him too I think. Not sure about any of the others. Come to think of it, I don't remember seeing Gina or Barry at all that day. Haven't they gone home by then? Lots of arrangements to make, I suppose; how sad, you know ..."

"Yes, quite," Collison said automatically, but then "now when you say that you saw both Angela Hughes and Tom Smythe come out of the session, did you see them go back in again? And can you be more specific about when this might have been, and where they went or came from?"

"Oh gosh," Fiona said desperately, "let me think."

There was an awkward pause while she gazed fixedly at the tape recorder and went, if possible, even redder than usual. Finally, she spoke.

"I remember Angela Hughes coming out of the session quite early, almost as soon as it began in fact. She ran into the loo opposite. To tell the truth, I don't remember her coming out again."

"But that must have been a good 30 minutes or so before the hue and cry of the body being discovered," Collison said incredulously. "Are you really saying that she went into the Ladies and was still there half an hour later?"

"Oh gosh," she said again, "yes, that does sound a bit strange doesn't it? Well, all I can say is that I didn't see her come out again. It's quite possible that she did but that I just didn't see her."

"Because you were serving people?"

"Yes, and we were jolly busy. Lots of people suddenly bought up all the unsold tickets after Ann died, and they all wanted to buy copies of her books. We had to have a special extra delivery just to cope with the demand. Ghoulish, I call it."

"You said "we" were jolly busy," Willis pointed out. "Does that mean that there were other people on the table with you?"

"Oh yes, like I said there was huge demand suddenly for her books. I think there were two or even maybe three of us. Oh gosh, I suppose they might have seen something, mightn't they? I'd better get you their contact details."

"Thank you," said Collison with a smile, "that would be helpful. But let's focus on you for the moment. You told us what you can remember about Angela Hughes, but what about Tom Smythe?"

"I definitely remember him coming out of the session. At about the same time as Angela, I think. But in his case I remember him coming back as well. Come to think of it, it was just before all the fuss started. I think that in both cases he used the staircase."

"Do you mean the service stairs?" Collison asked as he and Willis stared at each other.

"Oh no," she said quickly, "that's not allowed; they're only for staff. No, I mean the main stairs beside the lifts. Where it was a matter of only going up or down one or two floors, most people used them because the lifts could be very slow; I used them myself, for example."

"I see," Collison said. "Well, thank you. That's all been very helpful."

"Oh gosh," came the response. "Has it really? Oh gosh."

CHAPTER 23

"So it sounds like we need to get Mr Smyth back here for a little chat, Tom," Collison informed him as he and Willis reported back to the little huddle in the incident room. "Damn the man! That's the second time something like this has happened. Why can't he just tell the whole truth in the first place?"

"Villains rarely do," Allen replied grimly. "I'm old school. I believe that if someone has something to hide then it's usually something pretty iffy."

"I'm inclined to agree with you," Collison concurred. "Anyway, get him back will you?"

"Will do," the other acknowledged. "By the way, I think Desai has come across someone who knew our second victim. Apparently they shared a room together. She's working in a restaurant right here in Hampstead. We have her coming in after lunch. Would you like to sit in?"

"I will if I have time," Collison replied glancing at his watch. "I need to update Jim Murray on this new Tom Smythe angle and I'm also going to try to slip out for a coffee with Bob Metcalfe."

Allen raised his eyebrows and, taking Collison by the elbow, steered him gently away into an empty space.

"Bit risky, isn't it? Are you supposed to have contact with an officer who's been suspended?"

"To be honest, I'm not sure. I'm not proposing to discuss the case, or anything to do with the suspension. To tell the truth, Tom, I'm worried about him. I was speaking to Karen this morning and it seems that she and Peter believe he may be suffering some sort of delayed shock from a trauma he suffered years ago when he was just starting out in uniform."

"Really? How do they work that one out?" Allen asked dubiously.

"Bob told me that he had to attend a road accident in which a young girl had been knocked down and suffered a fractured skull. There was a big pool of blood around her head. Apparently exactly the same thing happened when that Gold woman clobbered the probation officer. They think the association may have brought everything flooding back for him."

"It's possible," Allen conceded. "I've known it happened before. I had a DS once who just started crying when he was sitting in the car with me. Turned out the song on the car radio was the same as one that was playing at a crime scene he'd attended – a sex murder, nasty one. Hadn't thought about it since, but suddenly it all came back to him."

"Well anyway," Collison concluded, "I just want to see that he's all right."

"I'd do the same thing in your place," Allen commented, gazing at him strangely.

"Don't sound so surprised, Tom," Collison said with a grin. "I am human sometimes you know."

So it was that a little while later Collison and Metcalfe sat slightly woodenly in their usual cafe looking out onto the King William IV pub, or The Willie as it was known to locals.

"Any news?" Metcalfe enquired without much hope.

Collison shook his head sadly.

"Nothing I can share with you I'm afraid, although of course you had a sneak preview last night of what that Fiona girl wanted to share with us."

Metcalfe nodded silently.

"I can tell you something, though it's not good news I fear. As anticipated, the probation service have put in a complaint. They feel they have to, since Lisa is unconscious and incapable of doing it for herself. The rules do provide for that; I checked."

Metcalfe nodded again.

"I am sorry about this, Bob," Collison said desperately. "If there was any other way of doing things, I promise you I would. But it's standard practice and there's really nothing I can do about it."

"Don't worry about it," Metcalfe replied quietly. "I understand. Anyway, there's nothing really for me to complain about, is there? I cocked up – that's all there is to it."

"Maybe, maybe not," Collison equivocated. "The more I think about it, the more I think you made quite a reasonable decision. After all, Lisa was supposed to be the expert on Sonia Gold and all you did was defer to her opinion. Anyway, it goes without saying that if it comes to a hearing I will speak up for you. I think the ACC is sympathetic too."

"How long will it be, do you think – until things get resolved I mean?"

Collison shrugged helplessly.

"I really don't know. It all depends on Lisa, whether she – well, you know, I mean how long it takes her to recover..."

Metcalfe smiled mirthlessly.

"I've just been to see her at the hospital. It's strange, she looks so peaceful lying there even with all those tubes in her."

"What do they say? The hospital, that is."

"They say it's impossible to know with a fractured skull. She may come out of the coma or she may not. And even if she does come out of the coma she may have brain damage. So it's all a matter of being patient, I guess."

"Well, at least you're not on your own," Collison said with an attempt at cheerfulness. "You're in good hands with Peter and Karen."

"Yes, I suppose so," Metcalfe said dully. "It's just difficult having nothing to do, that's all. There's the case going on just over the road there at the nick, and here am I hanging around aimlessly when I could be working."

"Surely there must be something you could do? What about tracing your mother? You've always been talking about it. I know it didn't work out for Karen, but maybe it would for you."

"Yes, I suppose so," Metcalfe repeated but without any real sign of animation.

Collison sighed.

"I really should be getting back," he said. "There's an interview I'd like to sit in on this afternoon and I have a few things to take care of first, but before I go tell me: have you contacted Adrian Partington?"

"Yes I have. In fact, I'm seeing him late this afternoon after he gets out of court. Thanks for setting that up, guv."

"You're very welcome," Collison said. "I know he's a bit pompous, but he's a good man. If I was in your place I can't think of anyone I'd rather have on my side."

"Except you perhaps," Metcalfe said simply. "Thanks for taking the time, guv – and the trouble."

"So he was okay, was he?" Allen asked later.

"No, Tom, not really," Collison replied heavily. "He was pretty much as you would expect, actually. The poor chap seems completely taken aback by what has happened, and I can't say I blame him. There you are wandering happily through life and suddenly something totally unexpected happens which completely tears your world apart. First there's the shock of what has happened, but also, in his case, the guilt of feeling that he was responsible for it."

"How's the girl?" Allen queried. "Do we know?"

"She's got a fractured skull," Collison answered simply, "and we all know what that means. Only a slim chance of coming out of the coma, and an even slimmer one of escaping without brain damage even if she does."

They both looked at each other without speaking. Then Desai put her head around the door and nodded to them.

"Why don't we do this together?" Collison suggested on a sudden impulse. "It's been a long time, hasn't it?"

As soon as the words were out of his mouth, he regretted them. Allen had the obvious rejoinder that the last time they had conducted an interview together it was he who had been the SIO, not Collison. Equally obviously, though, he was not going to use it. Nonetheless, the thought hung between them, no less potent for being unspoken.

The young black girl sitting in the interview room gave her name for the tape as Donna Mazewe and looked distinctly nervous.

"I'm sure DC Desai has already explained," Collison ventured, "that you're here simply as a witness. We very much want to find out who killed Peta, and we need you to tell us everything you know about. The slightest little thing might be important, no matter how trivial it might seem."

Donna looked around the room with an air of desperation.

"I really didn't know her that well," she protested. "We only shared a room together for a couple of weeks, and we were almost never there together. We both do shift work, you see – or did, I suppose I should say, shouldn't I? – so we were in and out all the time. And when she wasn't working she was taking drama classes; she was doing a part-time acting course, you know."

"No, we didn't know," Collison said with a smile, "so,

you see, you're being a great help already. Where was she doing it?"

"That drama school by Swiss Cottage station. I think it's famous, or something."

"If you mean Central then yes, it is. Now, what else can you tell us?"

Again the girl glanced around uncertainly.

"I dunno," she said hesitantly.

"Oh come on," Collison encouraged her gently. "You must know a lot more than that. How did you meet, for example?"

"At a party, of course. How else do you meet anyone?"

"When and where?"

"It was about five or six weeks ago at some posh pad in Notting Hill. I'm not sure whose party it was – I only met them for a couple of minutes to say hello. I think it was something to do with the drama school, though. The bloke who invited me had just finished a course there."

"It wasn't Barry Carver by any chance, was it?" Collison asked suddenly.

"The bloke who invited me? No. But I think the name rings a bell. Maybe he was the bloke giving the party. I think he was living with some bird there; can't remember her name, but she spoke posh."

"Interesting," Collison replied, glancing at Allen. "If you don't mind, we might ask you to glance at a few photographs before you leave just to see if you recognise anyone. Now, did you know anyone else at the party?"

"No, nobody. I was pretty bored in fact because most of the people there were all at the college together, so they knew each other. The bloke who took me disappeared early on, and I didn't know anyone else. I was just about to leave, in fact, when I got talking to Peta."

"Peter who?"

"No, Peter that was her. That's how she pronounced her name. Not the way you're doing it. Peter just like 'pee', not like 'pay'."

"Peter like pee," Allen repeated in jocular fashion. "Well, that's easy enough to remember anyway."

"There you are you see," Collison said with a smile, "that's two things we didn't know."

"Is it important? The way she pronounced her name, I mean."

"No, I don't expect so," Collison replied, "but we're just trying to build up a picture and every little helps. Now, what more can you tell us? What sort of person was she?"

"She was nice, I guess. Quiet though. Sort of difficult to get to know, if you know what I mean. Never really let you know what she was thinking."

"Did you ever see her with anyone else? Apart from at the party, I mean?"

"No, I don't think so, but like I said we hardly saw each other because we were going in and out at different times. I heard her talking on her mobile a few times and it sounded like it might be someone special because she was speaking very quietly with her hand over her mouth, but I never heard her mention a name or anything."

"Do you have any idea where her phone might be? She didn't have one on her when she – when we found her."

"No, but I can't imagine she wouldn't have had it with her. She had it all the time. She was always checking for messages, you know, the way people do."

"But you could give us the number, presumably?"

"Yeah, of course."

"Good, that's something else we can do at the end. We did try searching the networks but we couldn't find any record of her as a subscriber."

"No, you wouldn't, she used pay-as-you-go. Apparently she couldn't pass the credit check for a proper phone. She only had what she made from her shift work."

"I don't mean to pry," Collison said clumsily, "but do you have any knowledge about her sexuality?"

Donna stared at him for a moment and then burst out laughing.

"You mean were we an item?" she demanded.

"Yes, I suppose I do," Collison agreed, feeling himself reddening.

"No, we weren't. Like I said, we hardly knew each other. Anyway, I'm not gay, although I think she might have been, at least from time to time. I think the voice on the phone was a woman, though I never made out anything it was saying. I think I can remember her talking to some woman at the party as well, but I didn't get the impression they knew each other, more that they were meeting for the first time. So no, can't help with that I'm afraid."

Collison looked enquiringly at Allen, who shook his head.

"I don't think there's anything else we have to ask you," he said, "although we would like you to deal with those various matters before you leave, if you will."

"Do you know anything about her family, her mum and dad?" Donna asked unexpectedly. "She did talk about them quite a bit, you see. I can't help thinking about them not knowing what's happened to her. Doesn't seem right, does it?"

"Don't worry," Collison reassured her. "They are being contacted through the Estonian Embassy. But no, it's obviously going be pretty awful for them. I believe she was their only child."

Donna's lip started to quiver.

"Actually," Collison observed uncertainly, "talking of her parents, there is something you could do for them, and for us actually. You see, we need someone formally to identify her. Of course we could wait for her parents to get to the UK but, well, things are going to be difficult enough for them..."

"I see ... Yeah, all right then, I'll do it. Oh God."

Then she cried.

CHAPTER 24

"Hello," Peter Collins said cheerily as Angela Hughes greeted him at the door of her flat in Marylebone Village, "I saw you on breakfast television this morning."

"Yes, and I'm doing another interview later on today," she replied as she stood aside to let him enter. "Very busy, you know."

She led him into a small but exquisitely furnished living room. The walls were painted a light purple and on them hung what looked like some enlargements of old black-and-white photographs, but with curious metallic flecks of gold and silver. He stood and gazed around, lost in admiration.

"What a fantastic room," he marvelled and then, after a moment's hesitation, "I say, is it my imagination or is all the furniture smaller than normal?"

"How astute of you to notice," she said with a smile as she motioned for him to sit down. "Yes, you're quite right. Because it's a small room I really wanted things which matched the same scale. Would you like some tea or coffee by the way?"

"Some tea would be nice, but please don't go to any bother just for me. I know how busy you are right now."

"It's no bother at all," she assured him. "Why don't you

come into the kitchen with me and we can chat there while I make it?"

They walked the few steps from the small living room into an even smaller kitchen which was fitted out as Collins imagined the galley of a luxury yacht might be. She took a teapot from a cupboard and switched on the kettle.

"If you don't mind me saying so," she ventured, "I wouldn't have thought you were the sort of person to watch breakfast television."

"Actually, I'm not," he admitted. "Bob Metcalfe had it on while he was sitting in the kitchen and I was making myself some toast. I suddenly heard your voice so then of course I sat up, metaphorically speaking, and took note."

"Well, as you've seen, the world seems to have gone crazy since Ann's death. Every bookshop in the world wants a window display, every newspaper in the world wants to run a feature, and every TV and radio station wants an interview with her agent. I've never known anything like it."

"I hesitate to say this," Collins observed mildly, "and I'm not recommending it as a course of action, but getting killed in mysterious circumstances seems to be a wonderful promotional tactic."

She nodded sadly.

"You're right, of course," she agreed. "Dear me, poor Ann. If only she was here to see it; how she would love it so."

"But if she were still here then of course all the publicity would not be occurring," Collins pointed out pedantically. "But I understand what you mean."

She warmed the pot, put in tea (loose-leaf he noted with approval) and poured on boiling water.

"Would you mind taking that into the living room?" she asked. "I'll bring the milk and cups."

"No sugar?"

"Of course, if you'd like some. Somehow I rather assumed that you didn't take it."

"As a matter of fact you're quite right," he conceded ruefully, "but how on earth did you know?"

"I should say female intuition, shouldn't I?" she countered playfully, "but that would be cheating. If you remember we made tea together in the green room at the hotel and I noticed then that you didn't take sugar."

"Very observant. Perhaps you've missed a brilliant career as a detective."

They sat down on either side of a coffee table and carefully set down the tea things. She gave the pot a quick stir and then poured two cups, switching the tea strainer from one to the other in the process.

"It's really very good of you to come," she said as she handed him his cup, "particularly to the flat like this. I just had to escape from the office for a while. Things are so manic there."

"I was very happy to be invited," he said simply. "It's not easy to sit around quietly with not a lot to do while all your friends are dashing about solving murders you know."

"I'm sure it can't be," she concurred and then fell silent.

Collins waited for her to say something else, feeling

slightly awkward; after all, his tea was still too hot to drink.

"Was there anything in particular I can help you with?" he asked tentatively.

"Actually I was hoping to ask your advice."

"Willingly. Anything I can do."

"Well," she began uncertainly, "I know that you're a great authority on crime fiction, and I know that you're a great fan of the Bergmann books in particular. So I was wondering what you thought might be done for the best with this whole authorship problem. The news hasn't broken publicly yet, but I can't believe it will take long for the papers to ferret it out somehow."

"I thought you'd already decided to republish them under Goldstein's name," Collins replied. "Isn't that what you said? After all, Anne owned the rights didn't she? If so, then they will pass to her estate."

"Yes, that's all right," she said quickly. "There's no problem with the rights at all; I've checked with the lawyers. I'm more concerned with the presentational side of things."

"Then you're really asking the wrong person," Collins said in slight puzzlement. "Surely you want a PR expert don't you? I don't know anything about that sort of thing."

"Yes but I just feel I can trust you," she said awkwardly. "Please don't be embarrassed, but I have an instinct that you are a very good person, and that I can trust your judgement."

Collins felt a certain sensation rush through him. It was

not one he could define, nor even describe, but excitement was certainly one of its elements.

"Thank you," he said simply. "Then I hope I can prove worthy of your trust. What do you want my opinion on exactly?"

She sat back and gazed fixedly at the window, as though as an aid to concentration. As she tilted her head to do so Collins was struck by how very attractive the nape of her neck was.

"I suppose it all has to do with Ann," she mused, "her reputation, I suppose I mean. When the word gets out that she passed off another author's work as her own, albeit perfectly legally, what will her readers think of her then? As you know, she has a huge following all around the world. These are real fans; some of them travel huge distances to attend her events. Ironic really, given that she hated them really."

"The fans or the events?"

"Both," she said with a little mirthless chuckle. "She only did it because she had to, and she just play acted for an hour or two. Acted very well, mind you, but acting was all it was."

"Oh dear, how very sad," Collins murmured plaintively.

"And I have to be honest, there's the commercial aspect of things too. We are printing half a million of her books right now, believe it or not; all around the world. What happens to them if demand suddenly falls through a trapdoor?"

Collins considered the situation.

"But the timing of the media getting hold of the story is

beyond your control, isn't it? So if that's your concern then I would agree that there does seem to be a risk of exactly what you fear coming to pass."

"Oh dear," she lamented. "I was hoping you were going to tell me that I'd got it wrong."

"Well actually I think you may have done," he replied. "You see there is one situation in which you can control the timing, and that's if you announce it yourself. If you take the initiative you can pre-empt any media storm and make sure that the story is presented as you would wish it to be heard."

"With our spin on it, you mean? My, Peter, I thought you said you didn't know anything about PR?"

"Well so I don't," he protested, feeling himself flush slightly. "I don't have any of the jargon for a start. I would never have said 'with our spin on it' like you just did."

"Well, jargon free it may be, but it sounds like good advice nonetheless. You mean we should get ready to publish the books under Goldstein's name as soon as possible? Not wait as long as we can to harvest this huge popularity for Ann's books at the moment?"

"I can't advise on the commercial aspect of things, of course," Collins countered uncomfortably, "that's not my bag at all. I'm only suggesting that from a purely presentational point of view – and perhaps an ethical one as well – taking the bull by the horns and going public with the truth might make a lot of sense."

"Bless you, Peter, you're an absolute dear," she said, rising suddenly from her seat to lean over him and kiss him lightly on the forehead. "It shall be exactly as you suggest. I will drop in at the office on the way to the television studio and set things in motion. Stop the printing presses rolling on Ann Durham and start them rolling on Max Goldstein. Oh dear, not a very catchy name is it? These days an agent would get him to change it, preferably for something Nordic."

"Does that really happen?" Collins asked, still slightly taken aback by her sudden show of affection.

"Oh bless you, yes," she said breezily. "I expect half the writers of all this Nordic Noir stuff actually have names like Smith or Higginbotham and live in ghastly places like Watford or Cleethorpes. Publishers are funny like that, you see. They have an infinite appetite for pumping out more of the same, more of what everybody is already buying, and they're terrified of taking a chance on something new. So if you can tick the Nordic noir box, they know exactly which neat little compartment to fit you into and in all their marketing blurb they can describe you as the next Jo Nesbo. So much safer than having to promote you as an exciting new British talent."

"You're pulling my leg," Collins protested.

"Well yes I am," she said with a laugh, "but perhaps only slightly. What I just said was broadly correct. It's very difficult to get published if you're both an unknown author and writing something different, so there's an overpowering imperative to write books like those of already established authors. Sad, isn't it? Personally I believe a lot of readers are actually looking for something new, but they end up just having to take what they are given."

Collins rose and took the few steps required to take him across the room and inspect the artwork on the wall.

"I say," he called out over his shoulder, "I really like these. What exactly are they?"

"They're actually modern photographs taken on old metallic plates, but then treated in some way I don't pretend to understand to bring out those different colour effects. They're nice, aren't they? I bought them from the man who makes them."

"I wonder if you might give me his details? I'd be very interested in getting some for the house in Hampstead."

"I think that might be difficult, sadly. I haven't heard anything of him at all for a few years. Now I come to think of it, I think somebody told me that he had emigrated to Australia."

"That's a shame," Collins replied, "but not to worry. Now I know how it's done I can ask around. There must be other people using the same technique."

"Oh yes, I'm sure there are," she assured him. "I go to quite a few exhibitions and auctions and I've definitely seen very similar work for sale."

"Do you really? Go to exhibitions and auctions, I mean? So do I. Perhaps we could go together sometime?"

"What a nice idea, but I'm afraid that I could be very busy at work for quite some time. Exhibitions and auctions will have to wait."

"I'm sorry," he said in embarrassment. "That was much too forward of me. I do apologise."

"Oh, Peter," she said, openly bursting out laughing, "how wonderful you are. I'm not in the least offended. On the contrary, I would love nothing better than to spend some time in your company, but I am genuinely going to be tied to the office for the next few months. Can't we just put the idea on hold? I would so like to see you again."

"Oh," he said in relief, "yes of course, let's do that."

She glanced quickly at her watch.

"Now I'm afraid I really must be going. All those ideas of yours, Peter. I need to start taking steps to make them happen."

"Yes of course," he said again, "but let me help get these tea things out of your way."

She watched him gather together the tea cups and saucers. Noticing that one of them bore a lipstick stain, he tutted and, in a curiously old maid-like fashion, carefully wiped it clean with a paper napkin.

"Before you pick up that tray," she said suddenly, moving towards him, "I do hope that you're going to give me just the teeniest little goodbye kiss."

CHAPTER 25

"I've just cautioned Tom Smythe, guv," Willis said as she came into the incident room. "He's asked for a lawyer, so I'm afraid there may be a bit of a delay."

"Interesting," Allen commented grimly. "Innocent members of the public don't need a lawyer, do they? Nothing to hide."

"Oh come on, Tom," Collison chided him gently, "being cautioned can be a pretty frightening experience, you know. He probably just wants to make sure that he's taking all proper precautions."

Allen grunted, clearly unconvinced. Collison glanced at his watch.

"Since we have a bit of a wait anyway, why don't we have a quick discussion as to where we are? I was planning to do that today sometime anyway."

The others nodded and the three of them sat down around the table at the front of the room.

"First, Sonia Gold," Collison said. "She's clearly a very dangerous person, and I'm concerned that she's still out there apparently roaming around London somewhere. We desperately need to interview her to find out what happened when she met Ann Durham shortly before she died. Tom,

I'm sure uniform are doing everything they can, but why don't you go and have a chat with them anyway? If it's a question of resources, I can try talking to Jim Morris or even the ACC."

"Will do," Allen acknowledged.

"Second, Tom Smythe," Collison went on. "We need to get to the bottom of exactly what he may or may not have said to Ann Durham, and where he went when he left the conference session. Let's just hope that his brief allows him to play ball. If he won't, then I think we have to view that very seriously indeed. He's beginning to look like a natural and obvious suspect."

"So is Sonia Gold," Willis pointed out, "and we know only too well that she is capable of violence, whereas I'm not sure that Smythe is the type somehow."

"Everyone is capable of violence, young Willis," Allen observed with a sad smile, "it's just a matter of what it takes to push them to it."

"I'm inclined to agree," Collison remarked. "Logically, there must be a point beyond which even the most calm and peace loving person will feel compelled to resort to violence. Anyway, in the heat of the moment emotion can take over. I take your point though, Karen. It's strange in a way to have two such strong suspects."

"You don't suppose they could be in cahoots somehow, do you?" Allen enquired.

Collison shrugged.

"There's nothing to suggest they even knew each other,"

he replied, "much less entered into any sort of conspiracy together. Still, it's an angle we should investigate further."

"Suppose she's not roaming London as a fugitive?" Willis asked suddenly. "Suppose she does have an accomplice? They might have given her refuge somewhere."

"It's a long shot, but I suppose it's worth a try," Collison said. "Tom, when you speak to uniform why don't you investigate the possibility of them being able to put Tom Smythe's place under observation?"

"I'll try," he responded dubiously, "but they're bound to start moaning about available manpower. We are tying up a lot of bodies on this already, you know."

"Well do what you can, will you? Now, who else do we need to consider?"

"I think the second murder does make life simpler for us," Willis said thoughtfully, "just as Miss Marple said it would. Provided we assume, of course, that whoever murdered Peta also murdered Ann Durham, or conspired with Peta to kill her."

"Is that a reasonable assumption, I wonder?" Collison mused. "I'm not saying that it's not, you understand, but I do think we need to test it."

Alan looked vaguely irritated.

"If you're not prepared to assume that," he objected, "Then you're effectively saying that there was no connection between the two killings. How likely is that?"

"I'm not suggesting they are not connected," Collison said pedantically, "I'm simply questioning whether whoever killed Peta had to be directly concerned in the first murder. It doesn't necessarily have to be a conspiracy of only two people, for example."

Alan looked unconvinced.

"I think you're complicating things unnecessarily," he commented and then, as an afterthought, "with respect."

Collison smiled in obvious amusement.

"I'm just anxious that we shouldn't go heading down any particular path without fully considering all the possible alternatives," he replied. "In fact, we don't even know for certain that Peta *was* murdered. We haven't had the full pathology report yet, don't forget."

"You're saying she slipped?" Allen asked incredulously. "She was a slim, fit young woman, wearing flat shoes, not heels. She wasn't carrying anything. And, if she did slip, then who took her mobile phone? How many young people do you know today who don't have it on them at all times?"

Collison held up his hands in mock surrender.

"I'm not saying she slipped, Tom," he protested. "All I'm saying is that at the moment we can't be sure that she didn't."

He glanced down at his notes.

"Third, Gina Durham and Barry Carver, either alone or together. Well?"

"If we are continuing with the working assumption that the two killings are linked," Willis replied, looking at him a little uncertainly, "then we have no evidence from CCTV that either of them re-entered the hotel around the time of the second death. So, if they were to be in any way involved then there would had to be at least one further accomplice, and one who was prepared to murder at that."

"Sounds way too complicated," Allen said at once.

"Yes, I tend to agree," Collison concurred. "Unless something concrete comes up to link them with the second killing, Karen, let's put them on the backburner for the moment. Now, who else is there that we should be considering?"

"Miss Marple hardly seems the type," Allen observed dryly, "and anyway her story seems credible. Also, there's no evidence of her having been anywhere near the scene and time of the second murder."

"Yes," Collison agreed, "again, the backburner I think."

"There's Angela Hughes," Willis suggested.

Collison looked at her doubtfully.

"I suppose she had opportunity, in the sense that she was there when Ann Hughes collapsed and died, so she could just have easily have administered the poison as anybody else, but what possible motive could she have had? Ann Hughes was her friend as well as her client. You yourself said that she was distraught when it happened. And from what we know at present it seems that if anything Ann was preparing to alter her will in Angela's favour. So, if anything, surely she had every interest in keeping Ann alive, not in killing her off?"

"In the spirit of academic debate," Allen cut in with discernible sarcasm, "we have at least some evidence that the deceased may have been handed the poisoned glass before she ever got to the table, remember? In which case not only did the Hughes woman have no apparent motive, but she may not even have had opportunity."

"I still don't think we should take her off our list of suspects," Willis persisted. "For one thing, we know from Peter that the cyanide originally appeared on the scene out of her handbag. I know she says that it was Ann who obtained it and that she, Angela, doesn't know from where, but she's our only direct link to the murder weapon, and we've drawn a blank on all other enquiries about it."

"Okay," Collison replied, "but backburner again please, Karen. Let's pursue our two obvious suspects and see where that takes us. Agreed, Tom?"

"Couldn't agree more, guv. Aren't I right in thinking that the CCTV footage puts her in the Ladies when the second woman died? How do you think she got out to commit the crime, Willis – a secret passage?"

Willis looked mutinous but said nothing.

"But you raise an important point about the cyanide, Karen," Collison said quickly, seeing her expression. "It simply isn't good enough that we haven't been able to track down where it came from. Why don't you get together with the team members who are doing that and see if you can spot something which they've missed?"

The telephone on Willis's desk buzzed in peremptory fashion. She clacked across the room to answer it and then glanced back at them with a quick nod. Clearly, Tom Smythe's brief was now ready and waiting.

"You do understand, Mr Smythe, that this is an interview under caution, don't you?" Collison asked a short while later. "DCI Allen has just administered the caution. Do you understand it?"

Smythe nodded nervously.

"For the tape please," Allen intoned.

"Yes, I understand."

"Now then," Collison continued, "the reason we've asked you back is that once again we have suspicions that there are matters which may be highly relevant to this enquiry and which you have held back from us."

"My client can hardly be expected to account for anything he may not have said, Superintendent," his brief pointed out rather nasally, as if suffering from sinusitis, "nor to conjecture about what may or may not be relevant to the enquiry; only you can know that. So why don't you put this specific matter to my client and see what he has to say about it?"

Collison and Alan looked at each other and sighed.

"I was just about to, actually," Collison observed. "Mr Smythe, I have to put it to you that we now have evidence that you made what sounded like death threats to Ann Durham shortly before she died. What do you have to say to that?"

"When and where is it alleged that these statements were made?" the solicitor asked quickly.

"During the last day of Ann Durham's life, in what was called the green room where panellists waited before their session," Collison said evenly.

"And who else was present?" the lawyer came back.

"Hold on, let's not get ahead of ourselves," Collison cautioned. "Before we go any further, we'd be very interested in hearing whether your client has any recollection of this."

The two detectives gazed expectantly at Smythe, who moistened his lips and gazed uncertainly at his brief.

"Remember," the latter advised him, "that you do not have to say anything at all. The Superintendent has already made that clear. But, equally, if you choose not to answer but then advance an explanation in court, adverse conclusions may be drawn from that. Do you understand?"

Smythe nodded helplessly.

"I remember speaking to Ann a few times that day," he said slowly, "but I certainly have no recollection of threatening to kill her. If you could tell me who else was present, though, it might jog my memory."

Collison paused for effect. He gazed impassively at Smythe as if willing him to say more. Finally, he delivered his bombshell.

"The other person who was present," he said very deliberately and watching Smythe for any sign of reaction, "was Peta Lepik, who was subsequently found dead on the service staircase."

The solicitor looked shocked; clearly he had not been expecting this. His reaction, however, was as nothing compared to that of his client.

"Jesus!" cried Smythe, leaping to his feet and drawing

back from the table. "Not that girl? Surely you don't think I had anything to do with that?"

"For the benefit of the tape," Allen said without emotion, "Mr Smythe has stood up and retreated across the room. I must ask you to sit down again please, Mr Smythe."

"It's difficult to know what to think," Collison replied, "unless you are prepared to be completely honest with us. Surely you must see that if what we have been told turns out to be true, then you would have had a perfect motive to murder Peta Lepik."

"Only if my client had already murdered Ann Durham, surely?" the solicitor cut in looking suddenly grave. "And there's no evidence of that, is there?"

"Whether your client murdered Ann Durham or not," Collison responded, deliberately ignoring the lawyer's final question, "the fear of being incriminated for it would certainly constitute a motive for wanting to silence Peta Lepik, wouldn't it?"

"I don't understand," the lawyer said simply. "If the only people present other than my client were Ann Durham and Peta Lepik, and they are both dead, then where on earth can this evidence be coming from? Don't tell me the police are conducting seances now?"

"Not at all," Collison said, as if pretending to treat this enquiry seriously, "but the fact of the matter is that another person, a person who is still very much alive, overheard the conversation – or this part of it anyway – and has come forward to volunteer the information."

"And who is this person?" the solicitor persisted.

"I'm afraid I'm not prepared to answer that question," Collison said very calmly. "In view of what happened to Peta Lepik, whether or not your client was responsible for it, the identity of this new witness must remain confidential for their own safety."

"Well," the lawyer said, clearly weighing the situation in his mind, "I think our stance at this stage must be that if you are not prepared to tell my client who is accusing him, then I must advise him not to answer any further questions."

"Well now, that's a shame," Collison said mildly. "We were hoping to be able to eliminate your client from our enquiries. We can't do that if you won't give us a full statement."

"My client has stated for the record," the brief replied, gesturing towards the tape recorder, "that he has no recollection of making death threats to Ann Durham. Isn't that what you wanted to know?"

"Partly, yes. We would also like to ask your client where he was at the time just before Peta Lepik's body was found. We know that he was in one of the conference sessions which was running at that time, but we also know from CCTV footage that he left the session shortly before what we believe to have been the time of her death, and returned to it shortly before her body was discovered."

Again Collison and Alan stared unblinkingly at Smythe, who was breathing heavily and apparently on the verge of tears.

"I'm sorry," his brief said decisively, "but I don't think my client's best interest would be served by answering any further questions at this stage."

He gazed steadily at the detectives, who were now weighing the situation in their turn. They all knew the next issue which had to be faced. Finally, the lawyer took the bull by the horns.

"Are you proposing to charge my client, Superintendent? And, if so, with what?"

"Not necessarily," Collison said slowly, glancing at Allen who sat impassively beside him. "If mutually acceptable arrangements can be made to give us comfort about your client's continued availability, then I would be prepared to hold off any question of charging him, if only to give you an opportunity to take further instructions and perhaps reconsider your position as to cooperating with our enquiries."

The lawyer nodded.

"Suppose my client were prepared to surrender his passport, and not to leave the London area without your permission?"

Now it was Collison's turn to nod.

"If we are talking about police bail, and if you would be agreeable to your client not contacting anyone who is in any way connected with this investigation as an additional condition, then very well. You and your client to be ready to return to this police station on twenty-four hours' notice."

The lawyer glanced at Tom Smythe, but his client was clearly in no condition for rational discussion.

"Agreed," he said quickly, looking back at the detectives. "Shall we go and draw up the necessary paperwork?"

CHAPTER 26

"I think I made a bit of an idiot of myself today," Willis confessed moodily as she drew her legs up on the sofa.

"Really? How so?" Collins queried languidly, looking up from his book and laying it aside.

"Oh, I kept banging on about Angela Hughes when the guvnor was going through the list of suspects even though it's pretty obvious that she can't have had any motive for killing Ann Durham and she didn't even have an opportunity to kill Peta Lepik if the CCTV evidence is to be believed."

"You think there may be some doubt about the CCTV footage?" Collins asked curiously.

"No, not at all. There can't be, can there? That's why it's all so silly. I really don't know why I'm getting so obsessed about her. To tell the truth, I'm not entirely comfortable about excluding Gina Durham and her boyfriend either, the boyfriend in particular."

"Miss Marple had her doubts about the boyfriend, hadn't she?" Metcalfe chipped in unexpectedly from the other sofa, on which he had been curled up with every appearance of total detachment.

"Yes, that's right. I think she felt that he had an eye to the main chance: Ann Durham's money, that is. That he wasn't nearly as fond of Gina as she was of him. She was afraid that Gina may get badly hurt."

"That's not the same thing as suggesting that he may have murdered his prospective mother-in-law though, is it?" Collins enquired mildly.

"No, it isn't," Willis admitted. "Anyway, there's nothing to link any of them with the second murder. There is no record of any of them on the CCTV at the time. The only suspect we have who had a definite opportunity to kill Peta was Tom Smythe."

"Well now, I wouldn't be too sure about that," Collins said with a hint of mischief.

"What on earth do you mean?"

"I'm afraid I've been rather naughty," he said, sitting up straight in his chair. "You see I've been carrying out a few investigations of my own. I had time to spare after my meeting with Angela and I suddenly realised that there was something that needed to be checked."

"What was that?" she asked.

"The CCTV situation at the hotel. It occurred to me that if there was one area which was without coverage – namely, the service staircase – perhaps there was another as well."

"But there isn't," she said, puzzled. "All the public areas are fully covered, including the lobby. There's no way anyone could get in or out of the hotel without showing up on film."

"I don't think that's right," Collins stated blandly. "As a matter of fact I got both in and out of the hotel this very afternoon and I wouldn't mind wagering a small sum that I didn't show up on CCTV."

The others stared at him blankly, their minds racing. Suddenly Metcalfe got it.

"The underground car park!" he cried.

Collins nodded sagely.

"The underground car park indeed. All you have to do is walk down the ramp, ignoring the signs telling you not to, slide around the barrier and Robert's your father's brother, as I think Tom Allen says."

"So you're inside the car park," Willis ventured, trying to picture the scene. "Then there is presumably a lift up to the lobby, isn't there?"

"There is indeed, should you wish to use it."

"You mean –."

"I mean that there is also an access door to the service stairway, again with a prominent sign telling you not to use it, but I'm afraid I was very naughty and simply ignored it. I walked right the way up the stairs to the very top of the hotel and down again without being seen or challenged; jolly good exercise by the way."

"But Peter, do you realise what this means?" Willis asked, her head reeling.

"Of course. It means that all the people you have ruled out on the basis that they could not have been present when Peta Lepik died will have to be ruled back in again. Any of them could have agreed a rendezvous with her on a particular landing – or perhaps even in the car park – and have both entered and exited the scene undetected. Exactly as I did today in fact. By the way, doesn't that make the hotel shockingly insecure? You really must have a very stern word with the management."

"So Gina Durham, Barry Carver and Sonia Gold are still very much in the frame," she marvelled. "I can't wait to see Collison's face tomorrow when I break this to him. He thinks he's got everything tidily focused on the two obvious suspects."

"But they *are* the two obvious suspects," Metcalfe put in. "Don't let's forget that. I've seen with my own eyes that Sonia Gold is capable of committing murder – yes, and without giving it a second thought either – while Smythe is definitely hiding something about Ann Durham and had an opportunity to kill Peta Lepik."

"Agreed," Willis concurred, "but it does mean that we should still keep an open mind on the others."

"Even Angela Hughes?" Collins enquired naughtily. "And what about Miss Marple?"

Willis had the grace to laugh.

"I'm sorry," she replied in obvious embarrassment. "To be totally honest, I realised on the way home tonight as I was thinking about why I'd been such a complete twit about her that perhaps it was jealousy."

Collins raised his eyebrows.

"Yes, I know it sounds really stupid but I think that ever since I first met her I've been a little bit jealous of the way she looks at you and flirts with you. Like I say, it's stupid."

"It's not stupid," Collins reassured her awkwardly, the memory of a lingering kiss resting upon his lips, "it's just ... well, it's just human. No matter how much we may like to think that we are rational beings, the truth of the matter is that we are animals and, being animals, many of our emotions operate on a very basic instinctive level."

He broke off and looked at Metcalfe, as if for support, only to find that he seemed to be looking at least as awkward as he felt himself. Willis rose and, as if participating in some formal ritual, kissed each of them very gravely in turn on the forehead and then returned to her seat. Collins raised his glass and sipped thoughtfully, conscious of a feeling of guilt which he found frankly disturbing.

"And what about you, Bob darling?" Willis enquired. "What have you been up to?"

"I went to the hospital again, to see how Lisa was. There's no change of course. She's still in a coma and they seem to be preparing everybody for the fact that she may never come out of it."

There was silence in the room. Away in the distance the church clock could be heard striking the hour as if tolling the passing bell for the young woman who lay inert a short distance down Rosslyn Hill.

"I met her mother," he said suddenly. "It was awful."

"Why?" Willis asked, surprised, and then quickly as a thought struck, "she doesn't blame you for what happened, does she?"

"No, on the contrary, she told me not to worry about

it, that she was sure I had done everything I could. But I knew that wasn't really true. It made it worse somehow, her being so nice. In a way I wish she had come straight out and blamed me…"

She crossed the room, sat beside him on the sofa and put her arms around him. Collins took another sip of his drink, as much for something to do as for anything else.

"Bob dear," she implored him, "it's only natural that you should feel guilty about this, but it's just like me with Angela Hughes. It's not real, it's just some weird emotional reaction. You can't trust it. You have to focus on the facts, and the fact is that there wasn't anything you could do. It all happened in an instant, didn't it?"

He nodded wordlessly.

"I think it may have something to do with that awful experience you had with that schoolgirl in the road accident, Bob," Collins proffered quietly. "I don't know if it does any good for you to try to analyse it like this, but I think a lot of what you're feeling may be delayed shock, feelings which you repressed at the time but have been triggered now by seeing something similar. It brings it all back to you, as it were."

Metcalfe nodded again. Once more there was silence in the room.

"I've decided to trace my mother," he announced suddenly.

"Oh, that's wonderful news, Bob," Willis said at once.

"Not necessarily," he replied with a little laugh, "after all, it didn't work out for you, did it? But I got to thinking that at least it would give me something to do, something to take my mind off everything else."

"Yes, I'm sure that's good idea," Collins agreed, looking at Willis. "As you say, just because Karen had a bad experience it doesn't mean you will too."

"Well, we'll see," he said noncommittally. "I went along today and signed the papers. Apparently I may be able to see somebody in a day or two."

"Oh, I wonder if you'll get to see the same man that I did," Willis ventured. "He was rather a dear. I couldn't help being sorry for him, poor man, stuck in that awful little office and doing such a boring job."

"Well, I'm sure your presence brightened his existence anyway," Collins said gallantly, "at least for a while."

"You know, I found myself having exactly the same thought," she confessed. "In fact – this sounds awful, I know – but when I sat down I hitched my skirt up a bit so that he could get a good look at my legs."

Both men burst out laughing.

"Don't laugh!" she protested, "I'm being serious. I really did."

"We don't doubt your word, or at least I don't," Collins reassured her. "It's just the thought of some poor little functionary suddenly being presented with the vision of your legs. It's a wonder you didn't give him a heart attack or something."

"Well, I'm happy to confirm that he survived the

encounter unscathed," she said with mock seriousness. "Now, can we please change the subject? I'm sorry I ever mentioned it."

"You will be prepared for a disappointment though, Bob?" Collins asked. "After all, the odds of her being some ideal mother figure living in a country cottage somewhere are pretty slim, aren't they?"

"Oh yes," Metcalfe agreed. "Like I said, to be honest I'm really doing it as much to kill time as anything else. There's part of me that actually doubts whether it's a very clever thing to be doing at all. After all, she must have had good reasons for putting me up for adoption. Maybe some doors should remain closed, if you know I mean."

Willis, who still had her arms around him, patted his shoulder reassuringly.

"Going back to the case," Collins said, "I can't shake the feeling that somehow, somewhere, I've seen something that could provide the key. I've been over it again and again in my mind but I just can't spot what it might be."

The others looked thoughtful.

"What sort of thing?" Metcalfe asked. "Perhaps if you could get a sense of that it might help you to remember."

That's the problem," Collins said, shaking his head ruefully, "I haven't the slightest idea what it might be. Was it something I saw? Was it something I heard? If so, is there a connection to be made? I just don't know, but it's really niggling away at me."

"Why don't you try going right back to the beginning

and writing everything down that you can remember?" Willis suggested. "Blow by blow, as it were. You might be surprised by the level of detail you can remember. Perhaps doing that, and reading through it afterwards, might help things to fall into place."

"I wonder," Collins mused. "A bit like Patrick Leigh Fermor with 'A Time of Gifts' you mean? He wrote that decades after the events in question, and claimed to be able to remember quite small details."

"Yes, if you say so," Metcalfe agreed, though he had but the haziest idea of what the other was talking about. "A sort of recovered memory, I suppose."

"Well, it's not a bad idea," Collins said. "At the very least it can't do any harm."

He rose, took the bottle of Sicilian Chardonnay and carefully poured what was left into their three glasses.

"So Lisa's mother was nice, then?" Willis asked Metcalfe gently.

He nodded.

"She gave me her phone number," he said quietly. "Said I could call any time. That she'd like to get to know me whatever ... whatever happened."

"And did you give her yours?" she enquired softly.

"Yes, I gave my card. Asked to call me if there was any news."

"But you'll go back won't you? To the hospital, I mean? To see her for yourself?"

"Yes," he said after a pause. "Yes, of course I will."

CHAPTER 27

"I've got news," Collison announced as the team gathered in the incident room the next morning.

"So have I, guv," Willis returned with a grin, "but you go first because you might not like mine."

"How very tantalising," Collison commented, clearly intrigued, "but very well: I had a call at 3 o'clock this morning from the duty Sergeant at West End Central. Perhaps foolishly, I had left a note on the system asking to be notified as soon as there was any news of Sonia Gold. Well, she was arrested during the night after a disturbance near Leicester Square. Apparently she asked some man for money and got quite violent when he refused."

"Did she come quietly?" Allen asked.

"She did not. She resisted arrest very forcibly. Put one officer in hospital with a broken nose."

"She sounds like a complete nutter," Allen said dismissively.

"That's one way of putting it. Anyway, they're arranging for us to interview her there under caution with her lawyer later on this morning. They wanted to transfer here but we don't really have the cell facilities at the moment, given that we're supposed to be closing. That's the excuse I've used anyway. I'm sure the last thing the custody Sergeant here would want is a highly violent prisoner to have to control. I'm sure he's short staffed enough as it is."

Remembering, he glanced at Willis.

"So, Karen, what's this news that I may not like?"

"Remember that conversation we had yesterday, guv, about how nobody but Tom Smythe seems to have had an opportunity to get to Peta Lepik? Well we may have to revise our ideas a bit. It turns out that there is a serious security flaw at the hotel. It's possible to walk down the ramp of the underground car park and access the service staircase directly without being seen on CCTV at any time."

"Damn," said Collison quietly but with feeling. "That blows things wide open, doesn't it? But well done anyway, Karen, for checking."

"Actually it was Peter," she said, glancing uncomfortably at Allen. "He had a hunch and went and checked it out. He got right the way to the top of the hotel and down again without even coming across anyone on the stairs."

"Which means," Allen observed grimly, "that any of our suspects could have arranged to meet our deceased on the stairs, bumped her off, and have been clean away without anyone being the wiser."

"Exactly, guv," Willis confirmed.

"We'll have to re-interview Gina Durham and Barry Carver," Collison said, thinking quickly. "We'll also have to ask Sonia Gold if she was anywhere near the hotel on her travels. It might also be worth putting some of the troops on door-to-door enquiries at the houses opposite the car park ramp. We know pretty exactly at what time our killer would have needed to use it, if indeed that's what he or she did."

"Will do, guv," Willis acknowledged, jotting down a note.

"You know, on the whole I'm not sure that I do dislike your news after all," Collison commented. "After all, if Sonia Gold is indeed our most likely suspect for the Ann Durham murder then it means that she may also be in the frame for Pate Lepik, and the better view must be that the two deaths are somehow linked."

"But the only way that would make sense," Allen pointed out, "would be for the two of them to have been in cahoots together on the Durham killing. How likely is that? Do we have any evidence that the two of them even knew each other?"

"I'm assuming that the two deaths are linked," Collison answered carefully, as if thinking aloud. "That means that the Lepik girl must either have been an accomplice on the Durham killing, or have discovered something about it that she was trying to use for blackmail purposes. Either way, there must be another person involved and I don't see why it shouldn't be Sonia Gold. Put it this way: it's at least as likely that it was her as that it was anybody else."

"But we don't have any evidence of that, do we?" Allen persisted. "That's all I'm saying."

"And sadly, Tom, you're absolutely right. We showed her friend some photos of our various suspects to see if she could remember having seen any of them with Peta, but the only ones she could finger for certain were Gina Durham and Barry Carver, and that's hardly very incriminating since we know that she went to one of their parties."

"Well," Allen commented flatly, "then that means that the only hope we seem to have of getting her for either murder is if she's prepared to cough to them – and good luck with that, by the way."

The telephone on Willis's desk broke in at this point. She picked it up and, after listening for a moment, held it out towards Collison.

"Dr Williams for you, guv."

"Brian," Collison said, having taken it, "I hope this is about your report on that girl on the stairs. It is? Hang on then, I'm going to put you on the speaker. I've got Tom Allen and Karen Willis with me."

The pathologist's electronically distorted voice squawked at them from the loudspeaker.

"I'm sending my written report over this morning, but I thought I'd phone you just so I could summarise it for you. Briefly, my examination has been inconclusive. There's no sign of a struggle – nothing under her nails, for example – and the injuries which killed her could have been sustained in simply falling down the stairs, particularly if she fell more than one flight. However, given the degree of her injuries I think it likely that she was pushed. If that had been the case then she would obviously have fallen much more quickly, and her head would have hit the stairs with greater force."

There was silence at the Hampstead end of the phone.

"Are you saying that she wasn't murdered after all?" Collison asked at last.

"Not at all," Williams replied smoothly. "All I'm saying is that there is no direct evidence of her having been murdered. The head injuries are consistent with having struck the steps while falling downstairs. They would also be consistent with having been hit over the head first by some sort of blunt instrument, but there's no obvious profile to the injuries. If a hammer has been used, for example, then it's often possible to guess at that by the shape and depth of the impact, but here it's ambiguous."

"You say there is no direct evidence," Willis queried, wondering if she had caught a false scent, "but does that mean there may be some indirect evidence?"

"Yes," Williams answered with a chuckle, "there is: well spotted. In a case where someone has fallen down stairs I would expect there to be some evidence of them having put their hands out in front of them to break their fall. Here there isn't any. There are no obvious injuries to the hands, not even slight abrasions. That leads me to suppose that she was unconscious already as she began her fall. But as I say, that's supposition on my part and you'll have to come to your own view on what that might be worth in court."

"Thank you very much, Brian," Collison said. "That's quite clear. Thank you very much."

He handed the phone to Willis, who returned it to its cradle.

"Well," he said with as much cheerfulness as he could muster, "not as helpful as we might have wished, although we do have expert opinion on our side. It looks as though whoever killed her either pushed her down the stairs or knocked her on the head first. If the latter, though, what was the weapon and what happened to it? We searched the stairs and the adjacent hotel areas very thoroughly and found nothing."

"Which means," Willis concluded, "that if a weapon was used then the killer must have taken it away with them."

"It also means," Allen interjected thoughtfully, "that they must have got some blood on them, mustn't they? I mean, it's difficult to hit someone on the head without getting splattered to at least some extent. Maybe not enough to be immediately obvious, particularly if they were wearing dark clothing, but more than enough to show up for forensics."

"All true," Collison nodded. "The other thing which argues very strongly for murder is of course the missing phone. Can you imagine a young person today not having it ready to hand at all times? No, whoever killed her must have taken it, which in turn suggests that they had been in communication with her and didn't want us to be able to check up on it."

"If only it hadn't been a pay-as-you-go phone," Willis said regretfully.

"Well now you know why villains use them," Allen replied grimly.

Down the road at the Royal Free Hospital Bob Metcalfe

sat in a small individual ward staring fixedly at the seemingly lifeless form of Lisa Atkins. A brace encircled her head while another supported her neck. A large tube projected from her mouth while smaller ones ran away under the bedclothes. If he listened very carefully he could just hear the faint sound of her breathing.

After a while the door opened and Susan Atkins slipped into the room. She smiled at Bob and sat down on the other side of her daughter's bed.

"Hello, Bob," she greeted him gently. "No change, I suppose?"

"No, none, I'm afraid," he replied, trying not to sound as pessimistic as he felt.

"I'm glad you're here," she went on, looking at him closely. "You see there's something I want to talk to you about."

"Oh yes?" he asked warily.

"Yes. You see I was chatting to one of the nurses outside in the corridor yesterday. It turns out that her boyfriend is a policeman at the station up the road. That's your police station too, isn't it? Well he told her the other day that you'd got into trouble as a result of what happened to Lisa. Big trouble, he said. Is that really true, Bob?"

"Yes it is," he said, embarrassed. "The probation service have made a complaint. What it comes down to basically I suppose is that they're saying I didn't do enough to protect her."

"Can they do that?"

"Yes, it seems so. It's supposed to be the person who has actually been harmed in some way – injured in this case although it doesn't need to be physical harm – but where that person is unable to do it for themselves then it's okay for somebody else to do it for them."

"But shouldn't that be me? I'm her next-of-kin, after all. The probation service is just her employer."

Metcalfe shrugged helplessly.

"I really don't know. To be honest, I'm just letting it all wash over me. I still can't believe that any of this has really happened."

"Well you mustn't do that," she said briskly. "You must jolly well get yourself some good advice and fight this thing. It's absurd that anyone should be blaming you for what happened to Lisa. From what I understand she was attacked very suddenly by a disturbed young woman she was trying to look after and there was no time for anyone to do anything about it."

"That's true, of course, but I was there and I was supposed to be in charge of the situation."

"But how were you to know what was going to happen? It's not as if you have a crystal ball, is it? You couldn't see into the future."

"There's a complication you should be aware of," he said quietly. "There's a procedure in these cases. If you think that there might be any sort of trouble then you're supposed to take a uniformed officer with you. I didn't because Lisa asked me not to. At the end of the day, I got it wrong. If there had been someone else there it might have deterred her, or they might have been able to grab her in time. Oh, I don't know, but the fact is I didn't follow the procedure and she's lying here because of it."

"I don't believe that for a moment, and neither will your colleagues I hope. Lisa used to discuss her work with me. She was passionately committed to helping the troubled young people she was given to look after. If she asked you not to take anyone else with you then she must have had good reason. I can't believe she thought for a moment that anything like this might happen."

"You're very kind," he replied, trying to summon up a smile, "but I'm not sure the tribunal will see it like that."

"Then they'll have to be made to see it like that," she said firmly. "As I said, Lisa loved her work – she lived for it – and she would never have wanted to be responsible for anything like this happening to someone like you."

With a shock Metcalfe realised that she was now talking about her daughter in the past tense.

CHAPTER 28

Sonia Gold sat staring mutinously at Collison and Alan, her lawyer beside her. Collison sensed waves of blind hostility emanating from somewhere within her.

"You do understand, Sonia, that we are interviewing you under caution? Yes? DCI Allen has administered the caution and, even though your lawyer is present, I wish to ask you if you understand it."

"Course I understand," came the contemptuous reply, "but I ain't going to tell you nothing."

"That of course is a matter for you," Collison replied calmly, "and for your lawyer to advise you on, but I do urge you to consider your position. We have the eyewitness evidence of a police officer that you inflicted grievous bodily harm on a completely innocent young lady who was just doing her job; a job, incidentally, which consisted of trying to take care of you."

"Who asked her to?" she demanded fiercely. "Who said I needed taking care of anyway? The interfering bitch got what was coming to her."

Her lawyer, a slim young woman with a Home Counties accent, shifted uneasily.

"I see that you do not deny the attack," Collison said

with a sidelong glance at the tape recorder, "but that's not what we want to talk to you about. We are investigating the death of Ann Durham and we think you may be able to help us with our enquiries."

A look of sheer hatred flashed across Sonia Gold's face.

"That thieving cow! There she was giving herself all those airs and graces when all the time she was just a thief. She stole my grandfather's work and passed it off as her own. Did you know that? No, I bet you didn't."

"Actually we do know that," Collison countered, "and regardless of whether I approve of it ethically, the fact remains that it was perfectly legal. It was done with the consent of your family at the time – of your father in particular."

"He was desperate. My Nan was sick and he needed money for her treatment. That Durham cow knew that, and took advantage of him."

"Like I say," Collison replied, "clearly what occurred was very questionable, but that's not what we want to talk to you about. Our enquiries suggest that you met with Ann Durham shortly before she died. We very much need to know all about that meeting. When and where did it take place? What was said? How were things left between you?"

"Oh, and you think I'm just going to tell you, do you?"

"I'm hoping so, certainly, and I'll give you two very good reasons why I think you should. First, we are anxious to eliminate you from the Ann Durham enquiry. So if you know anything which might help us to do that then it's entirely in your interest to tell us. Second, if Lisa Atkins dies – and she very well might – then the GBH charge will automatically upgrade to murder, and in that case you could be looking at a very long sentence indeed. Any assistance you feel able to give us on the other matter is something we can tell the judge about or, in due course, the parole board."

Sonia Gold appeared deeply unconvinced. However, she glanced at her lawyer who nodded significantly. She folded her arms across her chest and stared fiercely at a spot on the wall above Collison's head.

"All right, what do you want to know?" she asked finally.

"What time did the meeting take place?"

"It was arranged for six, but I got there late, about six thirty I think."

"Who was there, was it just the two of you?"

"Yeah. I was a bit surprised as it happens. I thought that Hughes woman, her agent, might be there as well. I'd already had one run in with the old bitch."

"Yes, we know about that. The police were called to her office, weren't they?"

"Might have been," she said sullenly.

"Never mind that. Tell us what was said between the two of you."

"She offered me money to keep quiet. I was going to go to the papers, you see, with the whole story."

"How much money?"

"A hundred grand. That's when I got angry."

"Angry?" Collison queried innocently. "Why would you be angry at the prospect of being given a hundred grand?"

"Because it was a lot less than what I'd been asking for, that's why. I asked for half a million."

"That's a lot of money," Collison commented mildly.

"A lot of money?" she snorted. "Compared with what she's made out of the books all these years? Compared with what my family's been through? Compared with my Grandad never getting the recognition he deserved? I don't think so."

There were signs of growing agitation from the lawyer.

"I think your solicitor is a little concerned that you've just confessed to blackmail," Collison said gently, but looking at the lawyer and making it clear that his comments were addressed to her, "but let's not worry about that for the moment. As I said, we are focused on the death of Ann Durham. Now, what happened next?"

"I told her to sod off. I grabbed my bag and made for the door. She grabbed my arm and asked me to stay. She said she'd only offered what she had because that Hughes bitch had suggested it. That she was willing to give me what I was asking for, but that she needed guarantees that I wouldn't welch on the deal – you know, take the money but then go to the papers anyway."

"What sort of guarantees?"

"Yeah, that's what I asked her. She said that she'd like to have some papers drawn up by her lawyers for me to sign."

She shrugged.

"I said yeah, why not? As long as I got the money why should I care what I have to sign?"

"So what happened then?"

"Not a lot. She said she'd be in touch and then I left."

"And when you left her, how did she seem?"

"Calm, I suppose. Yeah, calm. OK. Normal."

"Now this may be very important so please think very carefully before you answer. At any time during your meeting did you see Ann Durham with a glass of liquid of any kind?"

"Yeah, she had a glass she was drinking from. In fact, she'd pretty much finished it. She asked me if I wanted anything, but I said no. I just wanted to get out of there, get it over with as quickly as possible."

"Do you have any idea what it was?"

"Nah, not really, but it was clear and had a slice of lemon in it, so I assume it was either gin or vodka."

"Now this is also very important. Did you leave the hotel as soon as your meeting was over?"

"Yeah, I did. Why?"

"Never mind why. And have you at any time returned to the hotel since leaving it that evening?"

"No. Why would I?"

"Do you know anyone called Peta Lepik?" Collison asked suddenly.

"No, I don't think so."

"Do you know anyone who works at the hotel, whether permanently or as a shift worker?"

"Not as far as I know, no."

"When did you hear about Ann Durham's death?"

"On the telly the next morning. I was well choked, I can

tell you. It was pretty obvious I wasn't going to get my half a million, wasn't it? Not now, with her having gone and croaked."

"One last thing. Can you cast your mind back once again to that meeting in Ann Durham's hotel room? Do you remember seeing a small bottle anywhere – a bottle like a medicine bottle or a large perfume bottle, perhaps?"

"No, I don't."

"Very well, interview terminated."

Allen reached across and turned off the tape recorder. As he was going through the formalities of initialling them and giving one to the solicitor Sonia Gold spoke again.

"So what's going to happen to me then?"

For the first time Collison thought he heard a note of uncertainty in her voice.

"You will be held here on a charge of inflicting grievous bodily harm on Lisa Atkins. I would imagine that the duty Sergeant here will be making arrangements for you to be held on remand somewhere; probably Holloway prison. Your lawyer can advise you on making an application for bail, but I must say that in the circumstances I think it would be unlikely to be successful. After all, it's a serious charge and you've already gone on the run once."

"And what about you lot – your investigation, I mean?"

"We'll be in touch if we need to speak you again," Collison said, and then could not resist adding "after all, we'll know where to find you."

Back in the house in Frognal, Peter Collins was busy with

his notes as Bob Metcalfe came into the room.

"How's it going?" the latter enquired.

"Well, I don't want to get ahead of myself," Collins replied carefully, "but I do at least have a few questions which require answers. I'm going to go through them with Karen when she gets back this evening to see if she can persuade Simon to let her do some work on them. How about you, by the way, what have you been up to?"

"I've been to the hospital. Met Lisa's mother again. She gave me something to think about, actually."

"Oh yes? What's that?"

"Well it's about this bloody disciplinary thing. She pointed out that she is Lisa's next-of-kin, so if anybody was going to make a complaint on her behalf then it should be her, not the probation service. They're just Lisa's employers."

Collins thought from moment.

"Sounds sensible," he concurred. "Why don't you speak to that barrister Simon recommended?"

"As it happens, I'm seeing him in an hour or two. I'd already arranged it but now at least I'll have something specific to ask him."

"And presumably – though this may be a silly question – Lisa's mother has indicated to you that she would not be minded to make a complaint were the matter left to her?"

"Yes, I suppose so. That's what I'm assuming anyway."

Collins toyed with his pen as if uncertain how to proceed.

"What is it?" Metcalfe prompted him.

"Well, this is a pretty wretched thing to have to ask," Collins admitted, "but have you asked yourself whether that might change if Lisa should actually die?"

"If Lisa dies," Metcalfe replied soberly, "then I'm not sure I would want the complaint withdrawn. Whatever anybody might say to the contrary, I'm responsible for what happened."

"Now we've been through that, Bob," Collins said at once, wishing desperately that Karen were there. "What you're feeling is just guilt; survivorship guilt, mostly."

"Yeah, well..."

"Since you're here," Collins went on, glad of a chance to change the subject, "perhaps you can help me with something. How would you go about getting hold of somebody's mobile phone records?"

"Provided it's a regular subscriber number, there's no real problem. A senior officer, usually a Superintendent or above, has to sign some paperwork and the Met's legal team then applies for a Court Order. Why, is that one of the things you're working on?"

"One of them, yes. I must say that all this is a fascinating puzzle, but irritating too. Different things suggest themselves as clues to different outcomes, but there is no consistent pattern. Everything seems to point in different directions. The most irritating thing of all, of course, is that I'm more convinced than ever that the answer lies somewhere inside my own head. Hence all this."

He gestured at the pages of spidery handwriting scattered

across the coffee table.

"But is it working?" Metcalfe asked, intrigued. "Do you find it's helping you to remember things?"

"Yes, I think so. Maybe it's just helping me to focus on what happened second by second. I get the feeling that whatever it is I'm looking for may be a very small thing, but that it will spark a connection or suggest a pattern of events."

"You know, talking of puzzles, there's one thing that's always niggled away at me about this case," Metcalfe commented, crossing to the window and gazing outside. "How did that Miss Marple woman know that there was going to be a second murder? Don't you find that very bizarre, Peter?"

"Yes, of course. But surely she's just a harmless old eccentric, isn't she? And she was right, you know, the second murder is a staple of Golden Age detective fiction, just as much as the gentleman detective or the ritual gathering in the library at the end when the solution is explained. She's acted in so much of the stuff over the years that it's become deeply ingrained in her. I speak with some experience, of course. As you know, I sometimes have problems of my own in distinguishing between the world of fiction and real-life."

"Yes I'm sure you're right," Metcalfe said. "I'm probably making too much of it. It just disturbs me when something happens which I can't explain."

"Then that's probably why you became a detective, old boy," Collins said smilingly in his best Lord Peter Wimsey manner.

CHAPTER 29

"So there we are," Collison concluded his report of the interview with Sonia Gold, "no further forward I'm afraid. I'm reluctant to eliminate Sonia as a suspect given her known propensity for violence, but there's nothing to link her with either killing."

"I'd go further," Allen observed. "If ever there was somebody who had absolutely no motive for murdering Ann Durham it's that woman. After all, she said it herself: once Durham was dead, Sonia's chance of a big blackmail payoff died with her."

"Agreed," Collison said. "But let's not be downhearted. After all, being able to eliminate someone from the enquiry is valuable in itself. Now, where are we with everything else?"

"We have a message from Tom Smythe's solicitor, guv," Desai informed him. "Apparently Mr Smythe wants to come back and give a further statement."

"Does he indeed?" Collison enquired grimly. "Okay, get him in ASAP, Priya. This morning if possible."

He looked down at his notebook, in which he had a few jottings from the previous day.

"I thought it might be valuable just to go through our remaining suspects once more," he continued, "as well as reviewing progress on outstanding issues: the cyanide, for example."

"Excuse me, guv," Willis cut in, "but before we start on that, I wanted to ask you if it would be all right to pursue a few points that Peter has come up with. He's been doing a sort of mind dump. He's still convinced that there is a vital clue hidden in his memory somewhere, and I've got all sorts of notes here that he's been making as he goes along."

Allen looked suitably disapproving at the idea of a gentleman detective interfering in a police investigation.

"I wasn't aware that Dr Collins was a member of the investigating team," he said sarcastically, looking hard at Collison.

"That's true of course," Collison said carefully, "but he is a key witness and anything we can do to help jog his memory of events can only be helpful, surely?"

"He's very conscious that he's not a member of the team, guv," Willis put in, reddening slightly. "That's why he's suggested asking your permission for me to look at a few things. To be honest, I'm not sure where he's going with this, and perhaps he doesn't know himself. None of the questions he's asking seem to make much sense, at least on their own."

"Well, do go ahead anyway," Collison decided. "After all, he's already come up with one key piece of information – the lack of CCTV in the underground car park – and if he really does have a key clue lurking about in his memory somewhere then let's do our very best to help him find it."

The first phone reserved for incoming outside calls began

to ring. They all knew that if it was allowed to ring more than three times then several others would automatically start up around the room. Evans, who was nearest, picked it up quickly, said "Hampstead incident room, DC Evans speaking", listened intently for a few moments, then said "right, guv, I'll tell him" and put it down again.

"That was DI Metcalfe. He's at the hospital. Thought we'd like to know that Lisa Atkins just came out of her coma, but she's still in a bad way. Can't speak, doesn't recognise anyone, and she's drifting in and out of consciousness. The doctor told the DI that she's still not out of danger."

They all glanced at each other uncertainly.

"Well, that's some good news anyway," Collison said with false heartiness, as the others looked unconvinced.

Allen went and stood by the board. He raised his eyebrows at Collison, who nodded.

"Yes, Tom. What do we have?"

"So, we are removing Sonia Gold from our list of suspects," Allen commented as he did precisely that on the board. "That leaves Tom Smythe as our leading suspect. We know that he was present at the first death, and that he could have been at the second. It seems that he had motive to murder our first victim, although it's as yet unclear what motive he might have had for the second."

He stopped, as if inviting observations. Desai duly obliged.

"Excuse me, sir, but is it necessarily right to say that he was present at the first murder, as opposed to the first death?

After all, wasn't there a suggestion that the poison was added to the drink earlier – you know, away from the table?"

"Yes there is," Allen agreed, "but it's worth remembering that the suggestion itself came from someone with a motive, and they could simply have been trying to shift suspicion away from themselves."

"You mean the boyfriend?" Collison asked with sudden interest. "Yes, you're raising a very interesting point, Tom, and you too, Priya. If Barry Carver was telling the truth then it's most likely that the poison was added to the drink by the person who gave it to her, which he thought was a waiter. But even if he was telling the truth, that wouldn't necessarily rule Smythe out. After all, if that waiter was Peta Lepik then the fact that she was acting in cahoots with somebody else, and the need to silence her about her involvement, would provide an obvious motive for her own murder."

"And that other person could quite easily have been Smythe," Allen said, continuing Collison's own thoughts.

"Yes, but it could equally have been anyone else," Desai went on doggedly. "What about Barry Carver, for example? We know that she knew him, or at least that she'd been to one of his parties."

"If that was the case," Allen enquired, again with more than a hint of sarcasm, "then why would he finger her as a suspect? Surely he'd be frightened that we would interview her and she would crack and finger him?"

"Perhaps that's what we're meant to think, guv?" Desai responded, unabashed.

Collison stared at her.

"That's not a bad thought, Priya," he said thoughtfully. "Especially as we now know that he, or indeed anyone else, could have re-entered the hotel unobserved at the time of her own murder."

"We'd need to show that he knew Ann Durham was about to change her will, wouldn't we?" Willis asked uncertainly.

"Maybe, maybe not," Allen said cryptically. "She'd already made it clear that she disapproved of him. He must have realised that sooner or later she was going to bring financial pressure to bear. Maybe getting rid of her just seemed the easiest way out. He presumably believed that if she died then one way or another most of her money would end up with Gina."

"This is all useful stuff," Collison said. "I think what we're saying is that both Barry and Gina are still suspects, whether jointly or separately. In addition, there seems a strong possibility that Peta was instrumental in the first murder, and was killed because of that."

"So we're down to three suspects then, are we?" Allen asked.

"I'm not sure," Collison admitted. "Somehow I just wonder if we're missing something. Maybe Peter's right. Maybe there is some connection somewhere which would make a pattern fall into place. Right now I find the picture rather confusing. Things point in different directions ..."

He tailed off as Allen gazed at him in consternation. He

had clearly never heard a senior detective admit to being confused before.

"I know Bob is not a member of the team anymore," Willis ventured hesitantly.

"Go on," Collison urged her.

"Well, I know we have all discounted this as the ramblings of an old eccentric, but Bob can't get his head around how Miss Marple was so certain there would be a second murder."

"I know, I was pretty shocked when she told me," Collison concurred, "but isn't that just exactly what it was? Her only experience of murder has been acting in the fictional kind, and in the fictional kind there always *is* a second murder. It's usually the only way the poor old detective manages to catch the criminal."

"I've looked through the notes Bob made when he re-interviewed her," Allen remarked, "and I must say that I didn't see anything which made me think twice. Yes, she was one of the eyewitnesses to the first death but where's her motive? If her evidence is to be believed – and there is nothing to contradict it apart from some vague recollection by Angela Hughes – then she had no reason to kill Ann Durham at all, let alone some poor kid she'd never even met."

"What about Angela Hughes, Sarge?" Evans asked mischievously. "I thought you fancied her for it."

Willis reddened again.

"I think I was mistaken. I was overreacting to ... to something or other."

"Yes, and as with Miss Marple where is the motive?" Collison asked, taking Evans's suggestion seriously. "After all, she *did* know that Ann Durham was about to change her will, and in her favour too. So, like dear Sonia, she had every interest in keeping her alive."

"I agree, guv," Willis said quickly. "Like I said, I was mistaken."

"Don't worry, Karen," Collison reassured her. "All questions are useful."

Allen looked less understanding, but then his own way of conducting an investigation was much less collegiate.

"I wonder if there may be someone else?" Desai queried. "Someone we've completely missed because we've been looking in the wrong direction?"

"You mean someone who may have had a completely different reason for killing Ann Durham?" Collison asked. "A reason which doesn't seem to have anything to do with what we know happened that night?"

"But we've been into every aspect of Durham's life pretty carefully," Allen protested, "and if there is anything which would provide a motive, surely it's the Bergmann angle, which would take us straight back to Sonia Gold – and we've just ruled her out."

"Hm," Collison said thoughtfully. "Yes, that's right, we have. That's what I mean about things being a bit confusing. We seem to keep circling back to the same people and ruling them in or out for the same reasons."

There was a pause.

"Open issues," Allen announced. "Where are we with the cyanide?"

"I'm sorry, guv," Evans replied rather desperately. "We've spoken to every business in the country who is licensed to supply it and none of them have any record of Ann Durham or Angela Hughes. In fact, they all say that they would never supply it to a private individual anyway, but only to trade customers who have a legitimate use for."

"They also all say," Desai added gloomily, "that it's something that could be made in a fairly basic chemistry lab by anybody who knew what they were doing."

"Well, since we have ruled out the former," Collison observed, "we have to assume the latter. Let's look for any of our suspects having a chemistry background, or a friend or relative with one."

There was another pause.

"Phone records," Allen said next. "We've obtained details of all the calls made by our suspects starting from a few weeks before the first murder, and we've cross-referenced them with the number given to us by the second victim's friend. There are no hits."

Again there was silence.

"Let's look at this logically," Collison said. "Possibility one: we are barking up completely the wrong tree and there is in fact no connection between the two deaths. Suppose, for instance, that Peta Lepik simply missed her footing and fell down the stairs by accident. It's possible, I admit, but it doesn't feel right."

"Agreed," Allen said with a nod.

"All right. Possibility two: there is a connection and there was contact between Peta and her accomplice, but we are looking at the wrong suspects and that's why we can't find any trace of it. Well, we've added Miss Marple and Angela Hughes into the phone records mix, as well as Sonia Gold and we still don't find any record of communication between them. So that takes us back to the same question: is there someone else, and are we missing something?"

"Possibility three – and this I think is my favourite one – is this: one of our suspects took the precaution of purchasing a pay-as-you-go mobile, presumably under an assumed name and topping it up where necessary with cash. Unfortunately, there are actually a lot of pay-as-you-go numbers on the record of Peta's calls, so that doesn't take us much further. I would imagine that most of her friends, like her, wouldn't have qualified for credit and so a pay-as-you-go was the only option."

"Then we'll just have to hope," Allen said with a grim smile, "that when Tom Smythe comes in later he's going to cough to both murders."

Collison shrugged helplessly.

CHAPTER 30

"Excuse me, guv," Willis said as Collison and Allen were heading down the stairs to interview Tom Smythe. "Can I just clear something with you while you're available?"

"Yes of course, Karen, what is it?"

"Well, I just wanted to check that you really are okay with some of the stuff that Peter has asked about," she explained in some embarrassment. "You see, to be honest, I'm not really sure where he's headed. For example, he's asking about DNA evidence, CCTV footage, and the hotel."

"What about the hotel?"

"He thinks there may still be some evidence there, and he's anxious that we should get there first before anyone has a chance to remove it."

"What evidence exactly?"

"Is it okay if I don't say?" Willis asked, more embarrassed than ever. "You see, his theory seems a bit fantastic and if I don't find what he's looking for then I'd rather just let the whole thing drop and not say any more about it."

Collison considered the position briefly while Allen bristled with disapproval.

"Very well, go ahead," he said, forestalling the latter who appeared ready to interject. "After all, Peter has always shown good judgement before, and I still owe him a big favour from our first case together. Yes, go ahead. But if any searching at the hotel is involved do make sure that you get the manager's consent first, won't you? Otherwise we'll have to wait and get a warrant."

"Thanks, guv, and yes of course I will. Leave the manager to me."

As she turned to leave, Collison, seeing that she was wearing a short skirt and a tightly belted jacket, realised that the manager was probably likely to offer little resistance to the peaceful existence of his hotel being disturbed yet again. Shaking his head with a wry smile, he caught Allen's eye and surmised that his thoughts were probably running along similar lines.

"Come on, Tom," he said quietly, "let's go and see what Mr Smythe has come up with now."

Smythe sat quietly with his lawyer while the policemen went through the formalities of starting the tape recorder, choreographing the announcements, and delivering a fresh caution. He seemed both chastened and nervous.

"Now then, Mr Smythe," Collison addressed him once the preliminaries had been completed, "I understand that there is something you wish to tell us."

"When we last spoke," Smythe said hesitantly, "I said that I have never made death threats to Ann Durham. That was strictly speaking true, but I realise now that some of the things I said that day may have been ... open to misinterpretation, shall we say."

"Open to misinterpretation?" Allen echoed incredulously.

Smythe squirmed visibly.

"Let's just cut to the chase shall we, Mr Smythe?" Collison suggested. "Specifically, did you say 'if you do that I'll kill you', or words to that effect?"

"Yes I suppose I did," he replied wretchedly, "but I didn't mean it. It was just something I said in the heat of the moment."

"If, as you say, you had no malicious intent when you said what you said, why didn't you simply admit it the last time we spoke?" Collison asked reasonably. "Yet on the contrary, you denied it."

"I was scared, and I panicked," Smythe said simply. "This is a murder enquiry after all, and you wouldn't have cautioned me unless you thought I was a suspect. I did it without thinking."

"I think my client has explained his position, Superintendent," his solicitor cut in smoothly. "He's acknowledged that he didn't tell the full truth last time. He's here today to put that right."

"And in the meantime," Allen pointed out, "he's had a lot of time to talk to you and get his story straight."

"My only advice to Mr Smythe," the lawyer said tightly, "has been to be completely open and truthful with you, as will be apparent from our request for a further interview. My client is innocent of any involvement with either of these murders and his only concern is to cooperate fully with you in the hope that you will be able to find whoever it was who was truly responsible."

"Very well, very well," Collison acknowledged, "but I'm sure you will agree that we still haven't really got to the bottom of this. Now then, Mr Smythe, why don't you tell us the full story this time? It really is very irritating that we have to keep re-interviewing you in order to hear everything you should have told us in the first place."

"What do you want to know?" Smythe asked, glancing sideways at his solicitor.

"What was it that you and the deceased were talking about? What was it that prompted you to threaten to kill her, regardless of whether or not you meant it?"

Smythe looked down at the table and drew a deep breath.

"She said that I no longer wrote my own books," he said at length, looking up at Collison, "or at any rate the television programmes which, as you know, are based on my books. She said that I had a team of ghostwriters who were being paid by the television company to create the scripts for me."

"And you took exception to that, did you?"

"Of course!" Smythe replied indignantly. "It was hugely insulting, and it could also have been hugely damaging had she started saying that sort of thing to other people."

"If you were concerned that she might start making damaging untruthful statements about you to third parties," Collison said mildly, "then surely the obvious thing to have said would be to threaten her with legal action if she were to repeat such allegations? Not threaten to kill her."

Even though Collison sounded more than ever like a headmaster rebuking a recalcitrant schoolboy, Allen found himself nodding approvingly.

"Oh yes, you're right of course," Smythe replied wretchedly, "but you have to understand the context. That awful woman had created so much bad feeling about the whole committee situation that everyone was just about ready to be at each other's throats. When she said that it was the final straw somehow. I could feel my face getting hot. I suddenly just lost my temper and started saying the most awful things to her. That must be what somebody heard. Looking back on it, I can understand that they would be concerned, knowing what happened next."

"But was there any truth to what she said?" Collison asked, intrigued. "I thought it was commonplace to have a team of writers once books were being adapted for television on a regular basis."

"There is a script team, yes," Smythe acknowledged stiffly, "but they report to me. I have full supervisory control over the script, so it simply wouldn't be possible for anybody to introduce any storyline or new character without my permission."

"Isn't that very unusual?"

"Yes, it is," Smythe agreed proudly. "Very few writers have that sort of clout, you know. Ordinarily once you sign away the rights to your book you're effectively selling your soul to the devil. The production company can do whatever they want with it then. Sometimes they only keep the name of the central character, and make everything else up."

"So what makes you so special?" Collison asked innocently.

Smythe bristled visibly.

"You may not be aware of this," he said fiercely, "but my books consistently outsell everybody else's. Even that wretched woman's little offerings – well, over the last 20 years or so anyway, after she moved on from the Bergmann stuff. That's why it always stuck in my craw the way she lorded it over the rest of us. The Queen of crime indeed! I'm the number one crime writer in this country, and have been for years. Not her."

"Without wishing in any way to wound my client's pride," the solicitor interjected gently, with a slight smile, "it may also be worth pointing out that the contract under which the current series of Mr Smythe's books is being made, is a seventh or eighth renewal of the contract which was first entered into many years ago. Things were different back then; there was more of an atmosphere of partnership between the author and the television people. Quite simply, in order to hang onto the contract each time it's been renewed they have been forced to agree to my client's demand for editorial control. It would be out of the question in any fresh contract entered into with a new writer today."

"So the deceased threatened to tell people – quite untruthfully, as you say – that you let other people write the Inspector Naesby television programmes, and then took credit yourself for their work?"

"Yes."

"And you then threatened to kill her if she did, though – as you say – without meaning it?"

"Yes."

"And you weren't aware until our last meeting that anybody had overheard you?"

"That's right."

Suddenly there came to Collison one of those completely random recollections whose origins defy explanation but which have a swift and startling impact. He sat up straight, gazed intently at the wall, then shook his head and carefully made a note. Allen gazed at him curiously.

"Now then, Mr Smythe," Collison went on, putting down his pen, "I'm going to ask you a couple of questions and I want you to think very carefully before you answer, because they are important."

"Very well."

"First, where did you go and what did you do between the time you left the panel session and the time you re-entered it? I'm talking about the day Peta Lepik died, by the way."

Smythe thought carefully.

"To be honest I was just feeling a bit bored and restless. I went up to my room and looked through some papers. Then I had a soft drink – a Coke I think – from the minibar and went back downstairs."

He looked nervously at Collison.

"So no actual alibi then?" Collison asked, stating the obvious.

"No, I'm afraid not."

"Okay, second question. Have you at any time procured any form of cyanide, or have you asked anybody to do so on your behalf?"

"No, I haven't," Smythe replied emphatically. "I don't think I would even know how to go about it."

"Very well. Then unless you have anything else to tell us I suggest we terminate the interview."

He looked enquiringly at the solicitor, who shrugged and shook his head.

"Just before you turn off the tape, Superintendent," he said quickly, "what is my client's status? Are you still proposing to treat him as a suspect?"

"Yes, I think I must," Collison said slowly, "but I would like to make it clear that our deepest wish is to be able to eliminate him from the enquiry. However, doing that is difficult if he cannot produce any corroboration of what he was doing at the time of the second murder."

"Thank you," the solicitor said without emotion.

He nodded at the tape recorder and Allen leaned across and switched it off. There was the usual ritual of initialling the tapes and securing them.

Once they had delivered suspect and lawyer together into the care of the duty Sergeant to be shown out of the building Allen turned abruptly to Collison.

"What was all that about then? You looked as if you'd seen a ghost."

"I suddenly had what might just be a revelation, Tom,"

Collison told him. "I suddenly remembered something which Angela Hughes told us. I'd have to check the notes but I'm pretty sure she said that Thomas Gold used to work as a lab assistant."

"What sort of lab, though?" Allen demanded at once. "Chemistry? Biology?"

"I don't know, but I mean to find out," Collison said determinedly. "Anyway, if it was at a school they are usually more or less next to each other, aren't they? I know ours were."

"Your school may not exactly be a good example of a local comprehensive," Allen commented sourly.

"Nonetheless," Collison went on, ignoring the dig, "it may well be that he operated across more than one lab, or that they shared a common chemical store or something. Let's get someone onto that straightaway, Tom."

"It shall be done," he promised.

"So what do you reckon to Tom Smythe now?" he asked as they walked upstairs together.

"I really wish I knew," Collison answered in exasperation. "Damn the man, why must he keep drawing suspicion onto himself by not telling us the full story straightaway? His story is plausible: I can quite believe that he lost his temper and shouted something which sounded dangerous but really wasn't meant to be. And the chairmanship of the CWA does seem an unlikely motive for murder, doesn't it? But what about you, Tom? You've had a chance to get under the skin of the case now. What does your copper's nose tell you?"

"For once, it doesn't seem to be working," he confessed. "I must say that I've always fancied Sonia Gold, like you. If her dad really does have access to a chemistry lab, and knows how to use it, then perhaps we should take another look at her."

"What about the daughter and her boyfriend?"

"Yes, I definitely get the feeling that there's something not right there. I don't see that there's anything to point specifically to them though, that's the problem."

"They are the only two key players whom we can fix as acquaintances of our second victim," Collison pointed out, "and they did have a pretty powerful financial motive to kill Ann Durham before she had a chance to change her will."

"All true enough," Allen conceded, "but what you asked is what my copper's nose told me, and the answer is nothing at the moment. It's strange. I know what you mean when you say this case feels different, special somehow, I'm starting to feel that way too. We need a break. We need something suddenly to fall into place. Who knows, maybe it will be this new idea of yours."

"Maybe," Collison agreed.

CHAPTER 31

"All right, gang, listen up please," DCI Allen called out the next morning. "We are going to be without DS Collison today. He rang me earlier to say that his wife's gone into labour. He's gone to hospital with her but hopes to be back sometime later today."

There was a murmur of appreciation, chiefly from the female members of the team.

"But we do have a possible break," Allen went on, "thanks to the Superintendent actually. He had a bit of a brainwave yesterday while we were re-interviewing Tom Smythe. He happened to remember that Angela Hughes had told us that Tom Gold worked as a lab assistant. I checked the notes of her interview afterwards and he was quite right."

This time a deeper, darker murmur ran around the room. It was moments like this, when a connection suddenly seemed to appear and point the way in a new direction, which made the hours and days of drudgery and frustration worthwhile.

"Now let's not get too excited," Allen warned, "but clearly this raises some very interesting possibilities. We need to find out as a matter of urgency exactly when and where Tom Gold worked as a lab assistant, what sort of lab it was, what access he had to chemicals, and so forth."

He looked across at Willis.

"Karen, why don't you take the lead on this?"

"Sorry, guv," she replied uncomfortably, "but I still have quite a lot of that other stuff to get through – you know, the things I mentioned to you and Mr Collison yesterday."

Allen drew breath heavily. Then he turned to Desai.

"Priya, what about you?"

"Sorry, sir," she replied equally uncomfortably, "I'm checking something on the CCTV coverage of the day of the second murder and I really don't know how long it's going to take. It's one of those things where you might stumble across what you're looking for straightaway, or it might take all day – or never."

"For God's sake," Allen said, controlling his irritation with obvious difficulty, "is there anybody who isn't already tied up on these ... new initiatives?"

It was obvious that he had lighted upon "new initiatives" as an alternative, albeit a tautologous one, to what he had originally meant to say.

"I'm free, sir," Evans volunteered. "I was working on the cyanide enquiries, but they've drawn a blank as you know."

"Fine," Allen acknowledged. "See what you can find out from his local authority. Chances are he hasn't moved recently, so presumably whichever school he was working at was local. They should have employment records and so forth. As soon as you've got something we can consider going to have a little chat with him."

"Does this mean that we ruling Sonia Gold back in, guv?" Willis enquired.

"For the time being, certainly," Allen stated firmly. "Apart from anything else, this may be the only link we've been able to establish between any of our suspects and a source of cyanide."

"What about motive, guv?" Willis persisted. "You said yourself that she had every interest in Ann Durham staying alive. After all, she'd just promised her a hefty payout, hadn't she?"

Allen shrugged.

"Who knows? Some of these nutters can be very smart you know. Perhaps she was never really interested in the money. Perhaps it was always just about revenge and she created this whole blackmail thing – the scene in the office and so forth – to put us off the scent."

Willis considered this.

"Well," she conceded, "it certainly might help to explain why she was so ridiculously protective of her father. Perhaps she was terrified what he might say if we really started to interrogate him."

"Well, let's not get ahead of ourselves," Allen cautioned her. "Let's get our facts straight first so that at least we know what we're talking about. Okay, everybody, we all have things to do so let's get on with them, shall we?"

At much the same time Metcalfe was sitting down in the cramped and dismal quarters of the Senior Clerk of the Family Division; occupying the very same chair, in fact, on which Willis had previously daintily perched, but offering no such diversion to the wretched official's daily calling as she had provided. If he minded, he gave no outward sign, but he did seem strangely nervous.

"Forgive me, Mr Metcalfe, but I understand from your paperwork that you are a police officer. Is that correct?"

"Yes, it is. I'm a Detective Inspector, actually."

His interlocutor shifted uneasily on his seat.

"I'm really sorry to have to ask this, but could you confirm that this is a genuine personal enquiry on your part?"

"Yes, of course it is. Why do you ask?"

"Well, as you know, our service is a strictly personal one provided only to private individuals. Our records are not available to anyone else – the police for example – without a court order, and that would normally only be provided in very special circumstances. So I just wanted to be clear that you weren't ..."

"Here under false pretences as it were?"

"Exactly, yes."

Metcalfe gave a weary smile.

"Being a police officer can be a bit of a curse, you know. People are apt to read an ulterior motive into just about any question. But no, I can give you my absolute assurance that I'm here purely as a private individual. I'm trying to trace my birthmother, Susan Rourke. I tried to do so myself – I applied for her name and address some time ago – but when I went round she wasn't there and nobody seemed ever to have heard of her."

"No, they wouldn't have. My understanding is that she moved away from Peterborough a long time ago. She changed her name at the same time; I assume because she'd taken up with a man and started using his name."

"And is that the end of the story?" Metcalfe asked. "Does the trail goes cold?"

"Not exactly. And that's really why I felt I had to ask you what I did. You see, Susan Rourke reappears in our filing system, and that later file was recently requested by somebody whom I believe may be a colleague of yours. That's why I thought – wrongly, obviously – that you might have come here flying false colours as it were."

"A colleague of mine?" Metcalfe repeated vacantly. "What on earth do you mean? Am I under investigation or something?"

The other man shrugged.

"Not so far as I am aware, although that would be nothing to do with me anyway. No, I was quite satisfied that the earlier enquiry was genuine, so my concern was actually the other way round. I wondered if you might be here as part of some investigation of her."

"Her?" Metcalfe echoed.

"Oh dear, perhaps I shouldn't have given that away. Her identity is of course confidential and I shouldn't be telling you anything which might help you discover it."

"Just a minute," Metcalfe said and then stopped, floundering.

The Senior Clerk fingered his folder nervously. Metcalfe's

mind was racing. Surely it was ridiculous – and yet ...

"Let me help you," he said, striving to keep his voice steady, "was her name Karen Willis?"

The other nodded unhappily.

"You're quite right," Metcalfe said after a pause. "She is a colleague of mine. In fact, I know her very well. We share a house together and I know all about her being here. She told me everything."

"Well, you're siblings as well as colleagues, as you've probably just guessed," the official said with a smile, "so now you'll probably want to get to know each other even better."

"Just let me understand this," Metcalfe implored desperately, the whole framework of his life collapsing around him, "are you saying that Susan Weedon and Susan Rourke are one and the same person?"

"Yes, that's exactly what I'm saying. I've got the records here for you to take away if you want them. She moved from Peterborough to the London area and a couple of years later she put a second child up for adoption: a girl. No details are given of the father, but I think we can safely assume that it was somebody different – which makes her your half-sister, of course."

Metcalfe tried to sit up straight. He put his hands on his thighs and breathed deeply in and out.

"Are you all right?" came the anxious enquiry.

"Yes, I think so ... Yes. It's just all come as a bit of a shock to me, that's all."

"I can understand that. Well look, would you like to take a photocopy of the records? Your colleague did, you know."

"No," Metcalfe decided. "I don't think I will if you don't mind."

"Not at all. It's entirely up to you of course."

Metcalfe stood up in a daze. Without really knowing what he was doing he shook hands and left the room. He started retracing the labyrinthine path which would take him back to the vaulted entrance hall redolent of a Gothic cathedral. Suddenly the bitterest of tastes swept into his mouth as a wave of nausea overcame him. Fortunately he caught sight of a welcoming toilet sign tucked away around the back of a winding staircase. Without even pausing to lock the door behind him, he knelt before the bowl and vomited long and hard, tears streaming down his face. Finally he reached up and pulled the handle, but the tears continued for many minutes after that. It wasn't until a long time afterwards that he stumbled out into the Strand on a darkening late afternoon with absolutely no idea of where he should go.

In a hospital on the other side of London, Simon Collison's firstborn – a boy – had just made a rather noisy and messy entrance into the world and was being cradled by his tired yet grateful mother, his father sitting beside the bed feeling rather useless.

"Nothing quite prepares you for the moment – this moment – does it?" he asked finally.

"No, it doesn't," Caroline agreed drowsily.

The baby seemed almost too small to be real, but he

reached out very gently with the little finger of his left hand and stroked one of its hands. Immediately, but without even opening his eyes, his son grabbed the tip of finger and held it tightly. They sat like this for a few minutes, contentedly together, until they were interrupted by a nurse bearing two green hospital cups and saucers.

"I thought you might both like a cup of tea," she explained.

"Now then, Mrs Collison," she added briskly as she put the cups down on the table beside the bed, "would you like me to take baby now? You'd probably like to rest for a bit, wouldn't you?"

"Well," Caroline replied reluctantly, "I do feel rather sleepy and it would be a shame to drop him, wouldn't it?"

"That's probably the after effects of the epidural," the nurse explained.

"Not to mention the gas and air," Collison added gently. He rather felt that he could have used some himself.

"Well let me take him then," she said, picking him up. "You just ask when you want him back."

As the nurse left the room with the first of the Collison line, Caroline smiled contentedly and took her husband's hand.

"Now tell me about Bob," she told him. "What on earth is happening with all that disciplinary nonsense?"

"I'm not sure that it's nonsense," he answered unhappily, "but hopefully it may go away. Alistair Partington seems to think that the only person who could properly bring a complaint would be Lisa's mother, not the probation service, and she seems happy to withdraw it. Of course, if Lisa were to regain consciousness – properly regain consciousness, I mean – then she could do so herself. But we just have to wait and see I suppose. Poor Bob, I do feel for what he must be going through."

Caroline nodded.

"And how is Lisa?"

"All I know is the message we had from Bob. She is out of the coma but not showing any obvious signs of being alive to her surroundings. Brain damage is very common where someone fractures their skull, you know."

"Yes, of course," she replied helplessly. "Well, as you say, we shall just have to wait and hope for the best, that's all."

"And how is the enquiry going?" she went on after a few moments, "or aren't you allowed to tell me?"

"I only wish I knew," he said thoughtfully. "I did come up with a new idea yesterday but I haven't heard yet whether anything has come of it."

"Then hadn't you better be getting back to the nick?" she suggested.

"No, I'll stay here with you of course," he protested.

She smiled and laughed quietly.

"Darling," she said gently, "your phone has buzzed at least three times in the last 10 minutes, and every time your hand has started towards it and then stopped. Why don't you get back to your investigation? You know you want to. And anyway, there's nothing more to see here. Isn't that what you policeman learn to say? 'Move along please, there's nothing to see here.' Well, there isn't, so why don't you move along, my dear?"

He squeezed her hand.

"Thank you. In that case I will. I can see you're going to have difficulty keeping your eyes open much longer anyway."

"This is true," she agreed softly, sinking back into her pillow.

He leant over and kissed her on the forehead, then got up and crossed to the door.

"Darling, haven't you forgotten something?" she called after him.

"What?" he asked over his shoulder, his hand on the door handle.

"A name, silly. What are we going to call our son? We said we'd decide on the day, if you remember."

"Oh Lord, yes, now you mention it I do remember."

"And?"

He stared at her helplessly.

"I really haven't the slightest idea."

"Oh Simon, you really are quite useless. Well, why don't you go away and have a little think?"

He nodded gratefully and opened the door.

"Only Simon?"

"Yes?"

"Don't wait too long will you, darling? It could be so awfully embarrassing when people say 'what a lovely baby, what's his name?' and I have to say that I don't know but I'm sure my husband will come up with something soon."

CHAPTER 32

Willis and Metcalfe sat on the sofa holding hands. They had been sitting there together for a long time and though it had long since grown dark neither had risen to switch on the lights.

"So what are we going to do?" Willis asked wretchedly at length.

"If you mean 'are we going to tell Peter?' then I was assuming that the answer would be yes and straight-away."

"Oh good," she said, stroking his hand, "I was so hoping you'd say that. Peter is so very wise. He always seems to know what to do."

"I was thinking more along the lines of he has a right to know," Metcalfe commented, looking at her sideways. "He does, doesn't he?"

"Yes, of course he does. I meant that as well."

As if on cue there came the sound of a key in the front door. Footsteps crossed the hall and Collins paused in the doorway.

"Hello, what are you two doing here in the dark? Is it okay to come in?"

"Yes of course, Peter," Willis said with a little laugh,

though laughing was the last thing she felt like doing, "do come in, and turn the light on won't you?"

Collins came into the room uncertainly, looking from one to the other.

"Forgive me if I'm being gauche," he ventured, "but you could cut the atmosphere in here with a knife. Has somebody died?"

Then, suddenly remembering, he looked deeply embarrassed.

"Oh, I'm so sorry. Is it Lisa? Has something happened to her?"

Metcalfe shook his head.

"No, it's nothing like that, but do sit down Peter. There's something I have to tell you."

Collins looked anxiously at Willis. He was only too aware that their living arrangements were highly unconventional, and that he had been the one to propose them. Ever since, he had lived in dread of the day that she might change her mind.

"Peter, there's no easy way to tell you this," Metcalfe said with quiet desperation, "so I'll come straight to the point. I've made a really horrific discovery this afternoon. It turns out that Karen is my half-sister. We both had the same mother who put us up for adoption a few years apart under different names. We had no idea of course."

"No, of course you didn't," Collins said automatically but then, as the full enormity of the situation sank in, "Christopher Columbus – what a mess!"

"Yes, it is, isn't it?" Willis agreed tearfully. "Oh Peter, I'm so sorry."

"We're both very sorry," Metcalfe put in. "Very sorry for everything this has done to you."

"Well, I don't see that either of you have anything to be sorry about," Collins responded. "After all, you had no idea. Isn't it more a question of what it does to you?"

"What you mean?" Willis queried.

"Well, I'm really not very good at this sort of thing, but isn't there a danger that unless you talk things through very carefully then it might damage your relationship very badly? You thought it was one thing but now it turns out to be quite another. That must have come as quite a shock, to put it mildly."

"Oh Peter," Willis said, shaking her head in irritation at the tears which would not stop flowing down her cheeks, "how very like you to be thinking of us at a time like this. You really are the most perfect man."

"Don't see that," Collins said awkwardly, "I'm just trying to be sensible, that's all. You need to think through the practical aspects of this. For example, haven't you told everyone at the nick that you're now an item?"

"I've been trying not to think about that," Metcalfe admitted. "Like you say, it's a mess."

"Actually, it may not be quite as bad as you think," Willis said thoughtfully. "The only person we've told officially is the guvnor."

"But that still means you'd have to let him in on the

secret, doesn't it?" Collins asked.

"I suppose we could just say that we weren't seeing each other anymore, and leave it at that," Metcalfe suggested.

"Well, like I say, it's a matter for you two," Collins replied. "I suppose it's just a question of how open you want to be about all this."

There was a silence while they all looked at each other.

"Actually, there is one good thing that's come out of this," Willis said brightly, blinking back tears determinedly, "and it's that I finally understand now what was happening to me. I knew that I was in love with you, Peter, desperately in love, and I just couldn't work out why it was that I could be so happy with you and yet so deeply attracted to Bob at the same time."

"Yes, I know what you mean," Metcalfe concurred. "I think we said at the time that it felt like meeting the other half of yourself, and of course that's really exactly what it was. Isn't biology amazing that we should somehow instinctively recognise that we were part of each other?"

"And I know it sounds an awful thing to say, Bob, but I feel somehow released, set free. All the old certainties are coming back to me. I feel settled again, grounded."

"I'm glad for that," he said simply. "To be honest, no matter what we said I always felt guilty about what I had done to you and to Peter."

"You'll stay here, of course, Bob?" Collins asked suddenly. "We all get on so well together and I really wouldn't want you to think that you had to leave. On the contrary, I'd love for you to stay."

"I really haven't had a chance to think about that," Metcalfe replied, "but thank you for the thought, Peter."

Willis had finally succeeded in staunching the flow, and was regarding a mascara stained handkerchief with dismay.

"I really must go and do something about my face," she acknowledged.

Letting go of Metcalfe's hand for the first time in a couple of hours, she stood up and walked rather unsteadily towards the door. She turned in classic silhouette, one hand on the door frame.

"Peter darling, why don't you get us all a drink?"

"Something special?"

"Yes, something very special. After all, at the risk of sounding corny, this is the start of the rest of our lives."

Metcalfe's thoughts flew to a hospital bed in the Royal Free.

"Corny works fine for me," he said softly to himself.

It was as a new father that Collison attended the regular team meeting the next morning. The inevitable congratulations over, Allen addressed the room.

"If I can have a bit of hush," he shouted and then, as the hubbub abated, "let's see where we are."

"First up, let's hear what DC Evans has come up with on Tom Gold. Timothy?"

"I managed to get quite a lot from the local authority, guv. Tom Gold was employed as a lab assistant at two different local schools: mostly physics but also quite a lot of chemistry, and he would definitely have had access to the chemistry store cupboard. Nobody there remembers him carrying out any unauthorised experiments, but he had keys so there would have been nothing to stop him making cyanide out of hours."

"Is he still employed there?" Collison asked.

"No, guv, he left about six months ago. He handed his keys in – I checked – but they're all ordinary Yales and Chubbs, so he could have had copies cut, no problem."

"Or he could have made the cyanide before he left," Desai suggested.

"All supposition," Allen commented tersely. "What we need is evidence, not ideas."

"Quite right, Tom," Collison agreed. "What do you suggest?"

"I think we have reasonable cause to support an application for a search warrant," Allen said, looking at him as if for confirmation.

Collison nodded.

"I agree. I'll happily sign off on it if you wish. Now, what else?"

"There's the other stuff we were looking at, guv, if you remember," Willis proffered.

"Yes, bring me up to speed on that."

"Well, it's all a bit inconclusive," Willis said slightly evasively. "On the plus side we might have a lead on the source of the cyanide, but we won't know for sure until after interviewing the guy. On the minus side, we were expecting – hoping I should say – to find something on the CCTV evidence which doesn't seem to be there after all. We haven't seen anyone new whom we recognise."

"What does Peter say about that?" Collison asked with interest.

Willis shifted rather uncomfortably.

"He reckons we should be looking for someone we don't recognise, or something unexpected, not part of the normal pattern."

Desai, who had spent much of the previous day running the CCTV tapes backwards and forwards, looked highly quizzical. So, needless to say, did Allen. He glanced at Collison. This had been the senior man's call, after all. The Superintendent thought for a moment.

"Let's do it one more time," he decided, "but with someone who hasn't looked at it before, someone who can come to it with fresh eyes. Now, what's this about a possible source for the cyanide?"

"It may be nothing, guv, but Peter saw some artwork in Angela Hughes's flat which he reckons was done using cyanide. He memorised the name of the artist: Christian Jarvis. Angela Hughes told him that Jarvis had emigrated to Australia, but guess what? He's never left London and I've got a meeting with him in an hour or so."

Collison whistled.

"If that's so, and his hunch is right then Angela Hughes has some explaining to do. If Jarvis does come up trumps then schedule another interview with her straightaway. I'd like to sit in on that, please."

"My guess for what it's worth," Allen interjected, "is that if she did source the cyanide for our victim then she got scared when she saw what happened and didn't want to own up to knowing anything about it."

"I tend to agree with you," Collison said mildly, "but as you say, Tom, let's have evidence not ideas."

When Willis and Collison interviewed Christian Jarvis shortly afterwards, evidence was indeed forthcoming. In his 50s or 60s with a neatly trimmed beard, he blinked nervously between questions.

"I'm not prepared to say anything which might get Angela into trouble," he said straightaway when asked if he had supplied her with cyanide.

Collison sighed heavily.

"If you did supply her with cyanide, Mr Jarvis, then it's highly likely that it was used to cause the death of Ann Durham, a death which we believe to have been murder. So I'm sure you can see why we are anxious to get at the truth. As far as Angela Hughes is concerned, all we're talking about at the moment is possession of cyanide which is not a criminal offence. Though we would be very interested to know why she didn't tell us about any of this for herself."

Jarvis considered the situation and then seemed to come to a decision.

"All right," he said quickly, "I did give her a small amount of the cyanide which I keep in my studio for professional purposes. She said that Ann Durham wanted it out of curiosity to see how it could be obtained, and to use it as some sort of curiosity piece at the big annual crime writers' bash where she was doing a session on poisons."

"It was in a bottle, I presume?"

"Yes, a small bottle which had previously been used for silver nitrate – I use that as well. A small amount, but highly dangerous nonetheless. I did warn Angela to be very careful about where she put it and what she did with it. Even inhaling it deeply could be fatal. It gives off hydrogen cyanide, you see. That's what the Nazis used in their gas chambers."

"Do you know what she did with it?"

"She said that she gave it to Ann Durham to show people at the convention. She says that she never saw it again. I believe that to be the truth."

"May I ask why you provided Angela Hughes with such a dangerous substance?" Willis enquired curiously. "You must have known that it was a highly irresponsible thing to do. Quite apart from what she might have done with it herself, there was always the danger of it falling into the wrong hands. Did she have some sort of hold on you?"

"I'm not sure what you mean," Jarvis replied guardedly.

"Then let me ask you straight out. Were you having some sort of relationship with her? Is that how she managed to persuade you to do it?"

Jarvis stared at her for a moment and then started to laugh.

"Oh, I see. No, not in the sense you mean anyway. You

see, Angela Hughes is my daughter. I brought her up. She was a bit of an accident to be honest, and her mother didn't want her, so I had her to live with me. We've always been together, until she moved out to her own place that is."

"Who is her mother?" Collison asked.

"Is that relevant?" Jarvis demanded, looking at him closely. "To your enquiry, I mean?"

"It might be," Collison replied equably, "you never know."

Jarvis thought deeply for a moment or two.

"I'm sorry," he said at length, "but I'm not prepared to answer that question. Not without Angela's permission anyway. It's a private matter for her."

"Very well," Collison said. "I can't force you to answer my questions anyway, but I respect your position. Well, if there's nothing else?"

He looked enquiringly at Willis, who shook her head.

"We'll get this typed up for you to sign, Mr Jarvis," he was saying as a uniformed constable took their visitor away when Willis's phone buzzed.

"It's Peter," she said, looking at it quickly.

"Take it," Collison urged her. "He may have come up with something else."

"Hello, Peter. No, nothing on the CCTV, I'm afraid. But you were right about the cyanide, so well done. And you were right about the DNA as well, though God knows what made you think of it."

"I didn't really want to do this," Collins answered at

the other end, "interfere too much, I mean. But in the light of what I now know then I think there's a rather obvious possibility which we should explore."

"Just a tick, Peter," Willis enjoined him, "let me switch the speaker on so the guvnor can hear too. Okay, now tell us."

So he did.

A few hours later a young detective constable looked carefully for the third or fourth time at an image of a woman in baggy clothes and came to a decision.

"Guv," he called out to Allen, "I think I've found something."

At the hotel later still somebody carefully lifted from beneath one of the ceiling panels in that ladies' toilet and, standing on the lowered lid, felt inside, first carefully and then in growing panic. Suddenly, groping fingers made contact not with what they were seeking but with a small envelope.

Hastily the panel was lowered back into position and a very bemused person sat down heavily, tearing open the envelope.

Inside was a note which read simply 'Please contact Superintendent Collison at your earliest convenience.'

CHAPTER 33

Dear Superintendent Collison,

I must say that I feel rather cheated. As an aficionado of detective fiction I had been expecting to be invited into a library and have Miss Marple, or perhaps that classic gentleman detective Peter Collins, explain exactly how the crime had been committed and point the finger elegantly in my direction. It's uncanny; he is so very like how I always imagined Lord Peter Wimsey to be.

I do compliment you, though, on your note which was an undeniably stylish gesture. Perhaps that makes you Rory Alleyn ...? He always had a sense for the right thing to do, didn't he? But no big 'reveal' then? Ah well, so be it. In the absence of any such classic confrontation I shall have to fall back on that other staple of the Golden Age, the deathbed confession.

My father has told me that you know about the cyanide. That was foolish, inviting Peter Collins to my flat. I should have realised that he would notice the artwork and put two and two together. Was it only that, I wonder, that put him on to me or was there something else as well? My father is completely innocent in all of this, by the way, so please leave him alone. His only mistake was to believe what I told him.

Ann Durham was my mother, as you will presumably know

by now; perhaps my father told you? Since you will presumably be curious as to how any daughter could bring herself to murder her mother, let me enlighten you.

First, I have never felt any great affection for the woman who until just a few years ago I knew only as a family friend. This lack of affection is mutual, incidentally. I do not believe that Ann Durham was capable of genuine affection for anybody. On the contrary, my father believes it is quite possible that she murdered both her husband and Tom Gold's mother. Certainly should you choose to look into these cases you will find that they seem to be consistent with arsenic poisoning. In my own case, she rejected me immediately after birth and wanted nothing more to do with me. It was my father who brought me up. She was finally persuaded to let me into the secret when she was looking for an agent whom she could trust with another great secret: the Bergmann affair.

Second, Ann Durham's world was falling apart and threatening to inflict a great deal of collateral damage on those around her. She was foolish to persist in playing the part of the grande dame of the CWA for as long as she did. There were others who were equally worthy, and who did not deserve the snide comments which she delivered both to and about them. She was universally disliked within a profession which is traditionally friendly and supportive.

Then of course there was the Bergmann affair. Having met Sonia Gold I knew she was completely out of control. I firmly believe that she would have gone public with the story no matter what she was promised or paid. Ironically, in a way, she and Ann were very similar people; they were both driven by rage. The difference was that in Sonia's case the rage was always bubbling about on the surface and threatening to break out into physical violence, whereas with Ann it was driven deep within her and festered in a horrible darkness and bitterness.

So on at least one level it was a mercy killing. I think Ann had got herself into a position which she was incapable of dealing with. The demons – all of her own making – which she had been holding at bay for so long were now threatening to engulf her. It was only a matter of time before she was dragged down by them.

The press, of course, would have been merciless, and understandably so. Ann had been very unpleasant about some of the poor reviews she had received recently, and of course she had given herself airs and graces for so long that the media would have delighted in bringing her low. She would never have been able to stand that. I know with complete certainty that she would have ended up taking her own life, so I was simply sparing her the trouble (and the intervening misery).

Yet on another level I think I was angry with her too. Not just angry for having made me miss out on having a mother, but angry about what the mess she had made of her own life might do to others, including me. There really was no good angle about the Bergmann affair. The best option I could come up with was that Ann's death would at least distance everybody else from it to a certain extent. After all, none of the original participants would still be alive apart from Tom Gold, and I *felt that he could probably be controlled to a large extent.*

So I decided that Ann should die, but that it should look like suicide. I asked myself how she would choose to do it had she once made that decision for herself, and hit upon the idea of a grandiose and melodramatic exit at the convention. That would have been very much like Ann. Those "little people", as she referred to them, who were trying to bring her down would be chastened. Her public would be devastated. Best of all, it would probably end up on the front page of every newspaper in the world.

The more I thought about it, the more I realised it would be much too risky actually to administer the cyanide myself. I had to establish some distance both in time and place from the evil deed. Yet I needed the cyanide to be back in Ann's possession either at or immediately after her death in order for the suicide story to work. So I needed an accomplice.

I met Peta Lepik at one of Gina's parties. I think she had come with some mousy little friend, but I didn't see her again after Peta and I got talking. Peta was really rather sweet. She was very lonely and very homesick. I genuinely liked her but once she told me that she sometimes worked waiting shifts at the hotel where I knew the convention was to be held, I spotted the opportunity at once.

She was gay and desperate for company, so it was really very easy to establish a close relationship with her very quickly. I explained that I had a friend who was terminally ill and who wished to kill herself, but amongst friends in a social setting. I said that I had promised to help her, and Peta in turn promised to help me. I don't think she really understood what she was letting herself in for. I think she was in love with me, or thought she was, and would just have done anything I asked.

When I heard that Ann was meeting with Sonia Gold that evening, I almost changed my plan. I thought about poisoning Sonia instead, but realised that wouldn't work. Suspicion would fall on Ann and myself, either jointly or together. No, the only way out was for Ann to die and for everyone to think it was suicide.

So we went ahead. I met Peta on the service stairs at about the time Ann was meeting with Sonia and gave her the cyanide. Ann was drinking very heavily by this time – almost the alcohol equivalent of chain-smoking – so there was a very good chance that if Peta handed her a glass of gin and tonic as she walked into the room she would simply assume that it was something which I had organised for her: as of course it was. I then went in search of an alibi.

When I saw Peter Collins I realised he was the obvious choice. He was waiting for that dramatically dressed policewoman, of course. Just when did policewomen become so glamorous and gorgeous? It was only for a few minutes, but it gave me what I needed. I made sure that I stuck close to them as we went into the room so that there could be no question at all of me having handed the glass to Ann.

Then things started to go wrong. I'm still not quite sure what or how. There was a disturbance on the other side of the table, which wasn't part of the plan at all and, though I didn't know it at the time, it stopped Peta from doing what she was supposed to do, namely slipping the bottle of poison back into Ann's bag or putting it by her place on the table. It also meant that Ann got distracted and didn't make it to her place in time anyway. What happened next you already know. If only that policewoman hadn't been there, and behaved so efficiently, there might still have been a chance for Peta to put the bottle somewhere sensible, but I suppose that was just my bad luck.

Of course I watched events pretty carefully after that. I was encouraged that, even with the cyanide bottle having gone missing, so many people seemed prepared to assume that it was suicide. So I decided just to hunker down and ride out the storm. But then things started to go wrong again.

Peta had been horrified by what she saw. Fortunately she had been one of the waiters whom the policewoman sent out of the room to guard the doors, and so when the rest of the police arrived – the uniformed ones – she was able to slip away unnoticed. I don't care to think what might have happened otherwise, as she was very upset.

I had several phone calls from her the next day. I had bought a pay-as-you-go mobile under an assumed name (wasn't that clever of me?) so presumably you were never able to trace the calls. She seemed to be coming apart at the seams. She said that she had never intended to get mixed up in anything so horrible, and she was crying about going to the police and telling them about what we had done; throwing herself on their mercy, as it were.

Naturally I had to do something about this, and quickly. I said that I was very busy at the office that day, and I was, but

I managed to slip out and buy a baggy top and jeans together with a nasty old brown curly wig. First thing next morning I went into the Ladies and hid them above the ceiling panel over one of the toilet stalls.

I had my plan, you see. Again what I needed was an alibi. This time I wasn't going to rely on anyone else to give it to me. I agreed to meet Peta at 2.30 on the service stairs. I left the conference session some time before that, went to the Ladies and put on my disguise, as well as changing my heels for flat shoes. I had to leave a decent safety margin in case the particular stall I needed was occupied when I went in, so I ended up being in there for quite a long time, hence the cover story of a tummy bug which I came up with.

I was pretty confident that nobody would recognise me, but just be on the safe side I adopted a rather shuffling walk, completely different from the way I normally stride about. I met Peta and she was no better. She was desperate to talk to somebody, anybody. I don't know whether it was because she was a Catholic, but she seemed to have an overpowering urge to confess what she had done. I grabbed her and kissed her and then said something like "all right, in that case I'll come with you, let's go downstairs". She turned to go with me and as she did I hit her very hard behind the ear with the big metal knob of my room key. I must have stunned her because as she fell down the stairs she never put her arms out to break her fall, and I saw her head hit the stairs two or three times. She came to rest on the first landing but half hanging over the first stair of the next flight, so it was a fairly easy matter to run down *and tip her over once more. Again, I saw her head bounce off the floor a few times.*

I followed her down again to where she had come to rest. I was pretty sure that she was dead but, just to make sure, I hit her very hard two or three more times, this time on the back of the head. Her head was a bit of a mess by this time, actually. There was blood everywhere. Luckily I kept my presence of mind. I felt inside her jacket with my hand wrapped in a handkerchief and took her phone and the cyanide bottle, which miraculously was unbroken. I ran into the hotel and took the lift back to the floor where the conference was happening. I was very lucky not to encounter anyone in the lift – I suppose because a session was going on – as I'm sure there must have been blood on my clothes.

When I got back into the Ladies I was shaking, but I forced myself to slip the disguise off and hide it back above the ceiling panel, this time with the cyanide bottle and Peta's phone. I even remembered to turn the phone off so that nobody would hear it if it rang.

But then you know all of this, don't you? Somehow – I'd love to know how – you worked it out and got to the ceiling void before I did. That was my one big mistake, I think. I was planning to wait a few weeks until things had really cooled down, but I should have taken a chance and tried to smuggle the stuff out straightaway. With it you have everything, since it's presumably covered in my DNA and Peta's blood. Without it, you wouldn't really have had very much, would you?

Oh, I know you could have shown that I lied about the

cyanide, but I think I could have explained that away as simply having panicked and then not felt able to change my story. And there would have been nothing to show that I was connected in any way with the second murder. No, I really don't think you would have got very far, would you?

I'm not sure why, but I sense the hand of Peter Collins in this. He is a remarkable man, isn't he? He's a gentleman – a real gentleman – and he's kind, and sensitive, and considerate, and all those other things which a woman seeks in a man so desperately. But he's deeply intelligent as well. My guess is that I made a mistake somewhere along the way and that he (not you, dear Superintendent) made a connection which ended up with you being able to substitute your humorous little note for the evidence with which I so clumsily supplied you.

I think that's everything, Superintendent, so I'm going to reach for the gin and tonic in a moment. Yes, cyanide naturally; I kept some. But I'm leaving a brief note for my father where you will find it with this one and since you too are a gentleman I trust you will feel able to make sure he gets it. I don't want to upset him by telling him on the telephone, and anyway I don't think I could face it. Will you try to explain, as best you can?

I suppose you'll need a signature on this to use it as evidence or whatever, so here you are.

Angela Hughes

Dearest Daddy, I've been a very silly girl. It's all gone wrong and I've been found out. I'm doing what I have to do, even though I really don't want to leave you. Forgive me. Love you always, Angie.

CHAPTER 34

"You know I really do wish that Angela Hughes could have been here to see this," Collison mused as he gazed around the booklined living room in Frognal. "It's pretty much a library, isn't it? And we're going to have our 'big reveal' after all."

"So it would seem," Collins agreed cautiously, "but I'm really not sure that I should be taking any of the credit for this. I just remembered something, that's all."

"And just what was it that you remembered?" Allen demanded. "How come we couldn't spot it? I went through the file dozens of times."

"Because it wasn't in the file, that's why. It was locked away in some dim recess of my memory."

Collins cradled his glass and gazed around benignly at the other four.

"In the end I went right back to the beginning, back to when I first arrived at the convention, and forced myself to try to remember every little thing that happened. In the event, it was actually a glass of wine which helped me to remember."

"With me it usually has the opposite effect," Metcalfe quipped.

"Oh no, not in that sense," Collins said quickly. "You see I had just opened a bottle of Pinot Noir and before I tasted it I raised it to my nose to smell it – the way you do, you know – and that's when I suddenly remembered Ann Durham doing the same thing with the cyanide bottle in the green room before our poisons session. Of course I was horrified, because I knew that just inhaling the stuff could be fatal, but there was more to it than that. There was something strange that had struck me at the time but which I couldn't remember thereafter. Suddenly I did. She sniffed the bottle and then frowned."

"Why on earth would she frown?" Willis asked.

"Yes, that's exactly what I asked myself, and suddenly it struck me. You see, I believe what happened was that she was expecting to smell almonds but couldn't, and couldn't understand why."

The others stared at him blankly.

"We all know that cyanide smells of almonds. Actually, that's not exactly true. It's more that almonds smell of cyanide since it occurs naturally in bitter almonds. Various other foods have it, incidentally. Apricots stones could prove fatal if you ground them up and ate them. But the most dangerous one of all is cassava. That could very easily kill you if you don't know exactly the right way to prepare it. But anyway, that's not the point. The point is that some people are incapable of smelling cyanide due to a genetic defect: a glitch in their DNA, you might say. That was what I initially asked Karen to have checked in the DNA evidence and it turned out I was right."

"But how did that help?" Collison pressed him. "How did it show you the way to take?"

"Well for a start it cleared up something that had been troubling me from the beginning. Why would anybody, let alone a crime writer, willingly drink from a glass which reeked of cyanide? That's why I originally favoured suicide, which was of course exactly what Angela Hughes wanted us to believe. Now I had my answer. Ann Durham couldn't have smelt the cyanide and therefore had no idea that she was drinking it."

"But by this time we knew it was murder," Allen pointed out. "That was obvious from the time of the second killing."

"Yes, indeed it was," Collins conceded, "but I was more concerned to think through what happened at the time of the first murder. In particular I got to thinking about what Angela Hughes said when Ann Durham collapsed. Do you remember, Karen? She said something like 'what's that smell?'. In other words, she was deliberately drawing our attention to the fact that cyanide had been used. She was rooting for everyone to believe that it was suicide, and of course the best way of doing that was to point out how obvious it was that the glass stank of cyanide. We swallowed it at the time, naturally – oh dear, no pun intended – but in the light of what we now know it was an obvious contrivance. Just as Ann Durham couldn't smell cyanide, neither could Angela Hughes. The genetic defect is mitochondrial; it's passed from mother to child."

"But you didn't know that at the time," Allen persisted.

"No, I didn't, but it became obvious later that it was something which needed to be checked. Oh dear, I think I'm getting ahead of myself, aren't I? Bear with me and I'll come back to that. Now, where was I?"

"Angela had just mentioned the smell of cyanide," Metcalfe prompted.

"Ah yes, thank you, Bob. Well, then there was quite a bit of 'oh, Ann, what have you done?' stuff to reinforce the suicide angle. I think you were on the phone by that time, Karen."

"That's right, I was, but now you mention it I do remember her saying something like that."

"But then I got to thinking about what she said next, and that's when my suspicions really got aroused. Again, it's nothing that I would have questioned at the time, just something that suddenly offered a connection in the light of something we discovered later. Do you remember what she said, Karen?"

"I don't think I can remember exactly," she said hesitantly. "After all, I was scrambling around on the floor at the time looking for a bottle of cyanide. It might have been something like 'oh, Peter, then it's murder' but I can't be quite sure."

"Actually you're pretty close," Collins said approvingly, "although I thought it was 'oh, but Peter, then it's murder' although she stopped after 'Peter'. However, with the greatest respect, old thing, you've just made exactly the same natural mistake which I did at the time. You've just remembered what you heard, which isn't necessarily the same thing as what she was actually saying."

For a few moments the others gazed at him blankly but then Collison broke in with a sudden flood of comprehension.

"Oh, you mean it was the girl she was talking about, not you."

"Absolutely. What if instead of 'oh, but Peter, then it's murder' she was actually starting to say 'oh, but Peta was supposed to put the bottle back'. Karen had just announced that she couldn't find it, you see, and that must have come as a bit of a shock. I think she may actually have started to give herself away, but then managed to stop, and fortuitously at a point where we all thought she was speaking to me."

"The other thing which was niggling away at me was the cyanide. It's such an unusual substance for anyone to have in their possession, and so difficult to obtain even illegitimately that normally you would expect the identity of whoever sourced it to be key to solving the mystery. But here it was apparent that the cyanide had gone missing – after all, we searched for it both at the scene and in Ann Durham's room but couldn't find it – but also that just about everyone at the convention had seen her with it and might have had the idea of taking it from her."

"That's why we were spending so much time and effort on finding out exactly what had happened to it," Allen pointed out heavily.

"Yes, absolutely, but the one thing we were never able to trace was how it had been sourced originally. It was when I saw the artwork in Angela Hughes's flat that a very real possibility suggested itself. You see, old-fashioned photography using plates is one of the few legitimate reasons for a private individual having cyanide in their possession; two different ones actually: potassium and ferric. Once we traced her father it became clear that she had lied not once but twice about the cyanide. First when she said that Ann Durham had obtained it somehow and just given it to her for safekeeping, and second when she told me that the person who created the artwork had gone to Australia. It was a silly lie because it was such an easy one to disprove, but she must have panicked and just said the first thing that came into her head. Once I knew that she had lied it was an obvious next step to wonder why she was so desperate to conceal the provenance of the cyanide. One possible explanation was that she had used it to kill Ann Durham, and had in fact always intended to do so."

Collins raised his glass and sipped reflectively.

"Then I'm afraid I did something rather underhand. I pretended to help clear away the tea things, but as I did so I made a great show of wiping her lipstick off one of the cups with a paper napkin. Fortunately she ... well, let's just say she was distracted, and I managed to slip it into the handkerchief in my pocket without her noticing. You see by then I was already thinking hard about what she had said at the time of Ann's death, particularly about the smell. I'd had a chance to do a bit more research and it turned out that many more people had that particular genetic defect than I had supposed to be the case. So all I was intending to do was to see if she could really smell cyanide herself. If she could then that wouldn't necessarily put her in the clear, but if she couldn't then that would look very bad because then she would have been lying, and why would she do that? More to the point, how could she have known it was cyanide if she couldn't smell it? The only logical answer to that was that she must have put the stuff in the drink herself, or have been party to someone else doing so."

"The outcome of that, however, was very unexpected, as you already know. Once my DNA had been eliminated what was left showed conclusively that she was in fact Ann Durham's daughter."

"But, Peter," Collison asked, intrigued, "how on earth did you get from there to the stuff in the toilet? That's what I really don't understand. For example, surely the fact that Ann Durham was her mother would make it less likely that she would have murdered her, not more?"

"Yes and no," Collins replied. "I gained two impressions of Angela Hughes. The first was that she was essentially quite a lonely person – she didn't seem to be in any sort of relationship, for example – and that argued for not having had any real sort of closeness with her mother. Certainly when I had seen them together it had seemed much more of a business relationship; I didn't get any sense of intimacy between them. The second was that she seemed completely wrapped up in the world of her job, the world of Ann Durham's books. I think she was genuinely horrified by the prospect of what was going to happen when the Bergmann affair became public knowledge. Incidentally, despite what I have just said about it having been a rather distant relationship, I think she was also genuinely very concerned about what it was going to do to Ann Durham herself."

"Certainly that comes across from the letter," Collison commented. "It sounds as though once she realised Sonia Gold was a total loose cannon who could not possibly be controlled or silenced then she proceeded on the basis that she really had no choice. Your last point chimes with the letter as well, Peter; she says that she regarded it as a sort of mercy killing."

"But that still doesn't explain how you got to the disguise in the toilet, Peter," Willis insisted. "How could you possibly know?"

"Actually, I didn't know," he confessed. "I just formed a hypothesis, thinking that I would run with it until something was discovered which was inconsistent with it, but of course that never happened."

"And what was that," Metcalfe asked him, "your hypothesis, I mean?"

"Well I remember saying to someone – actually, ironically I think it was Angela – that the second murder was always the key to solving the first, and so it proved in this case. Just as well, really. After all, would we ever have been able to prove conclusively that Angela killed Ann?"

"Probably not," Collison murmured. "All we would have had were the various lies about the cyanide, and that probably wouldn't have been enough for a jury."

A snort of derision from Allen expressed the DCI's opinion of juries.

"Well, there you are then," Collins continued, "but anyway, I got to thinking that whoever committed the first murder was likely also to have committed the second. To have two unconnected murders occurring in the same building within such a short space of time would surely have been too enormous a coincidence to be considered. It therefore seemed reasonable to assume that the second murderer was likely also to be either the first murderer or an accomplice in the first murder, and that the second murder had been carried out to prevent a witness, who might also have been an accomplice, from exposing them. Accepting that, I formed my hypothesis."

"I imagined Angela Hughes finding a way of introducing the cyanide into Ann Hughes's glass. From what I saw at the table, and from the later suggestion that she had been handed the glass as she entered the room, I knew that she could not have done so herself. Therefore she must have had an accomplice, and for my theory to work that accomplice must have been our second victim, Peta Lepik. I must confess that it was at that point that I had the sudden revelation of what Angela might have been saying as distinct from what we thought she was saying."

"Turning to the second murder, in order for Angela to

have killed Peta, she would have had to be physically present at the time and place of her death. That of course is where the difficulty arose. We knew from the CCTV footage that Angela had spent a lengthy time in the Ladies starting before the murder and not ending until after Peta's body had been discovered. The only remaining possibility, and the only possible way of saving my hypothesis, was if she had somehow found a way of leaving and re-entering the Ladies unobserved. That's when I asked for the CCTV evidence to be re-examined, but this time not looking specifically for Angela, but for any anomaly."

"And of course we found one," Willis said.

"We did indeed. We found that someone had come out of the Ladies of whom, running the tape back, we could find no evidence of them having entered it. Similarly when she re-entered the Ladies a little while later there was no subsequent picture of her leaving again. At that point it became clear that what had happened was that Angela had smuggled a disguise in there, either at the time or previously, and had thus created a completely false alibi."

"Of course that did not prove that she killed Peta, only that she had the opportunity to do so. But if the crime scene had been a messy one, which I understood that it was, then it was inevitable that the clothing of her disguise would have had some of Peta's blood on it as well as her own DNA. I suddenly realised that in that case we were engaged in a race to see who could get to it first, which is when I phoned Karen and explained my theory to her and Simon. Actually,

I wasn't that worried. I thought that Angela would have no idea that we were on to her, and would therefore be happy to leave it for a week or two, perhaps sneaking in early one morning. But of course there was always the possibility that I was wrong ..."

"But fortunately you weren't wrong," Collison said with a grin. "And your idea of the note was inspired. I would have given anything to see her face as she read it. I'm sorry she gave me the credit for that, by the way. Quite undeserved."

"It's all very sad in a way," Collins observed. "I think she was just an extremely lonely person who had never known any real human affection, and somehow it warped her moral compass. The real tragedy was that she involved Peta Lepik – another very lonely person I suspect – who was horrified when she found out what she had got into and tragically of course it was that – that essential decency – which sealed her own death warrant."

There was a pause and then Collison looked rather ostentatiously at his watch.

"I really must be going," he said and then, the phrase still sitting rather oddly with him, "I must go and see my wife and son."

CHAPTER 35

"So there's no doubt in your mind, Simon, that this Hughes woman was responsible for both murders?" the ACC asked.

"No, none at all, sir. But you've read the letter for yourself. Isn't it clear enough?"

"Yes, I think so. I just wanted to hear you say it, that's all. So we can officially close the investigation then?"

"Yes, sir, absolutely."

"Well it's a great relief I don't mind telling you," the ACC said. "Between you and me I was getting a lot of pressure from the Commissioner to clear this one up quickly, what with that Durham woman being all over the press and everything. I didn't say anything to you because I didn't think it was fair, but I'm heartily glad that you tied it all up so quickly. And a confession too! That always makes things tidier."

"Actually most of it was down to Peter Collins," Collison protested. "I really wouldn't want to take credit for somebody else's work. It was something which he remembered, and the hunch which he based upon it, which uncovered the vital evidence."

"Can't say that officially," the ACC replied gruffly. "You're the SIO so it's your collar. You take the credit whether it's due or not. But I'll happily write Dr Collins a letter if you like, thanking him for his contribution."

"Thank you, sir, I'm sure he'd appreciate that. But I'd like to commend my other team members as well. They all did a great job, especially Tom Allen who got parachuted in at short notice."

"Put it all in your report and I'll make sure that it gets taken care of officially," the ACC promised, "although in the circumstances it may be difficult to give a commendation to Bob Metcalfe."

"But why, sir? I thought that had all gone away."

"Officially, yes. He brought that fancy barrister of his in for a meeting with our legal team. Partington convinced them that the probation service had no – *locus standi*, is that the phrase? – to make a complaint in the first place. Only the girl's mother could have done that, and she didn't want to. So there was general agreement to treat the complaint as if it had never been made."

"Then I don't see the problem, sir," Collison ventured. "Bob Metcalfe did just as good a job as anybody else. So if there are any plaudits being given out then he deserves his fair share."

"Don't be naive, Simon," the ACC said briskly. "Whatever the record shows or doesn't show – and in my view Metcalfe is damn lucky that it won't show anything at all – he made a serious error of judgement as a result of which a girl who was as near as dammit a colleague ended up in intensive care. The Commissioner was minded to launch an internal investigation. Luckily I managed to persuade him that it would be in everybody's interest to keep it quiet."

"In that case I'm very grateful to you, sir," Collison said sincerely, "and I'm sure Bob will be too."

"Best if he doesn't know anything about it, I think. A shame though. I was hoping to put him on the next list for promotion to DCI but there's no way I'd get that past the Commissioner at present."

"I'm sure he'll understand, sir. After all, just a few days ago he was wondering whether he was going to have any future within the Met at all."

"Hm, well. How is the girl, by the way?"

"The signs are promising, I think. Bob had a message from her mother this morning that she recognised her on her last visit and tried to speak. For someone who wasn't expected to live, that's pretty good going don't you think?"

"I'd hope and pray so, yes. Head injuries are funny things though. Someone can appear fine and dandy one moment and then drop dead from a blood clot on the brain the next. I'd imagine that they'll keep her under observation for quite a while yet."

"What are we doing with Sonia Gold, if I may ask?"

"You may," the ACC said sardonically. "If I had my way we'd be charging her with attempted murder but the DPP seems to be going for GBH instead. Hopefully it won't make that much difference to her sentence. I've read the file and she seems an evil little bitch."

"I think she's very dangerous," Collison replied carefully. "She's prone to sudden violent rages and she doesn't seem to have any ability, or indeed desire, to control them."

"Sounds rather like my ex-wife," the ACC murmured.

He gazed into the distance for a moment, then shook his head sadly and looked down at a note on his desk.

"By the way, talking of hospitals, I haven't had a chance to congratulate you on the birth of your son. Please give my best wishes to your wife."

"Thank you, sir, I certainly will."

"Have you spoken to Jim Murray recently?"

"Yes of course, sir, I brought him up to speed on developments yesterday evening. Naturally, he's very pleased that it's all over."

"Did he say anything about your future?"

"No, sir. Why? Is there anything I should be aware of?"

"I only wish there was," the ACC replied, looking at him quizzically. "Sometimes I really don't understand you, Simon. The Met – the Commissioner himself – have got you marked out as a highflyer. We'd intended for you to be a Chief Superintendent by now in some high profile job on your way to the top, but you seem determined to hang on at Hampstead Nick even though there's no proper place for you there within the existing structure."

"I enjoy proper police work, sir. I'm sorry, I didn't mean that to sound derogatory of what other people do. What I meant was that I enjoy investigative work. I like solving cases."

"That may be, but the fact remains that SIOs are traditionally DCIs reporting to a DCS who himself takes no real active part in the enquiry. Seems to me that you're someone who should be a DCS but wants to be a DCI. And, before you ask, no I'm not going to drop you down to DCI."

"I wasn't going to ask for that, sir, just to be allowed to work a little longer as an SIO. I never really had that experience as a DCI, you see, and I really want to get it under my belt. After all, if I am going to end up as a senior officer – perhaps even a very senior officer – then I'm going to need the respect of the people who report to me. And I don't see how I can have that if all I've ever done are desk jobs, sitting on committees and putting up policy papers."

"Special Branch is hardly a desk job," the ACC commented sourly. "Very much up at the sharp end, I would say. Yet you turned down a job there, a job moreover which is a traditional stepping stone on the route to Commissioner."

"I really appreciated the offer, sir, but I didn't think I was cut out for it."

"It's important work the Branch does, you know. They've helped to foil several terrorist attacks already."

"I'm not ruling it out altogether, sir. I just didn't think I was ready for it. It all comes back to not having run many serious enquiries."

"Hm, well I've spoken to Jim and we are both agreed that you can stay where you are for the time being. You're getting so much coverage in the press over this Durham business that you can pretty much name your own terms."

"I hope you and Jim don't see things that way, sir. That's not my intention at all. At the end of the day I report to you and I'll go wherever you put me. I'm just expressing my personal preference, that's all."

"And we're going to respect it, at least for the moment. But you must understand, Simon, that it's not a permanent solution. It can't be. There's a system and a process and it needs to be followed. But until I can decide where you'd fit in best you can stay at Hampstead."

"Thank you, sir, I really appreciate it. I'm very happy there."

"Talking of the papers, I see the story has broken about those old books Ann Durham wrote. Rather a shock, isn't it? They're some of my favourites."

"Oh, but it doesn't make them any less good, does it? They will just have a different author's name on the cover. Personally, I'm rather glad that it's all come out. It's all about credit where it's due again, isn't it? She stole somebody else's work – oh, I know it was all legal and above board, but ethically it was completely wrong – and now justice has been done."

"But unless I've misunderstood the situation the original author's family won't benefit, will they? If the Durham estate owns the rights then all that will happen will be that Ann Durham's heirs will make even more money out of reissuing the books under Bergmann's name."

"That's true of course, but I happen to know that Gina Durham is considering cutting Tom Gold in on the royalties, so that will be something at least."

"And what about this damned paper of yours? I know

the Durham case got in the way, but don't forget you're supposed to be writing it."

"I haven't forgotten, sir, don't worry. You'll have it."

"What's it about?" the ACC asked curiously.

"I haven't decided exactly," Collison responded guardedly, "but something to do with organisational theory."

"Hm," said the ACC dubiously.

A few miles to the north-west of Scotland Yard Bob Metcalfe poked his head uncertainly round the door of Lisa Atkins's room. Her mother, sitting beside the bed, smiled, beckoned him inside and motioned him to sit down on the other side of the bed.

Lisa was still encased in bandages and braces. Unable to move her head, she swivelled her eyes in his direction. He could see that she was desperately trying to focus them. Then they seemed to settle upon him, but there was still no sign that she could recognise, or even see him. After a pause her throat started to flex as if she was attempting to speak. Finally, something came.

"Hello," she croaked weakly, "it's that awfully nice policeman."

GUY FRASER-SAMPSON is an established writer, having published not only fiction but also books on a diverse range of subjects including finance, investment, economics and cricket. His darkly disturbing economic history *The Mess We're In* was nominated for the Orwell Prize.

His *Mapp & Lucia* novels have all been optioned by BBC TV, and have won high praise from other authors including Alexander McCall Smith, Gyles Brandreth and Tom Holt. The second was featured in an exclusive interview with Mariella Forstrup on Radio 4, and Guy's entertaining talks on the series have been heard at a number of literary events including the Sunday Times Festival in Oxford and the Daily Telegraph Festival in Dartington.

THE FIRST THRILLING TITLE IN THE HAMPSTEAD MURDERS SERIES

£7.99, ISBN 978-1-910692-93-6

The genteel façade of London's Hampstead is shattered by a series of terrifying murders, and the ensuing police hunt is threatened by internal politics, and a burgeoning love triangle within the investigative team. Pressurised by senior officers desperate for a result a new initiative is clearly needed, but what?

Intellectual analysis and police procedure vie with the gut instinct of 'copper's nose', and help appears to offer itself from a very unlikely source a famous fictional detective. A psychological profile of the murderer allows the police to narrow down their search, but will Scotland Yard lose patience with the team before they can crack the case?

Praised by fellow authors and readers alike, this is a truly original crime story, speaking to a contemporary audience yet harking back to the Golden Age of detective fiction. Intelligent, quirky and mannered, it has been described as 'a love letter to the detective novel'. Above it all hovers Hampstead, a magical village evoking the elegance of an earlier time, and the spirit of mystery-solving detectives.

THE SECOND GRIPPING TITLE IN THE HAMPSTEAD MURDERS SERIES

£7.99, ISBN 978-1-911331-80-3

The second in the Hampstead Murders series opens with a sudden death at an iconic local venue, which some of the team believe may be connected with an unsolved murder featuring Cold War betrayals worthy of George Smiley.

It soon emerges that none other than Agatha Christie herself may be the key witness who is able to provide the missing link.

As with its bestselling predecessor, *Death in Profile*, the book develops the lives and loves of the team at 'Hampstead Nick'. While the next phase of a complicated love triangle plays itself out, the protagonists, struggling to crack not one but two apparently insoluble murders, face issues of national security in working alongside Special Branch.

On one level a classic whodunit, this quirky and intelligent read harks back not only to the world of Agatha Christie, but also to the Cold War thrillers of John Le Carré, making it a worthy successor to *Death in Profile* which was dubbed 'a love letter to the detective novel'.

Urbane Publications is dedicated to
developing new author voices, and publishing
fiction and non-fiction that challenges, thrills and
fascinates.

From page-turning novels to innovative
reference books, our goal is to publish what
YOU want to read.

Find out more at
urbanepublications.com